NICHELLE WALKER

WHEN A GOOD GIRL TURNS SHIESTY

Published by:
NWHoodTales
P.O Box 804782 Chicago IL, 60680
www.nwhoodtales.com

Publishing Consultant:
 Nakea S. Murray, Literary Consultant Group

Cover Design:
 Keith Saunders, www.mariondesigns.com

Editor:
 Todd Hunter, Literary Consultant Group

Typesetting:
 Shawna A. Grundy, sag@shawnagrundy.com

First Edition
Library of Congress Cataloging-in-Publication Data;
ISBN-13: 978-0979402821
ISBN-10: 0-0979402824

Money Over Men

Acknowledgements

Wow it's been a year already...I want to thank all my fans that rode with me and spread the word about *Doing His Time*. I know Money Over Men got pushed back more than Lil Wayne's CD. But just like Weezy I hope to deliver a hot project☺. Well I'ma keep this short and sweet, this shi* cost money. Thanks to the man upstairs for his blessings that he's poured on me. To my family I love you all. And I know all my cousin want me to print each and everyone's name but sorry paper cost went up lol. I love all of you!!!

To all the bookstores that stocked Doing His Time thanks so much for giving me a chance. And I'm sorry for your phone blowing up for part two. Special thanks to Black-N-Nobel thanks for the love...

To my friends I love all ya'll, Special shout out to my number 1 reader Kenwune (Keezy). Thanks for always reading all my projects with out being asked twice.

To my salesman and women who pushed Doing His Time for me. Francis Avilez thanks for pushing ya girl work love ya. Dreana a girl's best friend☺ Asian thanks for locking down the Cook County Jail for me I love ya. Gisela thanks for pushing my book at the shop, Dontane Farmer thanks for all the great ideas and encouragement you know when I start up my movies deals I got you. Steve's Mini Mart thanks a whole bunch for selling lots of copies of my novel outta your stores much love to you. Gomez Tires and Rims, Fresh Wear Clothing, Pinky and all the beauty and barber shops that I went into in the city of Chicago and ya'll showed me love thanks. And if I forgot some people please forgive me. My minds is messed up and plus I'm on cp time this is late sorry.

To my publicist Nakea Murray of the Literary Consultant Group thanks for believing in me and my project. You're the best agent there is and plus your funny lol. Thanks for words of wisdom and encouragement and always looking out for me. Dashawn (The Ultimate Hustler) nice meeting you stay grinding. Erick Gray love your book nice kicking it with ya and joking with ya. Treasure it was a pleasure to meet you and I took something back to the Chi with me. *Put the book in there face* it's been working. And Kwan you know you were supposed to come out and hang with us maybe next time stay grinding.

Everybody that worked on this project, Keith at Marion Designs, Todd thanks for the edit, Shawna and Nakea.

Well that's all I can think of right now I been up no sleep and can't think anymore. Thanks again to all my readers and I hope you all love it. The second book is really the hardest one to deliver everybody's watching now.

Oh I couldn't get out of here without thanking the most important people that keep me focus and on my grind. *Big ups to all my hater's* they know who they are.

Much Love
Nichelle

*This book is dedicated
to all the girls around the world,
please get an education and chase after your dreams
not a man!!!*

Girls do Rock!!!!

www.girlsdorock.org

At first she was Doing His Time
May 2007

Chapter 32
FINAL DETERMINATION

When I woke up this morning, I wasn't even scared; I was happy. I had fucked that bitch's face up real good. Roxy said she looked like Chucky when she left. I wished I coulda seen the look on Dollar's face when he seen his trick-ass baby momma. I bet he leave her ass alone quicker than he came and got her.

The closer I got to the courtroom, the more my stomach began to turn. I was scared now. What if he say we had to stay up in here? When I walked in, Ms. Peaches was sitting in the front row, which made me feel much better. I prayed to God and asked him to let me up outta here.

When the judge entered the courtroom, things became more serious. I knew this was it. The judge asked me and Angel to stand. "Emerald Jones, what can you tell me that you learned from this experience?" he asked.

I looked at my lawyer. We hadn't rehearsed anything to say. I wanted to say that the only thing I'd learned was to always put money over niggas, but instead I answered, "I learned not to trust people. I learned that a good education will take you anywhere you want to go. And I also learned to depend on myself and to take responsibility for my actions."

"Good, Ms. Jones. What about you, Ms. Davis?"

"I learned the same things too," Angel said. "And during my time in here, I completed my GED. If you release me, I going to school to be a chef."

"Ladies, I took into account all the evidence that was submitted to me. And in my reviewing, I do find that certain acts that you were convicted of were beyond your control. Since the state's attorney agreed to the appeal terms, my ruling today will overturn your sentences. Both of you will have time served thirty days from today. Thank you."

I didn't understand what he meant by time served or thirty days. I turned to my lawyer, who had a big smile on his face. "What does he mean?"

"He means that in thirty days you two will be free to go."

I looked at Angel and gave her a big hug. I'd be a free woman in thirty days! I looked at Ms. Peaches and smiled. "You gone be out there waiting?"

"Of course, bitch!" Ms. Peaches said.

When we went back to my cell, Angel didn't look as happy as me. "What's your problem?" I asked her.

"I don't have nowhere to go."

"You mean when you get out?"

"Yeah," she said. "I left my family for Dollar."

"Well, you can come stay with me," I told her.

"Can I?"

"Yeah, but before you make your choice, you see what I do to hos who cross me."

"How did we fall for Dollar so hard?" Angel asked.

"Good dick, money, clothes, cars, trips…I could go on."

"Yeah, that nigga got good game. I feel sorry for the next dumb bitch he get with."

"Don't be," I said. "I'ma fix his ass. He'll pay."

Angel just laughed and went back to her cell.

I don't mind having Angel with me; she's a hot bitch. And when I step outta here, the new me steps in. I need a hot bitch on my team because I'm getting money when I get outta here. I'm getting revenge and money, and everything else can fall back. Shit, Emerald is dead and Shiesty is born. Emerald was a good bitch; Shiesty's going to be a paid whore.

I thought about all the money I made for Dollar and realized I was bringing him a half-million dollars every week. That was two million dollars a month and I didn't see one red cent of it. Never again. I ain't falling in love with a nigga next time around; I'm taking two to three dicks at a time. I'ma fuck who I want, how I want, and when I want. And dem niggas gotta pay me too. The last time I checked before I went to jail, Summer's Eve cost $3.49 a bottle, and I ain't douching my shit for the next nigga to bust a free nut.

Dollar ruined the good girl in me, and now I'm all about making a dollar. In one month, Shiesty is gone seek revenge on four ruthless motherfuckers: Sissy, Dollar, Ginger, and Ms. Price. They gone pay for what they did to me.

From all the bullshit I went through, I learned a few valuable lessons:

1. Never trust a nigga farther than you can throw him!

2. Sometimes blood ain't thicker than water. I came in this world by myself, and I'ma die by myself.

3. Payback's a bitch.

4. One rule every bitch in America should live by: always put **Money Over Niggas!**

Stay tuned, because in thirty days I'll be free and it's going to be the big payback. And I don't give a fuck about getting them back neither. They already know that when you live by the sword you die by the sword. Karma's a bitch: I learned that the hard way and so will they. When I step outta prison on August 01, 2007, I'ma have a new outlook on life. I'ma do whatever I want and live and die by my new rule in life: **Fuck niggas, get money!** I'll always and forever put *Money Over Niggas*.

Peace,
Emerald ;)

Stay tuned for the sequel

Now she's just Shiesty!!!
July 2008

Revenge is a dish best served at the right time!

Niggas ain't shit but hos and tricks! "Fuck 'em," I say. The only thing a nigga can do for me is lick the crack of my ass and keep it moving. You hos better wake up and stop being in love by yourselves. These niggas only use you when you let 'em. They only play you when you let 'em. You getting sprung off the dick. You bitches better start reversing that shit! Don't let dem niggas dick-whip you—you pussy-whip dem niggas! The truth of the matter is, niggas hate a good woman and love the shit outta a ho. I'ma treat these cake-ass niggas just how they wanna be treated—like shit. And live by my new motto in life: *"Fuck You, Nigga, Pay Me!"* You bitches better step into the light and start seeing the truth about these niggas. They ain't looking for love. They looking for a good time. And if they run across me, they gots to pay me for mine! ***Break Bread, Bitches!***

SHIESTY

Money Over Men

PROLOGUE

June 29, 2008
7:00 PM

I PUT ANOTHER "X" on my LL Cool J calendar to mark another day I made it in this joint. *Only four more days in dis hellhole and I'm outta here.* It seemed like this last week took forever to pass by. I was going insane in there. Every time I closed my eyes, I pictured myself getting fucked by a nice, long, fat dick. "Damn, I'm horny!" I yelled to myself. I needed some dick fast. They were smart not to put male police officers in this joint, cause I woulda jumped on somebody's dick by now.

I lay back in my bed and stared at the poster of 50 Cent I hung on my wall. I was so hot and bothered that my pussy was flaming hot. Tonight was movie night and *Get Rich or Die Trying* was showing. Watching 50 Cent bite ol' girl's ass sent me into a daze. I wished that was me having my ass bit. I needed that shit; I needed it bad! I lay back in my bed and pushed my legs back. I needed to bust a nut, and frankly, I was tired of beating my own shit. If it wasn't for my posters of LL Cool J and 50 Cent, I'd have been stone crazy by now. Just looking at their bodies turned me on.

I pulled my panties to the side and started rubbing my clit slowly. I closed my eyes and imagined that one of them was fucking me, getting me right. I played with myself until I busted all over my fingers. My fingers were no longer doing the job for me. I needed to get out fast. I needed to feel a nice, long, fat dick in between my legs ASAP!

I was so anxious to get out in a couple of days so I could live my life again. Prison was no place for a boss bitch like me, and I would never wind up back here either. *Fuck love and a nigga. Niggas ain't shit. I'ma make dem cake niggas lick the pearl tongue and keep it moving. I'm glad Dollar showed me at a young age that a nigga ain't about shit. Now I know. I learned my lesson the hard way, but it's better to know now than to find out later. Fuck these nothin' ass niggas— I'ma treat they ass just like they wanna be treated. I'ma get they ass gone in the head, take they bread, and dash. I'll never slip again in my life. Fuck love! All I'm looking for is the big dicks! I'm walking through life wit my eyes wide open; I'm puttin' Money Over Niggas—fuck everything else.*

CHAPTER 1
FAMILY REUNION

July 1, 2008
6:00 AM

I WOKE UP in a cold sweat again. I kept having the weirdest dream about getting out of jail and Dollar killing me. I don't know why I kept having this dream, but every time I closed my eyes it was the same dream. I could just have been tweaking right about then. Our thirty-day sentence ended up being a year of time served. I had to celebrate my twentieth birthday in jail, and I wouldn't be able to party for my twenty-first birthday because I had to be low-key. I thought I was having some type of break-down. I felt like the four walls were closing in on me. *I don't think there is any other place worse than jail, not even the army.*

I always ran a mile and worked out in the morning to clear my mind. After my run, I took the long way to the Cook County Jail's so-called workout room. Just looking at the place made me sick. *Who in their right mind would want to be in and out of jail?* Roxy was pumping iron as usual. She swore she was a dude. All she needed was a sex change. She had bitches for days on her jock trying to be her bitch.

"Hey, cutie," Roxy said to me, rubbing the side of my face.

"Would you stop it? I don't wanna beat none of yo' bitches down today." Them bitches be fighting over Roxy like she's a nigga. I heard her tongue game was mean, but damn, they be busting each other's heads over her.

"Please, Emerald, they know better than that! You look like something's bothering you. What's on your mind?"

Them bitches was on Roxy's dick hard, but they all knew I had the juice around here. A bitch knew she'd get fucked up trying to test my gangster. I always slapped a bitch first and asked questions later.

"I had that dream again," I told her. Roxy was the only person I told about my bad dreams. I took a seat and started doing my sit-ups.

"I told you, Emerald. It's a sign from God telling you to move on with your life."

"Please don't start that shit with me today. I'm not even in the mood."

"Emerald, I'm just trying to talk some sense into you. You have a lot going on for yourself outside these four walls. You have a lot to lose. Why risk it on trying to make somebody suffer?"

Roxy got on my fucking nerves. She was such a hypocrite. I'd seen her beat a bitch head down to the white meat over her money. So how dare she tell me about my life? People always do that—tell you about your shit while they look at their shit differently.

"Roxy, spare me, okay?" I said. "It's the same reason why you beat a bitch down for coming up short with your money. It's the principle of things."

"To be perfectly honest with you, I don't have shit to lose. This is my life," Roxy said. "But you have a business to run. If you get locked back up, then what? You think you gone feel better once you hurt Sissy and Dollar?

"Bitch, hell yeah! I will be very satisfied!" I answered.

"Emerald Jones!" Officer Daniels yelled loudly, which surprised me, cause she knew I didn't like her ass.

"What you calling my name for?" I said, rolling my eyes at her.

"You have a visitor, bitch."

I looked at her and had to catch myself because I almost slapped her down for disrespecting me.

I followed her to the meeting room. When I entered, a tall brown-skinned older gentleman was seated waiting for me. His orange jumpsuit told me that he was an inmate like me. My first mind told me I knew him. He looked so familiar to me. I got a bad vibe from him; he looked at me and smiled too hard.

"What do you want with me?" I asked him as he stared me up and down.

"You're so beautiful, just like your mom," he said.

I took a good look at him. His slightly bumpy caramel skin and his gray eyes looked all too familiar. When he stood up his six-foot frame towered over me like a shadow. He reached out and rubbed his smooth hands across my face.

"Who the fuck are you?" I yelled as I moved back away from him. *He had a lot of nerve rubbing me and he doesn't know me like that.*

He smiled and laughed. "Just like Ruby," he said to me.

When he said my mom's name, my body started shaking and my heart was racing. I'd thought about this day since I was a little girl. What would I say or do? I'd prayed many nights that this day would come.

"Emerald Makay Jones, I've waited eighteen years to hug you."

I tried to hold back my tears and be strong, pretending not to care that I was face to face with my father. Here I stood, twenty years old, and I was finally looking at the one man I hated the most. He looked just like I last remembered him. His long arms embraced me and I could smell the Curve cologne he was wearing. He kissed me on the forehead like he did when I was a little girl. I felt like I was three again, back in his arms. Even though I hated my dad, I did miss him.

A sudden anger boiled through my blood when I thought about my mom. I pulled away from him.

"What do you want?" I said, walking away from him.

My dad looked at me. "It's me, baby girl. I'm your daddy."

"Correction: you're a sperm donor. I haven't seen you in years. So what do you want now?"

"I deserve that," he said as he took a seat, looking at me like a lost puppy.

As bad as I wanted to sit in his lap to cry about how much I missed and needed him, I couldn't. I wasn't gonna let any nigga come in my life and break me down again. *To me, he is just a man. I don't have a father.*

"Look, Emerald, when I found out you was in here, I cried for three days. I never thought that my Apple would be in jail."

"Don't call me that. How may I help you?"

"Emerald, I want to talk to you. I heard about what happened with you and your sister, and I know how you feel. I know you're getting out in a couple of days and I wanted to have a talk with you."

"About what? I don't need you to play daddy now." I was curious to know how he heard about me and Sissy. *I guess the streets do talk.*

"I know how you feel right now."

"You don't know shit! Don't try to come in here acting like you know me. You don't know shit about me."

"I'm your father, Emerald. I know you have a clothing store. I knew you were running drugs. I knew you dropped out of school. I knew about that nigga you was dealing with. I was praying that you wouldn't wind up in here, but when I found out a week ago, I had to come and see you."

I looked at him. *Who the fuck do he think he is, Ms. Cleo?* "Is there a reason you telling me this? Cause I was working out, and I don't have time to waste listening to you talk about nothing. So if you got a point, make it."

"You're full of mouth, just like me. You look just like your mother. I

7

really miss my Bella."

I became furious when he said that. I jumped into his face and muffed him. "Don't talk about my momma! You killed her. I know the truth, you *killed* her!" I yelled.

He hung his head low with shame. He took out a pack of cigarettes and lit up one. He stared deep into my gray eyes as he took one long pull of his cigarette, then exhaled a puff of smoke. "Is that what your grandmother told you?" he asked me as his voice cracked.

"No, but I ain't stupid. That's why you in here. So excuse me if I don't want to be your friend. You took everything away from me. You left me to fend for myself and Sissy. How could you do something like that?"

"Sit down, Emerald," he said.

"You don't tell me what to do."

"I understand. I know you. You're just like me. I met your mother when she was sixteen. She was the hottest girl on the block. I swear you look just like her. I fell in love with her. She was my everything. I was a street runner, but I made sure your mother had whatever she wanted. When you was born, I called you 'Apple' the very first time I held you because I had so much joy. Your mom never understood me needing to be in the streets and gone all the time. Then your sister came. It was perfect at first, but your mom wanted me to quit running the streets and go legit. I never saw it her way. I saw money, and I was making lots of it. Greed is what it's called. The more she cried for me to quit, the more I stayed out the house. I gave her a life of gifts, clothes, jewels, and money. But all she ever wanted was me and my time. Couldn't nobody tell me nothing…not my momma, my friends, nobody."

My dad stood up with his back turned to me so I wouldn't see the tears streaming down his face. "I was getting money, and that's all that mattered. I would sell to anybody that was buying. I didn't give a fuck. I didn't care if it was my momma. If she had her dime, I was selling her a pack. My brother was on my team, but he started smoking rocks, so I told him he couldn't get high for free. I started selling to him just like I didn't know him. I was in the streets so much I never noticed your momma losing weight."

He hung his head low and covered his eyes. I didn't know what to say to my dad at this point. "Listen, I'm not for sure where you're going with this talk," I advised him, cause I wanted him to get to the point.

"My brother started hanging around your mother. Once I found out he had her so strung out, it was too late to save her. I put her in rehab, but

I didn't think it was a big enough problem to stop selling drugs. When I looked back on it, I never knew what I was aiming for. Shit, I had made millions of dollars. You see, the problem with a lot of us is we don't know when we already won. So you out there fighting and fighting a battle that you already won. I put the streets before you, your mother, and our life. Once Bella came home, she went right back into her old ways. One day my brother came asking me for a hit and he'd pay me back. Nobody got a free hit from me, so I told him to take his five dollars and get the fuck on. Well, I decided to go home early that day. I saw my brother's car in the driveway. When I made it upstairs to the bedroom, I saw your mother laid across the bed with a needle stuck in her arm and my brother getting ready to leave."

My dad closed his eyes as tears started to pour down his face harder. I wanted to hold him at that point, but I couldn't. My feet wouldn't let me move.

"At that very point, I didn't think twice. I didn't think about you girls. I didn't think about what was gonna happen if I blew his head off. I was angry and I wanted him to hurt. You see, Emerald, the thing about revenge is that it only feels good for the moment. When I pulled out my nine and cocked it back, I made my brother fall to his knees. He tried explaining to me that it was an accident and that he tried to mix some drugs because I wouldn't sell him none. I wasn't trying to hear shit he had to say! He had to pay. He hurt me and my family. He took my everything from me…my wife. When somebody hurts you, you don't think clear; you want to get payback, and that's what I did. I shot him five times in the head. After the first bullet went through his head, I felt good. By the last shot, I felt terrible. What about my moms? What about my girls? I didn't think. I just reacted. I ruined my life and you girls' life in a blink of an eye, not thinking straight. When the police got there I got arrested for manslaughter. Your grandmother said I killed your mother because I was pumping poison into the streets. I sold my brother drugs and I was never home. In a way, she was right. I killed her. Even though my brother killed your momma, I helped him. I had to live with it for the last eighteen years. I have to live with that regret for the rest of my life. I think about it every day. What if I didn't kill my brother? What if I would have let him pay by calling the police?"

My heart sank. Big Momma had never told me about Momma being a crackhead, or that she was killed by an overdose. *All these years I thought my dad murdered my momma. How could Big Momma do such a thing?* "Well, I thought all these years that you killed my momma," I said. "Why didn't you ever write to us?"

"Emerald, I wrote to you guys every week and I sent money too," he said. "Big Momma always sent the money back. I always thought she gave you girls the letters, but that you guys just didn't want to see me. I tried to do the right thing by you girls, even though I wasn't out. But I understood she was hurting for her daughter and she didn't want the money. Your mother's culture was much different, with her being Filipino. Big Momma wanted her to marry her own kind, not me."

I was so angry with Big Momma. *How dare she ruin the chances of us having a father around?* "Well, I don't know what all this is supposed to mean. And why you telling me this now?"

"I just want you to think about your actions before you make your moves, Emerald. You're just like me. No matter how many times I tell you something, you're not going to listen and you're going to do what you want to do."

I know that's right. He can't tell me nothing. I'm grown as hell up in here. "Think about what?"

"All I'm saying is that I know you're hurting right now and I've been there. I lost everything for making a dumb decision. I just want you to think about what you have to lose. You're very beautiful, Emerald, just like your mother. You have my ways, and little do you know, Sissy does too."

"Fuck Sissy!" I yelled. "Don't mention that bitch's name to me." My blood started boiling when he said that shit. *I hate that bitch and she's gonna get hers.*

"I understand you," my dad said. "All I can say is, a lion studies his prey. He moves swiftly. He finds their weakness and picks up on it, and when they least expect it, he attacks. Now, a dog, he reacts when you walk past him. He barks and jumps around. He reacts without thinking. He thinks he can take anybody he sees. You know what I mean, Emerald? You can either be a lion or a dog."

I didn't have time to sit here and listen to this bullshit. I didn't need him coming up in here trying to run my show. I knew what the hell I was doing. I didn't need no help from this nigga. "Look, Otis, it's a little too late for a father-daughter talk. I know what I'm doing and I know you're just trying to protect Sissy. It's too late for her. She crossed me…locked me up in here to die. I paid outta my pocket for her to go to school. I kept her laced and with money. Sissy ain't my sister no longer. When she turned her back on me, I became an only child."

My father rubbed the sides of his smooth face with both his hands. He looked up at me with his gray eyes. He didn't speak, he just stared at me.

Finally he said, "Emerald, when I heard you was wrapped up into that nigga, I put the word out on the streets. But shit, things are different from when I grew up. When I grew up we had respect, loyalty, we cherished what the old Gs started. But these new niggas don't give a fuck. They have no respect. Shit, they look at you right in the eye and blow your fucking head off. I couldn't do nothing sitting here in jail. And besides, I know you got my blood pumping through your veins, so I knew you wouldn't listen to me. I'm goin' leave you with this, Apple: you can make a person pay way more by suffering. Killing people gives them the easy way out. Every day I've suffered, and my brother got the easy way out. I never knew why he did what he did at that point. It didn't matter. I wish I would have been a little smarter, a little swifter. I wish I would have planned my moves like a lion instead of reacting like a dog. Dogs get killed and lions dominate. Remember that, baby girl."

When my daddy stood up, his body was rock solid. My dad was very handsome. *His gray eyes are definitely getting him mad pussy from the guards. I know how they do in here.* "Wait," I said. "Do you need anything, money or something?"

"I'm cool, Apple." My dad walked up to me and pulled me close to his solid two-hundred-pound frame. He kissed me on my cheeks and whispered in my ear, "When it comes to money, I'm a lion. I'm good." He gave me a final kiss on my forehead. I felt like I was a little girl again. "I'll be getting out soon. I'll keep in touch with you."

"Wait, are you here in this jail?" I asked.

"Nope, I'm in the fed joint out in Wisconsin."

"Well, how can I get in touch with you?"

"I'll be out soon. I'll find you," he said.

"Well, you can find Big Momma and she'll find me."

"I will, Apple. I'll be home sooner than you think."

When they took my dad away, a part of me was relieved. I had needed to see him and talk to him after all this time. I made it back to my cell and thought long and hard about what he said…lion, dog, or walk away. *I'm confused about the whole situation, but the one thing I know for sure is that I ain't letting go. They're going to get what's coming to them.*

CHAPTER 2
LAST CHANCE

I HAD ONE more day until I was a free woman, and I couldn't wait. I had seen my dad one last time before they took him back to the feds. We had a long deep conversation. I wished I could remember my mother more. After speaking with my dad, I felt like letting go of what Sissy did to me and just moving on with my life. I'd been in jail for one year, two weeks, and three days. I was ready to get out and live my life.

I needed to make some phone calls, but not from the prison phone. I wanted to talk to Sissy again to see if she was sorry for what she did to me. It had been a while since I spoke to Sissy or Dollar. They both stopped taking my calls a long time ago.

The only way to get an outside line was through Linda. I needed her to let me use her cell phone. Her ass be acting scary sometimes. I knew how to loosen her ass up. When I licked that pussy good, she tended to see things my way.

"Linda!" I yelled. She came right away. She knew better than to have me waiting on her ass.

"What's up, Emmy?"

"Bitch, what I tell you about calling me that shit?"

"My bad."

This bitch keep stepping outta line wit me, she goin' see how strong my pimp hand is. "I need to see your cell phone."

"I'ma get fired."

"Bitch, relax," I said as I ran my hand across her pussy. "Mommy gonna take care of you."

"When?"

"When you think it's gonna be all good?"

"Tonight at movie time. I'll get you," she said.

"Cool."

One thing that can't be denied from bitches or niggas is *boss head,* and I was a motherfucking boss! I needed to talk to Sissy. The last time I'd called her, she was talking real greasy. I wanted to see how she really felt about this. I wanted to know why she'd stabbed me in my back like this.

Linda came and got me just seconds before they put the movie on. I knew her pussy was wet thinking about this mean head she fin to get. I straight played dis dumb bitch like a violin. She was always dancing to my tune.

"You ready?" she whispered.

I just shot a look at her ass. *Dumb hos really work my last nerve.* "What you think?"

I followed her to the same bathroom where we always went for her to get right. I knew I had to lick her before she let me use the phone, cause she be getting scary. *Once I relax that ass, she goin' be straight.* I pushed her against the wall and kissed her on her neck. I never kissed that bitch in the mouth. She was already sprung off the tongue; I ain't want the bitch thinking I loved her ass.

Once she got her pants off, I ran my hand over her pussy and it was wet as hell. *Boy, I'm a bad bitch. I get the bitch's pussy wet and the nigga's dick hard.* I fell to my knees, picked up one of her legs, and threw it over my shoulder. I buried my face into her pussy, licking her in all the right spots. *That's the key to licking pussy—you gotta lick all the right spots.*

I was licking that bitch so good, she was moaning too loud. "Be quiet, bitch!" I said. I didn't want nobody finding me in here with her ass. I wasn't ruining my chances for getting outta this joint. I knew I needed to hurry up and make her come so she could shut her fucking mouth. I stuck my finger up in her, reaching her G-spot. I fucked her with my finger and licked her clit. She was gone in 60 seconds.

She fell back to catch her breath. She was shaking like a crackhead. I know I whipped this tongue game on her ass. "Bitch, give me the phone," I said, and she handed me the phone. I dialed Sissy's number. I called private, hoping she would answer.

"Hello," Sissy answered.

"Hey, Sis, what's good?"

"Who dis?"

"Damn, you don't remember your sister no more?" I asked.

"Emerald, what the fuck do you want?"

"Thought I'd call you to see what's new and wait for your apology."

"Apology? Bitch, please!" Sissy said. "Whoever you had three-way me bet' not dial my fucking number no more."

"Or what? What you gonna do?"

"Emerald, please get a life! Ain't you playing cards or making some license plates or something?"

13

"Why would you do me like this?"

"Look, Emerald, that's why it's always wise to at least finish high school. Stupid people do stupid things. It ain't my fault—charge it to the game!"

"Charge it to the game?" *This bitch talking real gangster, knowing she can't bust a grape.*

"Bitch, I ain't got time for yo' games. Tricks are for kids," she said.

She had a lot of fucking nerve telling me tricks are for kids. *Bitch, you just got outta your pull-ups.* "Sissy, so it's like that? You let dis nigga lock me in here for ten years?"

"Bitch, you locked yourself up in there," she said. "I ain't have shit to do with it."

"So, water thicker than blood now?"

"Money is."

"Bitch, you ain't goin' never be me, no matter how hard you try," I said.

"Ain't nobody trying to be you! You a dumb dyke bitch. Me, I'm a smart paper chaser. Just face the fact that I'm the new baddest bitch now."

"Well, I hope you can hold that crown down, bitch. I'll see you when I see you."

"Bitch, enjoy prison! I'm pretty sure you licking mad hos in there, dyke-ass bitch! Fuck yo' dumb ass. That's why you doing Dollar's time. I'm out chillin', riding his big-ass dick." Sissy slammed the phone down in my ear.

I turned red. *I'ma wring her fucking neck when I get out. Emerald would be in tears by now, hurting because her sister turned her back on her. But Shiesty goin' slap that bitch with a backhand when I see her. I'ma get that wanna-be-me ho real good when I get outta here.*

My last phone call was to my ex-flame. He picked up on the first ring. "Who dis?"

"It's your long-lost love."

"Who?"

"You done erased a bitch that damn fast? You can't remember my voice?"

"Emerald?"

"Yeah, nigga, it's me," I said. "Long time no see, nigga."

"What you want?"

"So you living real hood rich right now? You played me, Dollar, after all I done for you."

"Save me the drama, Emerald. It's just business."

"Business?" I yelled. *Dis nigga done got me locked up and telling me it's just business?* "And Sissy?"

"What about her?"

"Is she just business too?"

"Sissy ain't your concern, Emerald," Dollar said.

"I don't give a fuck! She ain't goin' never be able to fuck you like me, nigga."

"I'ma train her, like I trained you."

"Nigga, you ain't train shit!" I said. "Dick-sucking came quite naturally to me."

"Well, I guess you just licking pussy now!" He laughed.

"Real funny. We'll see who gets the last laugh, nigga."

"Whatever," he said. "Don't call me back. Enjoy your time, baby girl. Maybe when you get out I'll let you ride the magic stick for old times' sake."

"Laugh now, nigga. I'll see you when I see you!" I yelled and hung up.

I was so pissed. *Just business, ha! I'ma show him just business.* I handed my bitch back her phone and told her ass to get outta my face. I ain't want to look at no-fucking-body, especially not her ugly ass.

I lay down in my cell thinking about how I'd get they ass back…how I'd make them pay for what they did to me. *All bets are off. I'm fucking people up when I get outta here. They can laugh now, but they'll pay later. Laugh on, motherfuckers, because Shiesty coming home and revenge is gonna be mine.*

(HAPTER 3
FREE AT LAST

July 4, 2008
12:00 PM

WHEN LINDA CAME to get me and Angel, I took one last look at my cell. I didn't want to see the inside of another cell ever again. I gave Roxy a hug and a goodbye kiss. I was gonna miss her.

"I'ma still come and see you, Roxy," I told her.

"Don't bother, girl," she said. "I'm getting out in a little while. You just make sure you take care of you and that body on the outside, because I'm coming to get y'all when I get out."

I busted out laughing cause I knew she was telling the truth. Roxy had been wanting a piece of my pussy for the longest. "You too stupid, Roxy. I will. If you need some money or anything, just holler at me and you know I got you." I gave her one last hug. I felt like I was leaving behind the only person I could talk to.

"Girl, don't be looking all sad. I thought you was a gangster? I'ma be cool. These bitches know who running this shit. You just make sure you hook up with my homey Slim. He can help you, cause I don't want you back in here."

"I will."

I turned and took one last look at my past, a place where I would never end up again. I walked down the long narrow gray hallway and took in a deep breath, smelling the cold damp funk that ran through the place.

I collected my items that I'd come in with and realized I had forgotten what brand-name stuff felt like. I pulled up my True Religion jeans that hugged me in all the right places. I put on a wifebeater that I'd purchased from commissary; it was too damn hot for the sweater I got booked in. My Gucci hobo bag felt so good under my arms. The smell of that fine leather filled my nose. Once I threw on my Gucci shades, I was ready to reclaim my crown as the **baddest bitch.**

I took one last look at Officer Linda. *I'm glad I'm leaving her ass. I'm tired of licking up in her stale coochie. She's Xed off my list. I don't need her ass anymore.* I threw her the peace sign and gave her my beat-it-bitch look.

"Emerald," she called to me.

"Yes."

"Can I come by and see you?"

"Hell no," I quickly replied as I stepped out into the hot Chicago air.

Peaches was waiting outside in a convertible CLK 550 Cabriolet Benz. I told Angel she'd better haul ass or she was going to be riding on the CTA. Shit, time waits for no one and I'd been locked in this joint for one year, two weeks, and six days.

The sunlight hurt my eyes. Inside the jail, it had been much darker. It was hot and humid outside; the air was stuffy, but it smelled so fresh. The wind hitting my face gave me chills. *I'm a free bitch now and I'm keeping it that way.* The sun beaming on my light-neglected skin showed how ashy I was. I smelled dick in the air and I couldn't wait to jump on one.

"What's up, bitches?" Ms. Peaches yelled.

"Shit," I said as I climbed into the car.

When we pulled away from the jail, my stomach turned. *That's one place I never want to go back to. People take for granted being able to go to the corner store when they want to. If I didn't learn one thing in there, I learned that there ain't nothing like being free. Shit, fuck the bullshit, I'm living my life and I'ma ride this motherfucker until the wheels fall off.*

"I guess you bitches have to come to my place for now," Ms. Peaches said.

"Of course. I need to get myself in order and go and see John," I said.

"I told him you'll be to see him."

"Good." I needed to go and purchase me a new ride. They had seized the cars Dollar bought me. I needed to get my hair done, visit the spa, and go and hurt the mall. I had to be careful about my whereabouts because nobody knew I was home, and that was the way I wanted to keep it.

Once we made it back to Ms. Peaches's house, he had two bags of clothes for me and Angel. Since I'd been locked in hell for a year, Ms. Peaches had to pick all of the summer styles. I was pretty pleased. The shit was hot to death. It couldn't have looked better if I picked the shit myself.

I pulled out some studded capris and a logo tank top, then went and ran me some bath water. I hadn't taken a bath in a whole year. I wanted to soak my body in my Carol's Daughter Peach Mango for at least an hour.

When I jumped into the tub, the hot water felt so good soaking against my skin. I lay back and tried to catch up on the latest tunes I'd been missing. *It feels great to be home, and it will feel even better once I get me some dick. Shit, it's been months since I got me some dick.*

The milk bath started to bring my dead skin back to life. My skin had been all fucked up using that cheap-ass soap. I rubbed my hand across my feet and noticed all the dead skin I had. *I gotta get that taken care of ASAP. Shit, I'm a bad bitch—my feet gots to be on point.*

I jumped out of the tub, dried off, and lotioned up my body. My skin was screaming for some A-list lotion. In the joint, all we had was some cheap-ass Jergens. I like to let myself air-dry, so I pulled my towel off me and walked around ass-naked. I went into Ms. Peaches's guest room and looked around. I needed to get my own pad quick—a condo in downtown Chicago.

I went in the kitchen where Angel and Ms. Peaches were talking shit. "What's so funny?" I asked.

"Nothing," Angel said as she stared at my body. My stomach was cut up harder than Beyoncé's and my ass was way fatter. My weekly work-outs helped me stay the top-notch bitch that I was.

Ms. Peaches's eyes stayed glued to me. Everywhere I moved, he was looking. I jiggled my ass into the kitchen and grabbed me a bite of cake. I brushed by Ms. Peaches and my hard nipples touched his back. I felt him shiver. I turned my back to him so he could peep out the total package I owned.

"This cake is good. Who made it?" I asked Ms. Peaches. His silence told me I had him speechless. I turned around and saw him turn away quickly. I walked over slowly and peeped his dick coming to life. *Now that's a bad, bad bitch when you can get them fun boys on rock.*

I looked at him and saw that he didn't want to look me in my face. "Peaches," I moaned, "it's okay. Can't nobody resist this pussy." *That's the truth. A bitch like me needs to be illegal, cause I get 'em up and can I get 'em down.* "Does Derrel want some of this pussy?"

He didn't say a word. I sized him up. His dick had to be at least ten inches. *I'll slap a condom on that big motherfucker and bounce on it. I don't be fucking for free no more, but since he did come through for me and hold me down, I think I owe him one. But just one free fuck. He still getting paid. Ain't no nigga pimping me twice.*

"Look, closed mouths don't get fed around here. Do you want some pussy or not?" *Shit, he needs to tell me something. I ain't got time to sit around and babysit his dick. Either he wants to feel this juicy pussy or not.*

18

"No, I can't do that," he said in his deep-toned voice. Shit, Ms. Peaches was out the door. He was Derrel now and he wanted a piece of this pussy. I could read his mind.

"I'll break you off," I said. "I might turn that ass back straight. I don't mind doing the Lord's work."

He just looked at me. I knew his dick was throbbing. I grabbed it, ran my hands over it, and told him to go get a condom and I'd hook him up. Shit, I wanted to feel them ten inches in me.

But he pulled away, and frankly, I had to go. I ain't got time for no crackhead games. I had a meeting with John. I needed to go and get me a Range Rover. *I know who will be getting fucked real good tonight. I'ma fuck John so good he goin' want to ice a bitch.*

I went into my room, got dressed, and made up my face. Then I made my way into the front, where I gave my orders to my new bitch. "Angel, have yo' pussy ready for tonight. We rolling over to John's house."

"Cool."

"And shave your pussy hair. It's Nair in the bathroom."

She knew to do as I said. *Tonight I'm getting fucked like never before. I hope Johnny-boy can keep that dick up, cause it's time to double up tonight.*

CHAPTER 4
JOHN

I MADE MY way into the bank. My appointment was set, and I'm not one who likes to wait. I went in and John was there waiting on me, looking extra-fuckable.

"Emerald," he said as he kissed me on my cheek.

John don't know nothing about my gangster; I'll fuck him right here. My pussy was extra-hot looking at his pretty brown eyes and dark hair.

"Hey, John, how are you?" I asked.

"Much better now that you're home."

"Good. I wouldn't mind staying here and shooting the shit with you, but I know you're busy and so am I. What do I need to control my money again?"

"Nothing, it's all handled," he said as he handed me a checkbook, a debit card, and a black American Express card. "Be careful with that black card, it's dangerous."

"Thanks so much, John, I owe you big." I owed John my life. If it weren't for him, I'd still be sitting in jail. While I was away, he maintained the stores, making sound business decisions and investing my money. John was a catch: smart, fine, and a gentleman. He'd be a perfect husband, if he only knew how to stroke the pussy right. *I hope he got in some practice while I was away, because I need my back caved in tonight.*

"No problem, Emerald. Right now your net worth is $1.5 million in assets and $1.3 in stock. The stores have been franchising very well—two more in Michigan."

"So how many stores do I have?"

"Nine," he said. "Isn't that great?"

"Yeah, that's hot." *Damn right, that's hot! I'm a rich bitch!*

"Stay outta trouble, Emerald."

"I am," I said as I walked over to his side of the desk and ran my fingers up his hand. I reached in and kissed him gently on his lips, then whispered in his ear, "I'ma show you tonight how much I thank you. Be ready for this pussy at seven."

He smiled and grabbed his collar. *Oh yeah, it's getting hot in here and it's gonna be flaming tonight.*

I grabbed my things and headed over to the Range Rover lot. *I need to floss like the rich bitch that I am.* I stepped into the lot and spotted a black-on-black Range, fully loaded, sitting on twenty-inch rims.

When I walked in, a tall, handsome black salesman approached me. "May I help you, ma'am?"

"Yes. I want that black Range that's out there."

"That's a seventy-thousand-dollar truck," he said.

"Excuse me," I snapped. *Dis nigga must got me confused. I can buy two or three of them.*

"No harm intended, ma'am. I just wanted to let you know."

I whipped out my black card. *This nigga must be sleepin' on me. You a fucking car salesman. Your pockets light compared to me. You lucky you getting commission off me, nigga.* "Just charge it."

His facial expression changed. "Ms. Jones, I'm sorry if I offended you."

"Nigga, just get me my damn car and fall back."

He ran off, got me the keys to the car, then he processed my paperwork. *I'ma be flossin' in this one. This is what I need. I need to be right back on top. That's where a bad bitch like me belongs!*

When the salesman finished kissing my ass good, I jumped into my new ride and took a spin. I stopped at a local Coconuts to repurchase some of my CDs that got left behind. When I found out all the Tower Records in the city of Chicago were closed, I was surprised and pissed. Where was I gonna get my Don Diva magazines from? I had to stay on top of my dick-sucking game.

When I entered Coconuts, I peeped this fine chocolate brother sizing me up. I got a weakness for chocolate brothers. I switched my big firm ass right by him to grab his attention.

"Excuse me, beautiful," he said as he flashed a smile at me.

I sized him up. He had some paper, and I was down for doing something strange for some change. "Hello."

"May I ask your name?"

"Sissy. What's yours?" My plan was to make Sissy seem like the biggest ho on the block.

"Mike. Can I get your number, ma?"

"Sure," I said as I wrote down my cell phone number. He took it and smiled. First thing tomorrow, I was going to get my hair done like Sissy. *I'ma be her twin. She fucked me and I'ma fuck her good.*

Angel was ready to go to John's house when I got there to pick her ass up. I freshened up, slipped into a bra and panties, and put on my trenchcoat and heels. I hadn't been fucked since Dollar stuck his nothing-ass dick in me and left me to die.

"So, what's the plan?" Angel asked.

"What you mean? We finna fuck the shit out of this nigga. And I hope you can throw yo' pussy good, cause I ain't got time to train hos."

"I can handle mines."

"You better." She was acting cocky, something like me. *I hope dis bitch ain't finna be biting my style. That will get her ass a one-way ticket the hell outta my life.*

We made it upstairs to John's condo. I rang the bell and unhooked my coat. He opened the door, and his eyes grew big when he saw me and Angel standing there in our panties and bras. "Wow, I wasn't expecting the both of you," he said.

"You can't handle it?" I moaned as I dropped my coat to the floor and Angel did the same. I walked over to John and pulled his shirt over his head. His body was cut up in all the right places. I ran my hand over his six-pack. It made my pussy tremble. I licked his fingers, sucking them one by one.

"You guys don't have to do this," John moaned. But that was his mouth talking. His dick grew bigger by the minute.

"Relax," I said as I rubbed my hand over his hard dick. Angel went to the back of John and I had the front. I unbuckled his pants with my teeth and pulled them down. John's dick was average, about seven inches. I prefer nine inches or better, but it would do.

We both licked him in slow soft strokes. His trembling body let me know he liked what we were doing to him. I licked down his legs into his inner thighs, and Angel licked from his ass cheeks down to the back of his thighs. His moaning told us both to give him more. I licked John's shaft slowly and teabagged his balls. As I shoved his dick in my mouth, Angel started to toss his salad.

John started to scream like a bitch. The more I sucked, the deeper Angel's tongue strokes went. He begged for mercy, but I wasn't taking no prisoners. *When I fuck a nigga, I give his ass a night to remember.* I was bobbing and weaving while Angel licked John's ass good.

"I can't take it!" he screamed.

I pulled off his dick and looked up at him. "You can't handle this?"

"No!" he screamed, but I didn't give a fuck. He was gonna have to take this pussy-whipping like a man.

"Sorry," I said as I shoved his dick down my throat. I could have swallowed him whole. John's dick was much smaller than what I was used to sucking, so it was easy for me to slurp his balls into my mouth.

I continued to suck all of him and Angel was still tossing his salad. He pulled the back of my hair and started screaming, "I'm coming, Emerald! Shit, baby, I'm coming!" He was getting rough with me, and that was turning me on. The more he pulled my hair, the harder and deeper I'd suck him. I liked that shit.

"Emerald, baby, yes, suck this shit, girl!" he screamed, and I sucked him even more. Sometimes I shock myself with how raw I am. After a few more strokes, I saw that he was at the point of no return. I pulled him out of my mouth and started jacking his dick off. His cum shot all over my lips—I know white men like that shit. I rubbed his dick and cum over my lips like lipstick and licked it all down.

John fell back and gasped for air, but he was just getting started for the night. I was fucking for at least two hours.

Angel went over and put John's dick in her mouth and started sucking on him again. Once she got his dick hard, she pushed him down to the floor and jumped on his dick. I didn't mind her bouncing on his dick first. She'd been without dick longer than me. Besides, I wanted to see how strong her fuck game was.

I watched her bounce on top of him for ten minutes. It was boring me, so I could imagine how he felt. *I'ma have to show her how a boss bitch throws her pussy.*

But first I needed my pussy licked from the front to the back. I went and sat down on top of John's face. He grabbed hold of my tiny waist, and I was riding his face like it was his dick. "Lick this shit, don't play games wit it," I commanded him.

He wasn't all that great; nobody could compare to that bitch Ginger. I pulled off of him because he wasn't doing nothing but spitting in my pussy.

"You didn't like it?" he asked me with concern.

"No," I said. "You suck." It was harsh, but I didn't stroke egos around here. His head game needed to be stepped up completely.

I looked at Angel, still riding his dick in the same position as when I

23

left her. She needed some serious help. I moved her out the way and slid down John's dick backwards. "Pay attention," I told Angel, "cause I don't train hos often."

I pushed my legs out to the side of me and bounced and rolled my hips every which way but right. I bounced, rolled, and sucked John's dick. I was trying to train the ho. You gotta bounce your ass, roll your hips, and suck the dick all in rhythm. John was screaming like a little bitch. I loved it. I knew my pussy piece a motherfucker!

I did an about-face on the dick and got that ass good from the front. I was feeling myself coming, so I started to grind my hips even more. "Shit!" I cried out. I hadn't had that feeling in almost eight months. I needed it.

Once I busted all over John's dick, I jumped off and let Angel get another turn. This time around, she did a much better job. I guess she wasn't scared no more.

I saw John's eyes on me, so I lay back and spread my legs apart. Niggas love to see bitches play with their pussies. I played with myself, rubbing my clit and sticking my fingers in and outta my pussy. John's eyes didn't move off me. He made Angel come and got up and came over my way, then turned me around and hit it hard from the back.

John fucked me and Angel in so many positions, I knew I was gonna be sore for at least a week. "Damn, Emerald, that was the best sex I ever had," he said with a smile. I looked at him and smiled. I couldn't say the same about him, because it would've been a flat-out lie.

"Yeah, I am a good lay, ain't I?" I giggled.

"Can you stay the night?"

"No, I have some things to do. Maybe I'll see you tomorrow."

I really wished I had somebody else to dip off with, because he didn't kill my pussy like I wanted him to. *I thought he would have stepped his game up by now. I ain't tripping; that only means he has to share me.*

CHAPTER 5
MY OWN PAD

I'D BEEN AT Ms. Peaches's place for three weeks, and I was ready to go. I mean, he didn't mind having me but I wanted my own shit—some fly shit dead in the middle of downtown. *Why should I be living with somebody like I'm broke?* I had plenty of money, and I needed my own space to do what the fuck I wanted to do.

I didn't know what I was gonna do with Angel. Some days I regretted getting her ass out. *I don't like bitches. I don't trust they ass as far as I can throw them. I mean, I know she not stupid enough to cross me; she seen firsthand how I treat bitches that cross me. But I ain't taking care of her ass, fuck that. If she come stay with me, she goin' have to lick my pussy or something. Shit, ain't nothing free in this world; she'll have to earn her keep some kind of way.*

I made my way to the Egyptian's to get my hair streaked blonde and cut into layers like Sissy's. Before I went to jail, I went to Mena's, who had shops all over the place. I got word that Sissy was going to him now, so I went to his shop out in Bolingbrook and got my hair done just like Sissy.

Me and Sissy are the same height, same weight, and same skin color. Everything about us is the same. That's why that bitch wanted to be me, cause I was living the glamorous life. Sissy thought she was so much smarter than me because she was in college, but street-smart and book-smart are two totally different things. Yeah, that bitch book-smart, but she didn't know shit about the streets. The mean streets of Chicago will eat you alive if you let them.

When I finished, I was looking off glass. *Shit, I get mad at my own damn self sometimes for looking this good.* I made my way over to Tip Top to get my feet did. I was well overdue. Getting my feet soaked felt great, but I wasn't letting the bitch put her razor to my feet. I heard that fucks up your feet even worse. She got most of my dead skin off, but I had to come back in two weeks. I got my feet designed, my French manicure done, and bounced.

I had a meeting with my real estate agent, Cindy, who wanted to show me a two-bedroom penthouse downtown. When I made it down to Loomis

Street, it amazed me how much they were building up down there.

The outside of the building was light washed brick. I was really digging the flow of the construction. I was definitely impressed, but one thing I didn't like already was there were no garages; I didn't want nobody scratching my fucking car up.

When I pulled into the underground parking lot, the spaces were pretty far from each other. They told me it was all heated and everybody had assigned parking. *If somebody hit my shit, I'll go to their door and beat the shit out of them.*

I met up with Cindy in the lobby. She was real perky all the damn time. I will never understand how somebody can be so happy all the time. That perky shit works my left nerve.

"Emerald!" she yelled. "I know you're gonna love this place! It's you, very high-class."

"Let's see," I said.

When she pressed the button for the thirtieth floor, I was a little excited. *Being on top of the world is where I need to be.* When the elevator opened, there were three doors. "It's only three penthouses on this floor," Cindy said as she opened one of the doors.

I entered the place and my mouth dropped. The deep oak floor that ran throughout the place was beautiful. The high vaulted ceilings were amazing. The place was me, and I was just in the living room, already wanting to buy it.

The oversized fireplace was almost as tall as me. The dining room was the perfect size. I went out onto the balcony, and the view was the best in the whole wide world. I could see all of downtown. When I came back inside, I went to the kitchen and admired all the Sub-Zero appliances. The marble countertop that graced the kitchen matched the floor. All the appliances were high-tech and top-of-the-line. My fridge had a TV on it. I wanted to run through the place and do backward flips, but of course I had to keep it pimping.

When I made it to the guest room, I was blown away. *This place makes me and Dollar's old crib look like we was staying in the projects.* The guest room had a bathroom and a huge walk-in closet. The foyer overlooked the family room, which was huge and had a fireplace. When I walked up the spiral staircase, there was another bathroom. The entire place had hardwood, which I loved, cause I hate carpet.

I opened the door to the master bedroom and felt like I was on MTV Cribs again. "Damn," I moaned as I looked around.

The master bedroom was bigger than Ms. Peaches's house. My bathroom was huge, like Ginger and S.L.'s. The Jacuzzi tub was big enough to fit six people. The bathroom had a shower that would fit at least ten people, and it also turned into a steam room. The view from the balcony was perfect. I saw the entire city.

It was perfect. This would be my palace. I walked through the place one last time, trying to take it all in. Getting this on my own gave me a sense of being. I felt so good knowing I didn't need nobody to get this for me.

"How much?" I asked.

"Six hundred and fifty," Cindy said.

"I want it."

I signed the papers and Cindy told me that it would take some weeks to close. I was so happy. I needed my own space. Ms. Peaches's place was cool and all, but ain't nothing like having your own.

CHAPTER 6
ANGEL

ANGEL TRIED HER best to befriend me but I wasn't having it. *Bitches ain't shit.* I told her that I would help her, and that's all. I already got her outta jail and let her run my store out in Bolingbrook, and I was paying her a nice salary. I ain't trying to be her friend. I didn't want any friends in my life. I didn't need nobody but me. Peaches was all the friend a girl could ever need, and I could do without him too if need be.

I was moving soon and I figured since Angel was working, she could get her own damn place. But of course, she ran me some bullshit about saving some money first. If she knew like I knew she had better get her pussy game together. I ain't letting her stay at my place long. I didn't even know her like that. In my eyes, I couldn't trust nobody.

"What you doing?" Angel came into Ms. Peaches's room and broke my train of thought.

"It looks like I'm packing, don't it?" *Damn, people ask the dumbest questions.*

"Emerald, I can't thank you enough for getting me out of jail and letting me work at your store. I could never repay you. I just want you to know that I want to be your friend. It's like you don't want to hang out with me or even talk to me. I'm not from here, so I really don't know my way around. I just want us to be friends, that's all."

"I mean, what?" I said. "I see you every damn day when I come in here. What more you want from me? I ain't looking to make no friends, Angel. Friends stab you in the back. Friends ain't shit! What you want to be, Thelma and Louise? Yeah, let's do that so we can tag-team some dicks. But the friendship thing is out the picture. I don't want one or never will need one."

Angel's face turned dark. *I don't give a fuck. I don't need her ass. She can bounce all I care. Friends will fuck your man, lie on you, and stab you in the back.* Shit, I didn't give a fuck about a bitch. Sissy crossed me—my own damn sister. Friends don't get no tighter than that. And if my own sister could do me in, I knew the next bitch would. The reality of it was, I was much prettier than her and I had shit going on for myself. Bitches are jealous. It's just a female trait.

Angel stood up and looked at me. "You know, Emerald, I had a best friend named Mary. We had been friends since the sandbox. When I met Dollar, I started to smell myself. I'm an only child so Mary was all I had. Everything moved so fast for me when Dollar came into my life. I stopped going to school. I rarely even came in the house. Dollar took me and up-graded me. I had everything—money, clothes, the hottest bags and jewels. Shit, I was the flyest bitch in the hood. Mary never once showed a sign of jealousy. She was concerned about me. She hated Dollar's guts. Of course, Dollar had me so dick-dumb that I believed she wanted him. I remember the last day I spoke to her. She got off the chain wit me. I slapped her so hard I know she seen stars. I was ready to kill her. She just wanted me to finish school. She never said leave him alone. All she said to me was, 'Don't let him take away what you worked so hard for.'"

Angel came in and sat on my bed like I really gave a fuck about what she was talking about. She continued, "Dollar had me hating her, feeling like she was trying to steal him. And I let him get into my head so tough that I fooled my own self. But when I looked back, she never did nothing to me. She was never around him. Sometimes people just want the best for you without wanting nothing in return."

"That's bullshit!" I yelled. Angel had been locked up a little too long. You can't get something for nothing. "This world was built off people pimping people. The whites pimped us and made us slaves. Please, girl, it's all about not letting nobody pimp you twice, cause we already got pimped once."

"So you never had nobody in your life tell you something just because they was looking out for you?"

"Hell no. That bitch-ass sister of mines was always in my ear. Oh Dollar this, Dollar that, and the bitch was all along sucking his dick."

"Well, I believe there are truly genuine people in the world. Look at John," she said.

"What about him? He making money off me. He getting paid to. You think he ain't getting his share?"

"He could have left you in jail, Emerald."

"First off, Angel, let me tell you this: John likes me. John knows I have really good pussy. John also knows I know how to make that paper, baby. I'm an investment to John. Now, do I think John likes me? Hell yeah! I fuck the shit out of him almost every other night, so I know he do. I'm not saying he's looking to do me in. All I'm saying is, he got his motives and reasoning for looking out for me. Everybody in this world does, including you."

"I'm not trying to get over on you, Emerald."

Angel was wearing thin on my nerves. If she knew what was best for her, she'd shut her fucking mouth while she was ahead. "Look, Angel, you don't know me and I don't know you. I ain't trying to make no friends wit you. Now I've been overly nice by getting you out of jail and letting you work in my store, and I'm letting you come stay with me for a month."

"You said I can stay there for four months," Angel replied.

"One month, four months, whatever. What I'm saying to you is that you and I ain't homegirls. And we will never be! I don't trust bitches and I don't trust you. I'm helping you out because I'm a woman of my word. I ain't no phony bitch. Now, if you want to get money together, that's fine. We can pull some threesomes and get some paper together. But being friends is out of the picture. *I will never have another friend.*"

Angel got up and walked out my room, looking at me all sad. I didn't care, because I'd been more than nice to her ass. *Fuck a friend...them bitches ain't good for shit.*

CHAPTER 7
PEACHES

I WORKED OUT for an hour listening to my iPod shuffle. Ms. Peaches's workout room was whack as hell. I couldn't wait till my place was ready. I was ready to move and start living the good life. I hadn't been able to focus that much since I'd been back home. I needed to get myself in order so I could start making other plans.

I jumped into the shower and turned the water up as hot as I could stand it. A hot shower after a workout always relaxed my muscles. As the water flowed out of the showerhead, hitting my nipples, it made me think about Dollar and how we used to make love for hours in the shower. A part of me still missed him for some strange reason.

It was probably because I hadn't been fucked right since I'd been out. John's dick was okay, but not long enough, and his head game was whack. I needed to get my back broke in like DMX did ol' girl in *Belly*. Just like that—nice and hard from the back.

I dried off my skin. I dreaded the thought of having to go sit in the crackhead meetings the judge ordered me to take. Like I smoked rocks. He knew I wasn't no damn junkie. But there was nothing I could do about it. It was part of my condition for release. Crackhead meetings once a week for six months…I had no choice but to attend. I didn't know how I'd make it. I hoped the instructor was some fine-ass bastard that I could put my pussy on. That would definitely get me outta the meetings. Shit, it could be a bitch too. I didn't care. Ain't no shame in my game. I'd break her ass off too.

"Emerald!" Peaches yelled my name as I walked out the bathroom, scaring the shit outta me.

"Damn, Peaches, you scared me. What's up?"

"What's your problem?" he said to me, rolling his head with an attitude.

"Excuse me?"

"Don't sit here and play dumb with me, girl."

"Peaches, for real, you tripping. I have no idea what you're talking about." He was confusing the hell outta me.

"You telling Angel you don't like her and she ain't your friend."

No, that little bitch didn't go back ratting on me! "And?" I said, rolling my eyes.

"And! What's yo' damn problem? You don't treat people like that."

"Firstly, the bitch just got on my bad side. If she has a problem wit me, she should have said something instead of running back to you like I'm some damn kid. And she ain't my friend. I don't even know her like that. I ain't trying to make new friends, and she should be thankful I got her ass outta jail."

"And you should be too, because without her, you probably be still in there," Peaches said.

"That's not true. I woulda got out."

"Girl, have you lost all yo' damn mind?"

Ms. Peaches was working my fucking nerves coming at me over some bitch. *Fuck bitches, they ain't shit but some conniving backstabbers.* "I ain't lost nothing, I'm just real with my shit. This is me now. I don't give a fuck no more about nothing. Bitches don't care about nobody but themselves, so why shouldn't I?"

"Emerald, there was a time when you didn't know me."

"Yeah, that was a different time and different place. I got my eyes wide open now. I finally know the truth about people. Everybody is only looking out for theirselves, and so am I. Shiesty ain't caring about a bitch or a nigga…fuck 'em."

"So, what you saying 'bout me?"

Peaches was taking this thing way too far. I wished my place was ready, because I would have left. "What about you?" I asked.

"So, you think I'm using you? Do you consider me a friend?"

"Peaches, do I think everybody got a motive? Yeah, and that includes you. I think you's real as hell and a rider, and I consider us friends. But shit, at the end of the day, I don't know who I can trust, and I gots to look out for me."

"You got some fucking nerve to fix yo' lips to say some shit like that," Peaches snapped at me. "I been busting my ass at them stores for you. Keeping your business afloat, making you money while you was gone. You don't know if you can trust me? How about I deposited every dollar since you hired me? How about I made sure you got yo' ass outta jail? How about I never thought twice about helping you? This Shiesty character that you supposed to be got you all fucked up."

"I'm fine, Ms. Peaches, and don't act like I ain't kicking you down either. I pay you a good salary, so you got yo' reasons for helping me. I'm not saying I ain't thankful, but let's be real. Nobody does something for nothing."

"Emerald, Shiesty, or whoever the hell you are, you don't treat people this way. You didn't like it, so you turn around and turn into the same type of person. Angel just wants to be your friend. And let me tell you something—using people, you can get yourself into a world of trouble, honey. You use the wrong person and you'll find yourself deep into some shit you can't buy yourself out of. You can't play with people emotions."

I started to get dressed, because I had to go to my meetings and I couldn't be late. Ms. Peaches was talking about a bunch of nothing. "Look, this is me, so deal with it."

"I ain't got to deal with shit, Shiesty, because Emerald wouldn't act like this...not towards me. I can bounce, Shiesty. There's plenty of places I can work."

"Well, do what you need to do," I said.

"So it's like that?"

"You making it like that. I want you to stay, but this is me, Peaches, and I ain't changing. I don't need no friends. I ain't taking shit from nobody. I'm looking out for me now. I let my life get fucked up, trusting people. That shit won't happen to me ever again."

Ms. Peaches stared at me, but I didn't care. I didn't need him or Angel. *I'm outta jail now. I can run my own shit. How dare he get off the chain with me over that bitch? I'll kick Angel to the curve so fast she won't know what hit her.* "Why you playing me for her anyway?" I asked him.

"Emerald, you need to learn to listen sometimes. That's your problem. I ain't playing you. I never played you. What I'm saying, child, is you can't walk through life alone. There's gonna come a point in your life where you're gonna need somebody. And it's gonna be the one person that you've been nasty to, and you better hope that they'll help you."

"I don't need nobody!"

"You gonna eat them words one day," Peaches told me.

Whatever. I don't need nobody but me, myself, and I. Shit, my own fucking sister backstabbed me and left me to die in jail. My best friend from the sandbox fucked my man and had a baby by him. Let's not even get on that nigga. Shiesty don't need no-fucking-body but me. I ain't letting nobody get close to me ever again.

33

CHAPTER 8
MEETINGS

I TOOK THE long way to my meeting. I needed to clear my head. Ms. Peaches had pissed me off. I'd tried to be nice to Angel and she went and stabbed me in the back like everybody else did. I didn't know what she was crying for. I wasn't being mean to her. I kindly told her that I would help her get some money and do some threesomes together. That was better than a friendship. Getting money was it. Everything else was irrelevant.

I'ma let her ass know about herself when I get back in. I don't play that shit. I'ma let her ass slide this time cause she don't know about my gangster. But if she fuck up again, she can get the fuck outta my life, cause I don't need her.

When I pulled into the parking lot, I dreaded getting out of my car. I mean, seriously, the judge knew he was wrong for this shit. *I ain't feeling this shit, period. I'ma just sit here and keep my mouth closed.*

The meeting was typically full of Black and Hispanic people. I gazed around the room and there were no cute guys in sight. I signed my name on the sign-in sheet and took a seat. The chairs were formed into a circle, like we was making friends tonight. *I have to sit through twenty minutes of dis bullshit? I need to have a drink later.*

Right before the meeting started, this crackhead bitch came and sat next to me, eyeing my Gucci bag. I saw her hype eyes checking for me to slip. *This bitch don't know nothing about my gangster. I'll slice that ass from A to Z. Shit, I just got this bag and spent 10 Gs on it. It will be going down up in dis bitch. She better fall back and be easy if she know what's best for her.*

"Hi, my name is Patty," she said as she reached her hand out for a shake. She had three teeth missing in her mouth, and her breath smelled like she licked some nasty ass before she came.

"Hi," I replied.

"How long you been clean?"

I just looked at her. *Bitch, do I look like I gotta crack habit?* "I ain't no crackhead."

"This meeting is for recovering drug addicts," she said.

"So, why don't you go talk to them women over there? I ain't trying to make no friends."

She smacked her teeth and went over there and talked with her other cracked-out friends. I kept my eyes on dem hos. *They probably plotting to get me for my bag. I'll take all three of them if they try.*

The instructor finally came in, and he was fine. He was tall and built. His skin was smooth and glowing. He had a sexy bread that lined up perfectly with his hairline. His caramel skin was slightly tanned like he just came outta the sun. He had long dreads, not the nasty kind. You could tell he went to the shop and got them twisted. He was dressed like a lame, but he had a pretty smile. I was feeling his geek ass.

"Gather around, everyone," he said. "My name is Joseph Wells. I'll be your mentor through your journey to a cleaner and healthier life."

All them crackheads got into the circle and was eating up what he said. He told everyone to introduce themselves. When it came to my turn, I just looked around. I didn't want to say shit.

"My name is Emerald Jones," I said.

"How long have you been clean?" he asked.

He acts as if I look like a hype bitch. He sees all this ass I got? "I'm not a crackhead. I always been clean."

"She thinks she better than somebody!" Patty yelled. "Coming up in here with all that expensive stuff on."

"I'm glad you noticed," I said. I knew that bitch was trying to clip me for my shit.

"All right, guys," Joseph said. "Maybe Ms. Jones doesn't want to open up today. That's fine."

By the end of the meeting, I was drained from listening to so many crackhead stories. I had to get outta there. *I need to find a way outta these meetings, cause this shit ain't for me.*

When I got ready to go, I heard Joseph call my name. "Emerald?"

"Yes?"

"I wanted to know if we can go get coffee and you can open up to me about your problems."

Bingo! I know just how I'ma get outta these meetings. My head game can get me anything I want. I knew his ass couldn't resist a bitch. Thank God for blessing me with good looks and a raw body. "Cool," I said. Even though this nigga was a geek, I'd show him a good time—make him feel like a man for once.

"Where you want to go?"

"I don't know. You're asking me, so you figure that out."

"Fine, just follow me," he said.

I followed him. He was driving a Dodge Magnum, so I knew he was a broke nigga. He couldn't even afford a Charger. *He's dirt broke, but today's his lucky day.*

I followed him to the Wild Hare, the hottest reggae club in Chicago. Luckily, I stayed looking off glass. I freshened up my Oh Baby lip gloss and followed him in. It was so loud in the club I could barely hear myself think.

Joseph spotted us a table and we sat down. When we took a seat, he stared at me. I knew he was probably wondering how a fine-ass bitch like me wound up at a crackhead meeting.

"So, what's your story?" he asked.

"No story. I ain't no crack fiend."

"So you just got drug rehab for nothing?"

"Pretty much. I got caught up in some shit and this was the only way out."

"Selling drugs?"

"You ask a lot of damn questions!" I snapped. He was working my left nerve.

"I'm just tryin' to get to know you."

I looked at him. He was a big geek and wearing thin on my nerves. "Well, Joseph, what do you want to know?"

"What do you do for a living?"

"I own a clothing line."

"May I ask the name?"

Dis nigga is killing me slowly with this nerd shit. "Icey," I said. "Look, you want to dance?" *Cuz frankly, I'm ret to go?*

"Sure."

When we made it to the dance floor, Shyne's song "Bonnie and Shyne" came on. That was my shit. We moved together with the music, and although he was a lame with a capital L, he was able to keep up with me while I threw my ass every way I wanted. I grinded my hips and ass on him as hard as I could so I could feel how big his dick was.

Lame boy was working with a Polish, but I didn't want to get too excited, cause you can never tell until you make 'em whip it out. I grinded, rubbed, and touched him in every place I thought would make him hot. The more places I touched him, the harder he grabbed me.

I knew I had his ass right where I wanted him. I took his hand and went out the back door of the club. It started raining outside, but that turned me on even more. I pushed his ass against the alley wall. I was excited. This shit was so gangsta. I'd always wanted to get fucked outside in the rain.

I unbuckled his pants and his dick was on hard. It was nice, about Dollar's size. I grabbed it and licked around the head of his shaft. He started shaking. "You want me to suck it?" I asked him.

"Yeah, please," he begged.

He rubbed his hand through my hair, now curly due to the rain. I sucked him softly and he was already gone, moaning and yelling and I hadn't put in my best work yet.

"What you goin' do for me?" I asked, cause I only fucked for cash and favors. I needed a favor, so I was goin' fuck him and fuck him good too.

"I'll do anything," he said.

And that's what I want to hear. You'll do anything for dis mean head. "Good," I said. "I need you to sign me in for them meetings saying I was there."

"I can't do that! I'll get fired."

"Fine, then," I said as I got up. "I'm 'bout to go." *Shit, he got me twisted, thinking I'm about to suck his dick for nothing.*

"Emerald!" he called to me as I walked away.

"Yeah," I said, knowing he wanted some ass.

"Fine, I'll do it."

I knew he'd see it my way. *I'm an irresistible bitch.* I walked back his way and got back on my knees. His dick was still on rock. It started raining harder, and the raindrops hitting his dick made it easier for me to slide him deep into my mouth. I was bobbing and weaving. The music coming from the nightclub silenced his moans. The rain pouring in my face made me want him more. I was giving him the best time of his life.

He was screaming like a little bitch. "Damn, Emerald, baby, this feel so good! I never felt this way!"

I know this lame-ass nigga ain't never got his dick sucked this good in his life. "I coming, Emerald!" he moaned. I gave him a few more strokes before I released him.

Once Joseph exploded, he picked me up and pinned me against the brick wall. My summer dress had me fuck-ready. He pulled my thong to the side, rolled a condom down his dick, and slid it in me. He felt so good to me. He hit me right on my G-spot. I needed this. It had been a while, and I need to bust as many nuts as I could to make up for lost time.

37

Joseph stroked his dick deep into my guts, and it felt so good. "Don't stop, keep it right there," I moaned as I pulled his wet dreads. He was beating my shit up right, hitting all my weak spots.

"Dis dick feeling good to you?" he asked me.

"Yeah," I moaned, because it was. I ain't goin' front, he was killing it.

"This shit feels so good to me too," he said. "Please say it's my pussy."

How he goin' ask me some shit like that? Nigga, I don't even know you like that. The dick is good and all, but this my pussy. I'm the owner and the operator! He kept on hollering and blowing my concentration. "Nigga, shut the fuck up and beat this pussy like you just was," I said, cause he could kill all that other noise. I wasn't tryin' to hear him.

He went back to work, better than before. I guess he was trying to get me to say this is his pussy, but I ain't. I just screamed, "Hit it harder!" cause I was coming and I needed him to hit it harder for me.

"Shit!" When my legs started to shake, I knew that was it. I came all over his dick hard. After ten more minutes, he dug so deep into me I could barely breathe.

He let me down and tried to kiss me, but I told his ass to be easy. He was already falling in love with my ass and I wasn't tryin' to be his bitch. "Fall back," I said. "We just fucking."

I walked off. *This nigga can beat it like Michael Jackson, all I care.*

He ran behind me yelling, "Emerald, the only way I'm going to keep signing you in for the meetings is we have to get together once a week or I'm turning you in."

I looked at him. Who did this lame-ass nigga think he was dealing with? It was kind of cute, he tried to get a little gangster with me. *He lucky he got a big dick.* I didn't mind fucking him once a week. The dick was good.

So I let him think he was bullying me, but little did he know, he was the one getting used. I didn't care about getting off the chain. As long as I didn't have to sit through them meetings, I'd do anything.

CHAPTER 9
SHIESTY

I PULLED INTO Peaches's driveway. *Damn, I wish my shit was ready. I really don't want to go in here, but I have no choice. I can't wait until my place is finished. Angel lucky I'm a woman of my word, cause I will leave her ass sleeping in the streets. Or maybe her new BFF Peaches will let her stay with him. Shit, I don't have time for people telling me what to do or how to think. I'm too grown and I don't give a fuck about nobody but me. So I ain't letting nobody get close to me. Fuck it. It's me against the world.*

When I walked in, Angel was sitting on the couch watching *The Wire*. I was so pissed with her, I could've slapped her ass. "I don't appreciate you running to Peaches like I'm a kid. Let's get this clear: if you gotta problem with me, come and tell me. I don't need to hear shit from a third party."

"Emerald, I'm sorry if you feel like I told on you, but he asked me why I was looking sad and I told him."

"What you sad for?" *She blowing the shit outta me.*

"Cause Emerald, I don't have nobody and I thought we was gonna be friends. I didn't know you hated me."

"Hate is a strong word, Angel. I don't hate nobody. I don't have a reason to. I don't give a fuck no more, Angel. My good girl is gone. Emerald is dead. I'm Shiesty now. I don't give a fuck about nobody but me. When I cared about people, they fucked me. I'm not letting nobody else fuck me. You, Peaches, or whoever. Nobody's gonna do me in ever again. So I don't have any feelings any more. I don't give a fuck about caring for someone's feelings, girl. It's hard to hear, but it's the truth. I'm out here fucking these niggas for whatever reason I want to. I'm getting money. Shit everything else means nothing to me. Money Over Niggas for me. And you should be just like me. Shit, you been in jail for two years because of trusting people."

"You know, Emerald, every day I sat in that cell I thought about my momma telling me about Dollar before she died or my friend telling me about Dollar. I wouldn't listen to nobody but him and that dyke-ass bitch Ginger. So I went to jail, cause I wouldn't listen. That was the major factor, thinking I knew everything."

When she called Ginger a dyke, I was curious to see if she was licking up in her magic box. "Well, I ain't got to listen to nobody," I said. "I know what's best for me. Anyways, you was dyking with Ginger?"

"Yeah, she slicked me."

"What that mean?"

"She was playing dirty, slipping shit in my drink. Then once she licked me the first time, I liked it. So we kept doing it. But I'm not gay, though."

"Slipping what into your drink?"

"Some type of date rape drug. S.L. told me."

"What!" I was furious. *That bitch!*

"Yeah, I was creeping with him on the low. His dick was much better than Dollar's."

I looked at Angel. *Damn, how dirty could one be? Creeping around with the man's friend...damn.* "Why would he tell you that?"

"One day I was over there, and we were creeping, and he was twisted already. He told me to get him a drink, so I grabbed the Grey Goose and brought it to him. He was so drunk he started running his mouth, telling me how she mixed a date rape drug with the Grey Goose to turn me out. He said she does it to all Dollar's girlfriends. I was pissed, but at the same time, so addicted to her that I looked over it. He didn't tell me nothing about them setting me up. I wish he would have slipped up and told me that. I mean, you know how serious her head game is. I really ain't even mad at the bitch. Her pussy game need to be illegal. But if I ever see her again, I'ma make sure to get her to eat my pussy, then I'ma rock her ass."

I couldn't believe it. When I thought about it, I did feel loose after those drinks Ginger had given me. I remembered being lightheaded and lying down. She turned me out against my own will. But I'm with Angel— Ginger's head was the best I ever had. *That sounds like a plan to me. I can get with that.* "How long was you and S.L. messing around?"

"Um...for six months, probably."

Angel was disloyal like a motherfucker. "Damn, how you manage that?"

"I think it was part of the plan, Emerald. We had a threesome and S.L. beat my shit up until I fainted. I had to get some more of that. At first we would sneak around; then we started to go over to his place when Ginger was out."

Damn, I was mad as hell. *How come S.L. ain't beat my shit up that good? I want me some dick that's gonna make me faint.* "Well, they did that shit to me too. I ain't faint or nothing, but I fucked him once when Ginger asked me to. They taped it and Dollar used that as the excuse to do me bogus."

"That nigga ain't shit. He goin' fuck over the wrong person and they gonna get him."

"He already fucked over the wrong person. That's what I'm telling you. That's what this shit is all about. Survival! Trying to make friends ain't goin' get you nowhere in this world. People can't be trusted no more. The only thing to live for is getting money. Live, eat, fuck, and get money."

"But, Emerald, you have money. What is the need?"

"Shit, you can never have too much money, Angel—and if I can fuck a nigga out of a plasma TV, then so be it. Why spend mine when I can spend yours? Fuck these nothing-ass niggas. It's all about me and getting my paper. M.O.N., baby girl. You better jump aboard. Just think, us together, we can hit these niggas' pockets hard. You need money? Why not use your pussy game to get it? It's the American way. Fuck being friends and being in love. Life is all about business. Me and you can be business partners, and that's better than friends."

"But you need somebody in your life you can depend on," Angel insisted.

"I got that, and his name is Benjamin Franklin and I love the shit outta him."

"What about playing innocent people? It ain't right."

"Girl, I'm Shiesty, baby, and so is everybody else," I said. "You can either be played or be a player! You choose."

"I mean, I just don't know. My momma always told me to believe in karma, and God don't like ugly. She said that he will make people pay in his time, and when you use the wrong person it can come back on you ten times worse."

"Girl, I ain't tryin' to hear that shit! I am God and I play by my own rules. I don't give a fuck! I'ma use who I want, how I want, and I don't give a fuck. You fuck with Shiesty, you goin' get dealt with."

"Well, I know you don't want to be my friend, but you can count on me for my word," Angel said. "I have your back."

Angel knew she better join in or she was gonna be on the outside looking in. I was in control of my life. I didn't give a fuck! *I'm taking what I want…and I'm coming for Dollar and Sissy…and they're gonna pay with their lives!*

CHAPTER 10
BIG MOMMA

I WOKE UP around seven and went to work out. I had to keep my body looking off the chain. When I got back, Ms. Peaches had cooked breakfast for us. Angel was up, looking sad as usual. I couldn't wait until my house was ready so I could move.

"Why you looking all sad for? Every time I see you, you looking sad."

"I need a car," Angel said.

I just looked at her. It sounded like a personal problem to me. She wasn't my bitch. I wasn't tricking on no-fucking-body. Now, if she wanted to lick up in my puss for a car, then maybe we could talk business. I could get her ass a Geo or something. "Well, I don't know why you looking sad. That ain't gonna get you a car."

"I know. It's gonna take me months to save my paychecks for one."

"All I can tell you is to get on your pussy game. Cause I can fuck a car outta a nigga in one day, so you should be able to fuck a down payment out of a nigga or two."

Ms. Peaches looked at me and twisted up his face. I didn't give a fuck! He could look at me all he wanted to. I was telling the truth. "Why you looking at me like that?" I asked.

"Nothing," Peaches replied with his hands on his hips. "I need to talk to you."

"About what?" I snapped because I was so tired of him telling me what to do.

"Bitch, don't get jazzy with me. I ain't finna put up with your attitude, Emerald."

"What's up? What's on your mind?" I said, being playful.

"Big Momma is in the hospital," he said as he sat down.

"When did this happen?"

"Three days ago."

"Why you just now telling me?"

"I tried to tell you, but you always gone. She had a heart attack."

My heart fell to the floor. The only thing I could think about was how

I'd never made peace with Big Momma. There was no question about it: I had to see her. "Well, I want to see her."

"I know. I went yesterday. I told her you were coming."

"Wait, she knows I'm home?"

"Yes she does, Emerald."

I looked at Ms. Peaches with his big-ass mouth. But Big Momma does have a way of picking what she wants out of you. I really wanted to see her and ask her about my momma. I wanted to know the truth. I had always wondered why Big Momma never told us what happened.

I sat down at Ms. Peaches's table to eat my food. My mind was all over the place right now. I didn't know if Big Momma had any money saved, or if she was getting the best care she could get.

My phone rang, breaking my thought. I looked at the caller ID and it was Joseph's stalking ass. I didn't feel like answering, so I ignored it. I knew it would only be a matter of time before he called back. Joseph was hooked on my crack rock and stressed me the hell out every chance he got. But right now, my mind was concerned about how Big Momma was doing.

CHAPTER 11
JOSEPH

JOSEPH WAS SO strung out on my pussy it was ridiculous. He even brought me a ring—like I would marry his broke ass. When the meetings were over, Joseph was gonna be a thing of the past. Every Tuesday he was on my ass, not letting me breathe. He even be crying and shit. I mean, for real, what man cries over somebody they barely know? Joseph's dick was cool, but he wanted to wife a bitch, and I wasn't tryin' get tied down.

When I got to Joseph's house, he was waiting on me by the door like the stalker he was.

"Damn, nigga, do you have to wait by the door for me?" I said to him as I walked in.

"I called you all day," he said.

"I know. I was busy. I know what you wanted."

"That's not all I want," he cried. *Here we go again. He goin' make me attend my meetings. I can't keep dealing with this extra stress.*

"Look, don't I fuck you good?" I asked him.

"Yeah."

"The best you ever had, right?"

"Yeah, but I want to be with you."

"I'm not ready right now for a relationship," I said. "So you can either lie down and let me put this fat kat in your mouth, or you can keep popping shit outta it. It's all up to you. It don't make me none."

I followed Joseph to his bedroom, and he opened the door. The smell of plumeria candles filled the room. Rose petals flooded the bed and the floor. In his master bathroom, he had a bubble bath waiting for me with candles burning and chocolate-covered strawberries around the tub. It was very romantic that he did all this for me, but I still would never be his bitch.

"I love you, Emerald," he said as he undressed me. I didn't have the energy to fuss with him. That was his business if he loved somebody that didn't love him back. *It ain't my problem, he can love me all he wants.*

I needed to be pampered, especially after that little-dick bastard wasted my damn time. *Lil' dick-ass nigga!* The hot water felt so good when I stuck my feet in the tub. I pulled my hair up into a ponytail, got in, and lay back while Joseph took his big hands and massaged my entire body.

I swear he sent me into a zone I'd never been in before. As his hands caressed each part of my body, I fell deeper into a daze. "I love you, Emerald," he whispered into my ear over and over again. I did my best to hold my concentration and ignore him being stupid.

When he picked me up out of the water and laid me on the side of the tub, I was ready for him. He licked my pussy lips first with soft strokes from his tongue. My body started shivering. Joseph licked me so damn right, I couldn't control myself. Joseph had me so open that I was losing control.

He licked up my juices, then turned me over and slid into me raw. I started to make him get up, but he felt so damn good, I didn't even care. I needed to feel all of his dick deep inside me.

I grabbed hold of his dreads and whispered in his ear, "Give it to me deeper." I needed to feel him in my chest.

Joseph laid his pipe game on me for an hour and a half. I could barely walk afterwards. He begged me to stay the night, but there was no way on God's green earth I was spending the night at his place. I put my clothes on and blew him a kiss. He looked like a lost puppy. I just laughed at his whipped ass. *Be in love by yourself, nigga.* I went home and went to sleep.

CHAPTER 12
TIME TO MOVE ON

September 15, 2008

MY CONDO WAS finally ready after months of waiting. I was glad; I'd been shopping for all the flyest shit I could find. I was gonna go for the look that DMX had in his house in *Belly*, but it reminded me too much of Dollar. That was the last thing I wanted to come home to—a memory of his no-good ass. So I passed on that idea. Instead, I picked rich colors for my theme.

I had been avoiding going to see Big Momma because I didn't want to run into Sissy, but I had to go and see if she was all right. I had tried to go see my dad the day before, but he had moved. I spent two hours out there getting the runaround. Nobody had any info on him.

When I made it to the hospital, my knees started to get weak. I'd never seen Big Momma sick, ever. She had always been so strong and a leader. She never needed nobody. When I walked to the front desk, I became frightened. I didn't know if I wanted to see her like this.

"May I help you, ma'am?" the front desk lady yelled.

"I'm here to see Jean Abham," I said.

"And who are you?"

I didn't like the bitch's tone of voice with me. "Sissy Jones!" I yelled.

She looked at me and rolled her eyes. She wrote Sissy's name on a nametag and handed it to me, then told me that Big Momma was in the ICU, room 202.

As I walked down the long narrow hallway, my heart started beating at a fast pace. I opened the door and my heart fell. Big Momma was laid on her back with tubes everywhere. Her chest was caving in and out every time she took a breath. I couldn't believe it.

"Big Momma!" I yelled. She looked over at me and held out her hand for me to come closer. I couldn't do nothing but cry.

"I'm glad you came, my child. I knew you would come."

"Do you know who I am?" I asked her.

"Of course, baby," she said as she rubbed the side of my face. "I could never forget my first grandchild."

"What happened to you?" I cried.

"Baby, I'm just old and tired."

"Big Momma, why didn't you tell me the truth about my momma?"

Big Momma looked at me and rubbed the side of my face. "Sometimes you hide the truth to keep from hurting people."

"But you lied and kept us from our dad. Why would you do that?"

"Emerald, your dad was just as much at fault for your mother's death as his brother. He was out there selling poison. He killed a lot of people too."

"But he didn't kill my mother." Big Momma pissed me off, trying to make up excuses for what she did.

"Emerald, I never forgave your father for what happened to your mother. She was my only child, so I erased him, and doing so, I took him from you girls. I never thought about how much you two needed him, or how important it was for him to talk to you girls about men and this so-called street life. When you started talking to that boy, my heart broke. I saw your father's ways in him. I knew that it wasn't gonna turn out good. That's why I fought so hard to get you to stop talking to him. Every day I blamed myself for what happened to you and Sissy."

"Fuck Sissy, Big Momma. How could you not tell me she was messing with Dollar?"

"I didn't know. I told you she was acting funny, but I never knew who he was. Soon as I found out, I told her to stop, but he had her far too gone. She wouldn't listen to me, so I told her to go and never come back. I disowned her."

"I hate her. I'm gonna make her pay for what she did to me."

"That your sister, child. People make mistakes. You can't walk through life with hatred."

"Like hell if I can't. You always liked her better than me, anyways. 'Oh, Sissy so smart…Sissy so this.' You always thought she was better than me."

"That's not true, Emerald!" Big Momma managed to raise her voice and yell.

"Whatever," I said as I rolled my eyes at her.

"Emerald, I won't lay here on my deathbed and let you fill the air with lies."

When she said deathbed, my heart started beating faster. "What do you mean, deathbed? You gonna be all right, aren't you?"

47

Big Momma turned her head away from me and looked away. My body began to shake. My heart started pounding so loud it drowned out the TV that was quietly playing in the room. "No, I ain't got long, Emerald."

"Big Momma!" I cried as I kneeled down at the side of her bed. "Tell me you're lying…tell me," I demanded.

Big Momma looked me in my eyes. I didn't notice at first, but her eyes had changed from her light brown to a worn-out blue. The bags under her eyes showed me how deprived of sleep she was. She ran her fingers through my hair. "Child, you're my firstborn granddaughter. I remember when you was first born. I was so happy to have a grandchild. You went everywhere with me. I never loved Sissy more than you. Both you girls took after your father, very stubborn. I stayed on you more because I knew you would be great someday. Sissy was always a follower. Whatever you did, she followed you. I knew if I got you to do the right things, Sissy would follow. But…." Big Momma moaned as she took in a deep breath. "I never got to tell you how proud I am of you. I been in three of your stores, and my friends' kids wear your clothes. I tell everybody my grand-baby made them clothes. I want you to forgive me. Forgive Sissy. Forgive your father. Forgive life. Baby, life's too short not to forgive. I'm leaving here soon, and I don't want you back in jail."

"Big Momma, don't say that. What is it? I can get you transferred to a better hospital. I have money."

"Baby, I'm so tired. I'm ready to go. I'm tired of the needles and the doctors. This chemo is making my bones too weak. I'm tired. I've been sick ten years now. I'm tired now."

Tears started pouring down my face. I just couldn't believe it. What was I gonna do? Big Momma was the only family I had left. I didn't want her to die. "Ten years, why didn't you say something?" I cried. I laid my head on her chest as tears fell down my cheeks. How could I be so selfish? I put my grandma through all that pain when she was sick with cancer. I was running around with Dollar, making her even sicker. "I don't want you to die, Big Momma!" I cried.

"Baby, in my closet I have a shoebox full of letters that your dad sent home from jail. I want you to go get them and read them. I want you to promise me that you will."

"Big Momma," I cried. "Please, I can pay for a better doctor for you. Please, Big Momma, don't give up on me. Don't leave me. I'm so sorry for all that I took you through. I'm so sorry, Big Momma." I couldn't stop crying. The more I thought about it, the more tears fell.

"Baby, I'm tired. I'll always be with you, through your spirit. Take this," she said as she reached over into the drawer and handed me a locket with a picture of me, her, my momma, and Sissy. "I always believed in you, Emerald. Cherished this...cherish life, baby."

"No, I won't let you die!" I buzzed the button for the doctor to come in. I was getting her transferred to the best cancer center in Chicago. The cost didn't mean nothing.

"Emerald, it's too late for me. I need you to make me a promise." I reached over and buzzed the button again. *This cheap-ass hospital is taking too long to see what I want.* The nerve of Sissy's ass—having Big Momma in this ghetto-ass hospital when she could've been getting better treatment.

"Emerald, listen to me," Big Momma said as she started coughing. "Promise me you'll make peace with your dad."

"Okay," I cried as I hugged her hand.

"Tell him how sorry I am for taking his daughters away from him. Tell him I forgave him for what happened to your mother. I was too damn stubborn to admit it. Let him know that my life has been full of regrets and I wish I could take it all back. I wish I never turned him away from you girls."

"Big Momma," I cried. "You're gonna live. I'm gonna get you outta here, you're gonna live."

"Promise me, Emerald," she demanded.

"I promise. I promise. I'm gonna get you out of here!" I yelled as I buzzed for the damn doctor one more time.

"Promise me you'll make peace with Sissy. That's the only blood you have now. Promise me that you will make peace with her."

"I won't do that, Big Momma. Look at what she did to me."

"Listen, Sissy is a follower, like I said. She don't know no better, baby. I need you to forgive and move on with your life. If not, you're gonna end up like me with a life full of regrets. Promise me you'll forgive her and move on with your life."

I looked at Big Momma. She was asking me to tell her something that I didn't feel. I wanted to hurt Sissy like she hurt me. I wanted her to pay.

Big Momma started to cough really bad. Her monitors started to beep. I didn't know what was going on. "Big Momma!" I yelled. "Somebody help me!" I cried. "Somebody help me!"

Big Momma grabbed my hand and looked me in the eyes. "Promise me." She caught her breath just enough to cough up the words.

"Okay, I promise!" I screamed, hoping it would bring her back out of this stage.

"Excuse me, ma'am!" the doctor yelled as he pushed me out of the way.

"Help my grandma," I cried.

"I need you to get out."

"No, help my grandma."

"Clear!" was all I heard as the doctor pressed the machine against Big Momma's chest. "Clear!" they yelled again, but the line on the monitor went straight. I knew what that meant. I'd lost her. My grandmother was dead. I fell to the floor because my knees gave out on me.

"Ma'am, what's your name?" the doctor asked.

"Huh?" I said as I looked up at him, spaced out.

"Ma'am, what's your name?"

I looked up at him. I couldn't believe it. My grandmother died right in front of me. I didn't have nobody now. I picked myself off of the floor and grabbed my purse.

"Ma'am, your name?" he asked me again, more firmly.

"Sissy Jones," I said as I took in a deep breath, grabbing hold of the chain Big Momma left with me.

When I walked outta the hospital, I felt so lonely. I'd never felt this lonely before—not even when I was in prison. I had made big promises to Big Momma, and I hoped I could keep them.

I drove around for hours before I ended up at John's door. I needed for him to hold me. I didn't even call him. I just stopped by. I didn't know if he had company or not. I just wanted to see him. I knew he could make me feel better.

I rang his doorbell twice before I heard his deep voice tell me he was coming. My face was bloodshot red from crying my eyes out. When John opened the door, his face grew big. "Emerald!" he yelled as he pulled me into his home. "Baby, what's the matter?"

I couldn't hold back the mountain of tears I was carrying inside. "Big Momma died today," I cried out as I buried my head into his chest.

"Emerald, it's okay," John consoled me as he ran his strong hands up and down my back.

"She's gone, John…she's gone."

John lay back on his couch and pulled me onto his chest. He held me so tight until I cried the last tear that would come out.

"Can you make sure she gets the best funeral? Can you do that for me?" I asked him.

"It's already done," John reassured me.

I didn't know what Sissy had planned, but judging by how she had Big Momma stuck in that ghetto-ass hospital, Big Momma wouldn't get buried like she should be.

"I need you right now. I need you inside of me," I said to John.

John took off all my clothes. He licked me from the bottom of my feet all the way to the top of my head. I needed this from him. If he could have done me like that all the time, I would have had no problem settling down with him.

John stroked me right for two hours, and I went right to sleep after we were done. I needed him and he was there for me, physically and mentally. He made my feelings for him grow so much deeper.

After I left John, I felt so lost again. What was I to do? Should I make up with Sissy and move on with my life? I made Big Momma a promise. I was always a woman of my word. I hated phony-ass people, but I also hated people who crossed me. Sissy didn't deserve another chance. I was too good to her. I made sure she had everything, and she did me like that.

I just wished I hadn't made that promise. Big Momma had died on me anyway. Maybe if I saw Sissy face to face, we could talk things out—just me and her, no Dollar around. Maybe we could pan this thing out, because I still loved my sister. That could never change.

CHAPTER 13
JOSEPH

JOSEPH HAD BEEN calling my phone all day with his stalking ass. I didn't feel like being bothered with him today. My nerves were too bad. But I had to pick up and say something to him, or he would try to go and rat on me. Lord knows, I didn't need no extra drama. "Hello!" I screamed through my phone.

"Where are you? You trying to break our agreement?" he asked me in a nasty tone.

"Excuse me, nigga. You better watch your tone. I'm busy."

"Emerald, you know I'm getting sick and tired of these little games you playing with me. Now, I've been real good to you, and I don't appreciate you giving my pussy away. I want it to stop." He demanded this of me like I was his bitch and he owned me.

Once I finished laughing at his dumb cake broke ass, I had to let him know whose pussy this was. "First of all, Joseph, you can't even afford pussy like mine. That's first. Secondly, I'm the owner and the operator of this pussy. I do what the fuck I want with it! Third off, I was only fucking you to get outta them meetings, and guess what? Boo-boo, they're over next week, so I could care less about what you want, nigga." *This nigga has a lot of balls wit his broke ass—getting off the chain with me after I've been kind enough to suck the life outta his dick and give him some free mean pussy. The nerve of some people. It's a shame how ungrateful people are these days.*

Joseph took in a long pause before he spoke. "So you think you get to say when it's over?"

"Yup, I'm the head bitch in charge."

"But I love you, Emerald. You said you loved me too."

"I ain't never told you that shit. I might have said I love the way you lick my ass, but that's about it. I never told you I loved you. This was just a good business decision."

"What about us?"

"Joseph, you can't be that slow. There is no us. Now, I know you sprung on the kat and the head, but check this out: use the same speech you use on them crackheads for yourself. You too can kick your addiction to my pussy."

"But I love you," Joseph stuttered. "I wanted you to be my wife. I wanted us to be a family."

"Joseph, go get a clue."

"You used me, Emerald."

"Don't act like you didn't know what time it was. It was fun while it lasted, right?"

"Emerald, don't do this to me. I need you."

"Look, Joseph, my grandmother died last week and I'm not in the mood. Have a good life."

I hung up the phone on his ass. *Goodbye and thank the Lord.* I didn't need him or would see his ass ever again. I could use my grandmother's death to get me out of my last classes. I was glad we were over and done with. *It ain't my fault I got good pussy. What can a bitch do? Niggas can try to lock us up all they want to. I ain't having it.*

CHAPTER 14
THE FUNERAL

IT FELT LIKE I had been lying awake with my eyes closed. I was very restless when my alarm went off. I couldn't believe I was burying my grandmother today. My stomach was turning upside down, thinking about facing Sissy. What if she got slick at the mouth? If she did, I would kick her ass dead in her fucking teeth and beat the shit out of her.

I knew Dollar's stank ass would be there. I still had to man up and do the right thing. I promised Big Momma I'd make good, and I was a woman of my word. *If you fall back on your word, than you ain't worth shit.*

I had stayed at Ms. Peaches's house, because I didn't want to be alone right now. I had also purchased a black Chanel pantsuit to look perfect for the funeral.

I jumped out of the shower, washed my face, and brushed my teeth. I felt a little better once I got dressed. I walked into the kitchen to get me something to eat.

"How you feel?" Ms. Peaches asked me as he rubbed my back.

"I'm okay. I'll be glad when this is over with."

"You goin' be fine, child. Don't worry."

"What if Sissy doesn't want to make back up? Then I'll look stupid and my plans will be ruined."

"Girl, when you make promises, you have to keep them or at least try. If you at least try, then that means you kept your word. If she act all stank, we goin' ride down on her ass, okay?" Peaches laughed.

I couldn't help but laugh at his crazy ass. I needed a good laugh anyway. "Okay. Don't be punking out on me when it's time to ride."

"Now, you know I'm a five-degree pink belt. I will Jet Li the both of them, okay?"

Angel walked into the kitchen and gave me a hug. "Emerald, some cute guy is in the front room for you, girl. He's cute," she said while smiling like a hyena.

"Guy? Who is it, John?"

"Nah, he black."

When I stood up, I didn't know who the fuck it could be. Nobody knew where I stayed. I made my way to Ms. Peaches's front room, where Joseph stood up and handed me some flowers.

"What the fuck are you doing here?" I asked, all nasty. Ms. Peaches and Angel came in and took a seat.

"I came to see how you were doing," Joseph said. "I know you said your grandmother passed, and I know you need me."

"What?" I yelled. "You been following me, nigga? How you find out I was here?"

"Emerald," Joseph whined as he moved in closer to me. I backed away. "I know you're hurting right now and not thinking clearly. I got your address off your paperwork. I never followed you."

I guess Ms. Peaches sensed my resistance toward him. "Emerald, you goin' introduce us to your friend?" he asked me.

"No, he ain't nobody," I said as I handed Joseph back his flowers.

Joseph looked up at me like a lost puppy. "Nobody?" he shouted. "Emerald, we've been dating for the last six months. Was I a nobody when you was sucking on my dick and making love to me for hours? Was I a nobody when I helped you? How could you say I'm a nobody when you said you loved me?"

Joseph had lost all his damn mind, rolling up in here and trying to front on me. "You need to leave," I told him as I escorted him to the door. "Don't ever come around here trying to front on me. You hear me, nigga? I never told your dumb ass I loved you, so stop lying on me! I hate when people lie on me. I never said that to you, wit your crazy ass. Yes, I sucked yo' dick for six months, and a couple other guys too! I was never your bitch, and we damn sure wasn't dating. I only saw you once a week. Jesus, get a life and a clue. I'm not feeling yo' geek ass! I never did. I only fucked with you to get me outta them meetings. Other than that, you would have never even got any of this mean pussy. So go get some help and break yo' habit. I don't want you!"

"Emerald," Joseph cried as tears started pouring down his face. *He's a little bitch for real.* "I love you. I need you. Please don't do this to me. I'll do whatever you want."

"Okay, I want you to leave me the fuck alone!" I yelled as I slammed the door in his face.

"What was all that about?" Angel asked me.

"Nothing…some pussy-whipped nigga trying to wife me. But you know my motto: Fuck niggas, get money."

Ms. Peaches stood up. "Girl, listen to me. I might look like a girl to you, but I'm still a man," he said. "You better watch him, cause he'll try to hurt you."

"I ain't worried about his geek pussy-whipped ass. If he wasn't so stupid, he could have still got some pussy. He was packing a big dick, but it's his loss."

"All right, Emerald," Peaches said. "It would pay to listen sometimes."

I looked at Peaches. I didn't give a fuck about nobody but me. It was my world, and everybody else didn't matter. If Joseph's ass knew what was good for him, he'd better move on and get a life.

My knees began to shake as I reached the stairs to the church. Me and John both agreed that having her service here was the best choice. Big Momma had never missed a Sunday at church. I made sure she had the best casket, flowers, and tombstone. I didn't care what the cost was. She raised me, and even though I didn't have the best of everything, she did her best.

I told Ms. Peaches and John that I would sit in the back of the church to keep chaos down. I wanted Big Momma to be buried in peace. The church was jam-packed from the front to the back. Everybody came out to pay their respects to Big Momma. She was loved by everyone.

But I just couldn't stop thinking about arguing with her over Dollar's stank ass. I had put her through all that stress for nothing. As the preacher preached, I couldn't hear the words he was saying. Instead, I kept thinking about how I'd walked out of Big Momma's house without even saying goodbye to her. All that over a man—I was just plain stupid.

I thanked God I had been able to patch things up with Big Momma before she left here. I was so glad I apologized to her for disrespecting her. Lord knows, I couldn't have lived with myself without making peace with my grandma.

My view of the church was perfect. I could see everybody and everything that was going on. Sissy's seat had been empty since the service started.

The funeral went on for three hours. After the choir sang "Love" by Kurt Franklin, the preacher called for us to take one last view of the body. I put on my shades and hat so nobody would notice me. I had to see Big Momma one last time before we laid her to rest. The choir sang "His

Eye Is On The Sparrow," which made me cry even harder. This was Big Momma's favorite song.

When I had made it to the front row, Sissy's seat was still empty. She didn't bother to show her face. I couldn't believe it. How could you not come to your own grandma's funeral? I knew John said he tried contacting her and had no luck. But damn, this was beyond dirty.

I made it to her casket and leaned in to kiss her on the lips. She looked so pretty. I had made sure they didn't put too much makeup on her. Big Momma never wore makeup. I wanted her to look like she always did.

I rubbed the side of her face for the last time in my life. "I'm so sorry for everything I ever done to you," I said to her, because I knew she was listening to me. I walked off from my grandma and I wiped my tears. I knew she was in a better place. It was better for her to rest in peace than to be alive and suffering like she was.

After the funeral, I met up with Ms. Peaches and Angel. They had both helped John with the funeral. "You okay, Emerald?" Peaches asked me.

"Yeah, I'll be fine."

"The service was beautiful," Angel said as she gave me a hug.

"Yeah, it was perfect. Sissy didn't even show up," I told Ms. Peaches, like he didn't know.

"I see. Well, maybe it was for the best. It's just time to move on."

"Yeah, I guess so," I said. I felt a strange hand rubbing my back. I turned around and threw a mean mug because I thought it was Joseph's crazy ass.

"I'm sorry. Did I scare you, honey?" John asked. "I just wanted to know that you were okay."

"Yeah, I'm cool. You wanna come see my place?" I asked him, because I didn't want to be alone tonight.

"Yeah."

When we made it to my place, John's eyes grew big once he saw how I was living. My crib was much fatter than his. "Wow! Emerald, this is beautiful." He went to my balcony and looked at the view. "I want a place like this," he said to me with his sexy dimples, making me wet.

I reached in and gave him a kiss on his cheek. *John's a really good catch. He's handsome, got a hell of a body, smart, a gentleman, and he's paid. If only his dick was bigger and he stepped his fuck game up, I could see myself with him. I could be John's wife. We would be good together. Maybe I should settle down with him? I think white men treat their women better anyways.*

"How you feeling?" he asked me, breaking my thought.

"I'm fine," I said, looking off the balcony and letting the wind hit my face.

"You know I care about you," he said as he stepped behind me and kissed my neck.

"I know. I care for you too."

"Well, when you're ready to be serious, I'm here."

I just looked at him and smiled. Even though I liked him and thought about settling down, I wasn't ready to be nobody's girl. I was doing me now right now. *His ass will be there when I get ready, and if not, fuck it! I'll find another one.*

I showed John to my bedroom and we got it in a few times before I fell asleep. When I closed my eyes that night, I vowed to let the past be the past.

(HAPTER 15
ALL BETS ARE OFF

Six Weeks Later

ME AND ANGEL hit a mad lick on this lame-ass Jamaican vic. He had deep pockets and a big-ass mandingo dick—just how I like 'em: long, hard, and thick. Shit, my house was completely furnished thanks to him. I didn't mind fucking him, cause he knew how to blow a bitch back out. He was on my permanent fuck list. He had a wife, so I knew it was only about the dick and paper.

We'd fucked him into a coma last night and made ten grand apiece. Shit, it didn't get no better than this. *Free money and good dick. Shit, I think I'm back in love again.* I only had odds and ends left to finish up my house; I needed to run out to The Great Indoors to get the last pieces in my set.

After I finished cleaning up and got dressed, I went into my guest room where Angel was staying. "Angel, you coming with me?" I asked her.

"Where you going?"

"Do it matter? You ain't gotta come if you don't want to."

I grabbed my Spy bag and the keys to my newly purchased BMW 745 and headed out the door.

"Here I come," Angel yelled as she grabbed her purse. I knew she was coming.

I got in my car, put in my Ciara CD, and started jamming. "*You changed the game, I like your thug style,*" I sang to the beat.

"Girl!" Angel screamed out loud in my ear as she turned down my radio.

I shot a look at her ass. She knew better than to touch my shit. "Bitch, is you tweaking?"

"My bad, but look, I got a lick on this sweet vic over East."

"Hell naw," I said. *Shit, after fucking with that cheap-ass nigga, the eastside is Xed off my list.* "Dem niggas is cheap as hell. They want you to pop yo' pussy for five hundred dollars…fuck that."

"Naw, I'm telling you this nigga got big chips, I'm talking bout. He ain't no drug dealer. He's an Italian, older guy. He owns like six, seven car lots. He just like him some black pussy, that's all."

"How much?"

"I hit him for six stacks by myself. You know if it's the two of us, we can rack up."

"Is his dick little? Cause my patience is running low with these little-dick niggas."

"Yeah, but his head game is mean. So, you in?"

"Let me think about it." *Shit, the truth be told, every time I cock my legs open for these little-dick niggas, it ain't worth it.* I wasn't hard up for no money like Angel's ass. I could pass on them little dicks.

I stopped at the mall first; I wanted to hit up the Bebe store. I shopped with the competition sometimes. *I ain't no hater.* I picked out everything I wanted and headed to the fitting room. I slipped on a pair of Carmen jeans in my size, but they were too small. I went out and yelled to Angel to get me a bigger size. *I swear, these people will have you thinking you fat, making this shit too small.*

"There go that bitch," I heard coming from this four eyed bitch and her friends. I looked at her. I didn't know who she was and she damn sho' didn't know shit about me. The bitch was ice grilling me hard. She ain't look like shit. She had a pig nose and big pop-bottle eyes that stood out from her thick-ass glasses. Her bushy eyebrows were in need of a serious wax. She was plain ugly.

Her girls stayed posted up next to her like they were securing the president or something. Their mouths were running a mile a minute, popping mad shit.

I went back to the dressing room and got dressed. I figured they must think I was Sissy. *Damn, Dollar getting thirsty as hell, sticking his dick in these raggedy bitches.* I grabbed my Spy bag and got my blade ready just in case something popped off. This bitch would be going down if need be.

When I came out, I went to Angel and gave her that look for her to get on her A game. "Dem bitches don't want none!" Angel yelled.

Everywhere I went, them hos followed me like a lost kid. I could already see that she was nothing but Dollar's jump off. She wasn't rocking nothing name brand.

I got tired of these broke hos' bullshit. *They popping all that noise, knowing they ass can't back it up.* "Bitch, you got a problem with yo' four eyes?" I yelled at her.

"What you goin' do about it?" her ugly-ass friend spit back at me.

"Bitch, was I even talking to you?" I yelled at her ass.

"She tryin' to get all tough today." The other friend smiled.

I evaluated the situation and decided they must have rolled up on Sissy and scared her. *They got the right bitch today. This bitch is begging to get slapped. I don't let hos get away with disrespecting me.*

"Bitch, if you got a fucking problem, then let it be known. Other than that, fall yo' ugly ass back!"

"Bitch, you tryin' to get all tough today cause you with ya girl?" she said. "When I rolled up on you by yourself, you was shaking in your boots."

What? I thought Sissy was the new baddest bitch. Sissy's fake ass was out here letting these bitches punk her. She was trying to walk a mile in my stilettos and couldn't even fill 'em.

I started to walk off, since I was putting all that behind me. But Sissy was talking real greasy over the phone to me, and she out here letting bitches punk her ass. I might've been moving on, but I could still make her suffer. *Bitches need to stay in their lane. If you ain't gangster, then this shit ain't for you.*

"Bitch!" I yelled at this pig-faced ho as I stepped into her face. "You talking real tough shit! Ain't nobody scared of yo' ugly ass. You ain't shit. Dollar ain't giving you shit!" I spit on her.

"Bitch, I'll kick yo' ugly ass," she replied. *She must need her glasses cleaned.*

"That's the problem with the world, bitches like you—fucking haters. Ugly bitch, you need to take off yo' thick-ass glasses, cause you know I'm that bitch."

Frankly, I never been the one to argue with hos, and I wasn't finna start that day. I was going to show her how Sissy should have done her ass and her mouth. I took my backhand and slapped her ass down to the floor.

She was so shocked. She looked up at me. Angel got posted up, letting them bitches know to be easy.

She got up and jumped into my face like she was tough.

"You better beat it, bitch, or you gonna piss me off even more," I said.

"I got you, bitch. Wait till I find you coming outta the beauty shop. I'ma get your ass."

"Whatever!" I yelled. I coughed up enough spit to land a big one right in the middle of her eyes. I ain't run off neither. I hadn't kicked a bitch ass since I'd been home. I was ready to get it popping.

Her friends took her and ran off. I fell out laughing. Sissy was sure to get her ass kicked good. I wished I could see it.

I paid for my clothes and continued with my shopping spree. *Fuck a bitch! I ain't never scared.*

I loved the Great Indoors. Their look was different. You could pick out some fly shit and not worry about too many people having your shit. I liked to be different. I was finishing off my bathrooms and needed to pick up the last pieces to my set.

"Them bitches gonna kick your sister's ass," Angel laughed.

"I know. That's what that bitch get for trying to be me. Besides, if I can't do it, then somebody needs to kick her ass."

Me and Angel searched the towel section for the towels that matched my set. All of a sudden, I felt a cold chill shoot up my spine. I felt like I was having déjà vu or something. I heard a familiar voice headed toward me. I couldn't believe it. It was coming closer and closer. My heart started beating so fast. "Angel," I whispered.

She looked at me.

"I think that's Ms. Price!"

"I think so too," she said.

I hid in the cut so she couldn't see me. Angel put on her hat and shades to hide her face.

She had that same ghetto-ass laugh that irritated the shit outta me. As she came closer, I swore I was looking in a mirror. I saw me, but it wasn't me; it was Sissy. Her six-thousand-dollar Bogri hobo bag matched her leather jacket and boots. Her Bogri deep denim jeans and wifebeater fit perfectly, and her makeup was flawless.

She took my style and ran with it. She walked like me and talked like me. She had turned into me. I swear, all the anger that I'd tried to forget came back tenfold. I wanted to run out and slice Sissy's face up.

Sissy was worse than a drag queen trying to be Beyoncé. She was out here acting like she me, but she was letting raggedy bitches punk her. I couldn't believe my eyes. I felt all the hate I had inside of me come back with a vengeance. My blood was boiling, seeing her and knowing she was out here trying to be me.

"Momma, look at this," Sissy said to Ms. Price.

"That's nice. I came in here to get me some towels, girl."

My eyes followed them everywhere they went. I was so angry I felt like throwing up.

"Sissy, did you get that insurance check from your grandmother yet?"

Ms. Price asked.

"Yeah, I put it in the bank. Dollar is gonna use the money for something."

"Oh," Ms. Price's manipulating ass moaned.

My knees became weak, almost giving out on me. I couldn't believe it. *What the fuck she mean, insurance money? She didn't even come to Big Momma's funeral or pay for it. The nerve of this bitch.*

"Yeah, they paid it out with no problem. I had been paying on the policy for two years when I found out she was sick," Sissy said.

"I'm surprised they insured her, being sick and all."

"Well, you know, when you got connections you can do what you want."

"I know. Well, easy come, easy go, right?" said Ms. Price.

"Right."

"How the funeral get paid for?"

"I don't know. Some white guy called me and left a message saying he knew Emerald. He wanted to know was I going to help pay for the funeral. I didn't call his ass back. I'm like, first of all, don't call my phone talking about that bitch Emerald. Don't nobody give a fuck about Emerald or Big Momma. They both where they need to be…the hell outta my life." Sissy laughed.

Angel walked over to me. I was at my last straw with Sissy. I was finna kick her ass. That bitch didn't even know how I would slice her throat with my blade and Ms. Price's too.

"Girl, you so silly!" Ms. Price laughed like Sissy said something funny. They both was sick in the head.

"I'm so serious," Sissy said. "I been waiting for Big Momma to croak over for two months now. Dollar been needing that insurance check so he can flip it to make us some more money."

I threw down all my shit. That was it! *You let your own grandmother die for a nigga.* Angel pulled me back. "Emerald, no," she whispered. "Not here, not right now, but we goin' get their ass."

The more Sissy and Ms. Price ran their mouths, the more angry I got. *Fucking bitches, I swear, they're gonna get theirs.* Watching Sissy switch her ass around the store made me sick. She talking all tough now, when she was just shaking in her boots letting bitches run over her and talk shit.

"You want to eat at Lee's? I love their mashed potatoes," Sissy said.

"Girl, hell naw. The last time I ate there, I almost died. I'm allergic to nuts and they put nuts in their bread and gravy."

63

"You'll die from eating nuts?"

"Yes, I'm allergic. My throat closes up and I can't breathe. I have it really bad. I have to carry around an inhaler just in case I eat some on accident."

"Well, let's go to Webber Grill."

Ms. Price and Sissy walked off with their stank-ass perfume trailing behind them, making me sick again.

"I swear I'm going to kill her!" I yelled to Angel.

"That's messed up that Dollar can have that much mind control," Angel said. "It's crazy."

"Well, all bets are off! I know I promised Big Momma, but promises are made to be broken."

I paid for my items and headed straight to my car. The only thing on my mind right then was payback. *Sissy's ass is mine, and they better believe when I come for them,* **I'm coming like a thief in the night.** *Ain't no more Ms. Nice Bitch. Shiesty is in full effect!*

CHAPTER 16
LETTERS

I COULDN'T SLEEP or eat all week thinking about Sissy and Big Momma. I thought I was going to be okay with her being gone, but I wasn't.

I took a ride over to Big Momma's house to get the letters my dad wrote. I hadn't been in Big Momma's house in years. It looked the same way it had looked when I was sixteen. I walked past Big Momma's fireplace and she had a picture of me, her, and Sissy. I still couldn't believe she was gone.

I took a couple of pictures, went to her room, and opened the closet. Big Momma told me that the letters were at the top of her closet. When I pulled down the shoebox, letters were falling out.

Damn. All these years, I'd thought my father killed my mother and didn't love me and Sissy. I never would have imagined that Big Momma would hate anybody or keep us from our father. She was so loving and always got along with everybody. Big Momma went to church three times a week and still managed to do something wrong. *I guess you never know people like you think you do.*

I took a seat in Big Momma's favorite chair and shuffled through the letters. There were at least four hundred. It would be months before I finished reading these letters.

I found a picture of my momma and daddy hugged up and smiling. I had never seen any pictures of them together. They made a cute couple. Momma looked just like Sissy and me. *My daddy was fine as hell. No wonder Momma was on his jock. Man, I wish I could remember more about her.* I took all the pictures and letters and put them in my Louis Vuitton bag.

I still couldn't find where they had moved my dad. It was like he'd vanished in the system. I wanted to get my lawyer to look over his case so I could get him out. I hoped he would find me.

I told John that I wouldn't sell Big Momma's house and he should cover the cost out of my expenses. Big Momma had lived in this house for thirty-five years. I knew she wouldn't want me to sell it.

I got into my car and I took a look at the pendant necklace Big Momma gave me. Every time I took a look at the locket, I heard her voice in my head telling me to forgive Sissy, but I couldn't. I just couldn't get past the betrayal. Seeing Sissy had only made it worse. She was out there having a good ol' time being me. I couldn't let that slide. "Sorry, Big Momma." I looked up to the sky and cried. I had to do what was right. Sissy couldn't get away with what she did.

CHAPTER 17
SLIM

I NEEDED TO get my plans in order to go and meet that guy Roxy told me about. I hadn't talked to Roxy or seen her since I'd been out, but she'd told me all that I needed to know while I was there. Slim wanted to take over Dollar's turf, and I was just the bitch to help him get it.

Roxy told me about a couple of places I could find him, and I was going out looking. My first stop was Neal's car wash. Roxy said he went there every Friday at one.

When I made it up to Neal's, it was packed like they was giving away free food. The workers scrambled to get my keys. I've always wondered why most of the workers at a car wash are crackheads. I guess they're the only people who will work for cheap. My Range needed washing anyway, so I gave the man the keys. "I know how much change I have and how many CDs I got in my car," I scolded.

He smacked his three teeth. "Ain't nobody trying to steal from you." He could talk all that shit he wanted, but I knew how crackheads do. I just brought back my CD collection, and I'd be damned if he stole my shit to go and sell it for two and five dollars.

All eyes were on me when I went into the waiting area. I stepped back and searched the room. There was only three nice whips that was getting washed, so it shouldn't be too hard finding this guy.

I walked around the waiting room and took a closer look. Thank God I knew how to sniff out money. I spotted two prospects, both tall and chocolate. One was G'd and the other guy was low-key. My gut was telling me that the low-key brother was Slim. He was way finer than the other guy, so maybe I just wanted him to be Slim. I walked up to him and smiled. "You got change for a hundred?" I asked.

"No, baby girl, I don't," he said. "The owner might." *Maybe I'm wrong. What kind of drug dealer don't have change for a hundred?*

"Can you show me the owner? It's so many guys in here."

"Sure…" he said as he looked for me to give him my name.

"Emerald," I said.

"Emerald, I'm Slim." *Jackpot. But dis nigga broke. He ain't even got change for a hundred.*

"Hi, Slim. How much does a car wash cost here?"

"What do you have, a car or a truck?"

"A Range," I smiled to let him know a bitch is balling.

"I like that," he said as he flashed a smile at me.

I was impressed with Slim. His name didn't represent him well. I thought he'd be tall and thin, but instead he was tall and built. His wife-beater showed his strong tattooed arms and his six-pack abs. *Shit, I need that in my life.* His chocolate skin was smooth and buttery. His mustache was lined perfect. He had a classic smile with pretty white straight teeth. His low-cut caesar with the deep waves showed he was blessed with some good genes. This brother was serious. He was much finer than Dollar. He had on no jewels, no ice, nothing. He was just plain. He didn't look like no drug dealer to me.

"Fourteen dollars," he said, knocking me outta my daze.

"Thank you," I said.

"You from around here?" he asked me

"No, I stay downtown."

"You came all the way out here for a car wash?"

"No, I came to meet you."

"Me?" he said as his eyes looked me up and down.

"Yeah," I said. I could tell he was trying to read me. "Be easy. I'm just messing wit ya."

"Really?"

"Yeah, what, you scared of me?" I asked.

"Scared is not a word I use in my vocabulary."

"I'm glad to hear that, cause I hate scary-ass niggas. My Range is ready. Take my number and call me when you're free."

He looked at me and smiled. "What is it?"

I took his phone and stored my number as "New Wifey." When I gave it back to him, he just stared at me. *Niggas love a bitch that knows she all that.* "I'ma call you tonight," he said.

I waved my hands up at him like it didn't matter whether he called or not. I hoped he would call me. I hoped my plan worked.

When I jumped into my car, I checked to see if my change was still there and I thumbed through my CDs. "I told you I don't steal!" the guy yelled at me.

I took out twenty dollars and handed it to him. "Make sure you do the right thing with that," I said as I pulled off.

My Plies CD was playing loud as I snapped my fingers to "Shawty." I didn't notice my phone ringing until it started vibrating on my lap, scaring me. When I looked at the phone, it was an unknown number, so I knew it was Slim. I wasn't gone a good ten minutes and he was calling me already. "What's up, Slim?"

"How you know it was me?"

"Because I knew."

"You're real sure of yourself."

"I am," I said. "I have no reason to second-guess myself."

"I feel you, shorty. Can I see you tonight?"

"What time?"

"Is seven good for you? I have to take care of some business first," he said.

"Yeah. Where you want to meet?" I asked him.

"Anywhere you want."

"Well, meet me at my place," I said. "I'll figure something out by then. I stay downtown. I'll text you my address."

"Cool," he said then he hung up. I was happy he'd called me. I told him to meet me at my place because I had business I wanted to discuss with him. I needed him to feel like he could trust me.

My doorbell rang just before seven. I'd just finished fixing myself up. My house was so fucking fly, I knew it would impress him. I had all fly shit in my crib, nothing but the best. I'd fucked the shit out of Mandingo to get this shit. Selling my pussy really paid off. My house was picture-perfect.

I fixed Slim some dinner—stuffed chicken breast with rice pilaf—so we could stay in. I wasn't sure what kind of food he ate, but I figured all black people eat chicken. I took one last look at myself in the mirror. I was looking off glass. I had my hair blow-dried and my feet redid just in case it popped off. It was still hot outside, so I slipped into a summer dress that showed every curve I owned.

When I made it to the door, Slim was standing there looking sexy as hell. He had on a G-Unit short set, the matching G-Unit sneakers, and a Rolex watch, and he smelled like Puffy's cologne Unforgettable—that shit smells off the chain. He still wasn't iced out. He couldn't pass as a drug dealer to me. *I hope he ain't no wanksta, because he don't represent a baller at all.*

"Come in," I said as I waved my hand for him to enter.

"Your house is just as gorgeous as you."

"Thank you. Please have a seat."

He took a look around, seeing how my house decor flowed from one room to the next. I knew his ass was impressed. He probably dealt with only tackheads.

"I cooked us dinner, if you don't mind," I said.

"You can cook?"

"Of course. I can do a lot of things. I'm bad."

He just cracked a smile at me. I walked over to the kitchen and I felt his eyes searching my body. *Yeah, it's off the chain, ain't it?*

I fixed him a plate of food and set it on my dining room table. "Go wash your hands and come sit down to eat." He got off my couch and I pointed him to the guest bathroom. When he entered the hallway coming back my way, he looked so damn good to me I coulda ripped his clothes off. His aura was so smooth; he was so low-key, it made me want him more.

"Sit down here," I said. "What would you like to drink?"

"Juice would be fine."

I brushed past him so he could catch a whiff of my Be Delicious that trailed behind me. I brought him a Snapple, sat down across from him, and ate.

"You know you didn't have to cook for me," Slim said.

"It's cool. You never had a girl cook you a meal before?"

He smiled at me. "So, Emerald, what was your real purpose for coming all the way out south today?"

I just looked at him and smiled. "You were my reason." I'd just met him, and maybe it was too soon, but I just didn't have time to waste.

He put down his fork and looked at me sideways. I could tell he was unsure about being here. That's a drug dealer's mentality...never trust a bitch.

"Look, Slim, I'ma keep it real with ya," I said.

"Please do," he said as he backed away from the table.

"Be easy, nigga. Ain't nobody tryin' to set you up. Chill."

His facial expression changed from low-key to "Bitch, pull it and I'll wet your ass." *I guess Slim has two different sides to him.*

"Look, can I trust you to tell you something private without you running your mouth?" I asked him.

"You don't know me," he said.

"That's true, but you need to know me."

"Why is that?"

"Look, I heard about you from Roxy."

He gave me a confused look. "How you know Roxy? She's in jail."

My face turned red and I hung my head low. I was too embarrassed to tell Slim that I was in jail with her. "Look, never mind," I said, all sassy. I got scared and turned into a chicken for the first time in my life.

"No, finish. Don't get scared now. Tell me what the hell's going on!" He looked upset with me.

He probably thinking I'm tryin' to stick him for his paper. "Look, Slim, I want to show you something." I got outta my seat and went to my balcony.

Slim didn't move. He was trying to peep my action…read what was on my mind. "Can you please just come here?" I asked.

After five minutes he got up and walked my way. "Look, Emerald, I don't know what type of games you're playing, but I ain't wit it."

"Just look at all the girls down there." It was hot as hell in the Chi and downtown was packed. It was a comedy show at the Chicago Theater.

"What am I looking at?" he asked me, frustrated.

"Those clothes. Look at all those clothes." And he did. Every other chick that walked by had on my shit, Icey. "You see, I got every bitch in the hood rocking my shit."

"What, Icey? That's your store?"

"Yeah, that's my shit. I'm that bitch."

He just looked at me not knowing what to say.

"Look, I'm filthy. I don't need a dollar from ya," I went on. "I don't need to be your bitch. I own eleven stores. My security strap's in the millions, so I ain't looking to set ya ass up for some paper."

"Well, what do you want from me?"

"I know you're trying to take over Dollar's spot, and I'm just the bitch to help ya."

He walked back inside, sat back down at the table, and continued to eat. I knew he was wondering now…was I Five-O? He was too difficult to read.

I walked back in and went into the kitchen. He came in behind me and pushed me against the refrigerator. He grabbed me by the cheeks and took his other hand and searched my body. Once he saw that I wasn't wearing a wire, he let me go. Truth be told, I loved the way his hands touched me.

My pussy was flaming.

"What's your deal?" he asked me.

"Look," I said as I turned away from him. "I want Dollar to go down. I owe him one."

"What's that got to do wit me?"

"His turf. I ain't running it."

"What's yo' beef?" Slim asked.

"It's a long story," I said as I brushed by him and sat on the couch.

He walked behind me and sat beside me. "I'm listening."

"Look," I stuttered as I searched for the words to say to him. I didn't know him from a can of paint. How could I tell him my business? He might go and spread the word about me being out and everything would be ruined. I knew I couldn't lie. I knew that at first daylight break he was going to see Roxy to check out my story. "Look, I don't know if I can trust you with my personal business."

"But, you want me to trust you enough to agree to set up a nigga, when all I know, you could be working wit him."

"Please," I said as I rolled my eyes. He took a good look at me. He grabbed my face again like he was having déjà vu. He got off the couch and made a phone call, whispering so I couldn't hear him. His motions were fast as he paced my kitchen floor.

"Bitch, you's a liar," he snapped as he pulled out his strap that I had no idea he had. He went to my bedroom and kicked in the door. I got scared. My heart started racing fast as hell. *I shouldn't have done this here. This motherfucker is crazy.*

"Where he at?" he said as he cocked back his gun.

"Where who at?" I said as fear went over my face.

"That nigga up in here."

I looked at him in the eyes. He felt like I was setting him up. "Slim, chill! It's just me and you up in here. I swear on my life. It's just us."

"No, I seen you wit that nigga."

"No, that's my sister," I said in a low voice.

"You think I'm stupid?"

I got off my couch and went into the hallway closet. Slim's eyes never left my body. "Look," I said as I handed him pictures from my birthday party. "That's me and that's my sister. We look like twins."

He took the pictures outta my hands and looked through them. "What kind of games you playing?"

I knew then that I needed to come clean. "Look, Slim," I said as my voice began to shake. "I met Dollar when I was sixteen. I fell in love with him. I moved in with him and tried to be all the woman he needed, but I was just dumb enough to believe he loved me too. I was his ride-or-die chick. I did everything for him. I carried dope across state lines for him a countless number of times."

I saw him loosening up and listening to me. "I let him put all his properties in my name foolishly. I believed it wasn't a big deal. I opened my clothing store legit—that didn't have nothing to do with the drug sales. I started stacking my money and hiding it from him just in case. One day I made a drop and he claimed I stole fifty thousand dollars from him."

I got off the couch and walked to the balcony because I needed some fresh air. Slim followed me. "Well, afterwards, he beat the shit outta me and told me to go and get his money back. I had money in the bank that I took out and gave him back. I thought that would make him love me again. Instead, he said shit wasn't working out. He told me if I ran some dope to California for him, we could get back together. I loved him so much, Slim, I thought that was gonna bring us back together. But the drop went bad and police got there and I got arrested." Tears started rolling down my eyes. I began to shake as a chill ran up my back.

"Don't cry, sweetie," Slim said.

I just looked at him. "Well, when it was time to fess up, Dollar promised me that if I took the blame, he would marry me when I got out. He said I would only get six months in jail. I wanted him so bad that I took the stand and lied for him, and when the gavel came down, I got ten years in prison." Slim looked shocked.

"That's nothing," I continued. "After time went on and I hadn't seen or heard a word from him, I started to feel like he was moving on with his life. Three months passed and he didn't call or see me, no money on my books, nothing. He left me to die in jail. And when my sister came to see me, she made it clear that she was fucking him now—that he had set me up to go to jail and do his time. My own sister crossed me and turned her back on me. When I got a hold of Dollar, he told me it was just business and not to take it personal." I started to breathe heavy. Just thinking about it made me lightheaded.

"Well, how you get out?" Slim asked.

"My money. I owned six stores at the time. They all thought I was broke and would die in jail, but I had mad cash. My gay friend paid a lawyer for me to get an appeal, and the judge overturned my sentence and let me out with time served."

"Word. That's heavy."

"Yeah," I said. "They don't know I'm home, and I want to keep it that way."

"I got you," Slim said. "So where do I come into play?"

"Dollar gots to go down, period. I'ma make that motherfucker pay."

"Revenge?"

"If that's what you call it."

"Look, I've been reading my Holy Koran and I think you should just move on with your life," he said.

Koran, who give a fuck about a Koran? Dis nigga got me twisted. "Well, I tried that. I was just gonna leave well enough alone and live my life. But my grandmother passed, and I kind of ran into my sister and she was making fun, saying how she was glad my grandmother died and she couldn't wait to get her check."

"That's fucked up. I'm sorry to hear about your loss. I know how you feel. I lost both of my parents."

"Yeah, I gotta make her pay. She walking around here trying to fill my shoes, and I ain't having it. If you ain't down, I know dis nigga name Black tryin' to come up too. Maybe he'll be down."

"Naw, squash that, little momma," Slim said. "What you got planned?"

"I don't know. I'm still working that out," I said. "So, you in?"

"I guess I'm wit that…but, no killing. I ain't going to jail for nobody."

"Good." I was glad Slim was down for me. It would be that much easier to make Dollar pay.

(HAPTER 18
JOHN

IT WAS 85 degrees outside and it was only seven in the morning. My head had been pounding all night. I jumped into the shower to relax my mind.

I'd thought about Slim fucking me all night long. My pussy was soaking wet thinking about him last night. The warm water hitting my nipples was making me hot. I needed to be fucked right.

John wanted to hang out today. I liked spending time with him. He could get on my left nerve sometimes, sweating me about being together, but other than that, I liked kicking it with him. *Everybody wants to wife me. Damn, I'm a bad motherfucker. I guess I'm something like J-Lo. I ain't getting tied down to nobody. I'm living a single life.*

I jumped outta the shower and lotioned myself up. It was so hot outside, I really wanted to stay in and relax. I put on a short set and some flip-flops. I didn't know what John had planned, but I wanted to be comfortable.

I went to the kitchen to fix me something to eat and Angel was at the table watching the news.

"Why you watching that depressing shit?" I asked

"To see what's going on in the hood."

"Whatever," I replied as I sat down and ate my Honeycomb. "How's the store coming along out there?"

"Good. It's doing well. We're running neck and neck with Wet Seal."

"Good." That's what I wanted to hear. Making money...that's music to my ears.

"What you doing tonight?" she asked me.

"Why?"

"Cause I got us a lick. This nigga got big chips and money to burn."

"Is this nigga dick little?" I said.

"It ain't big like we like, but his pockets deep."

"What you want with me?" I asked her.

"He asked for a threesome. He's been lacing me. Shit, that's the quickest dollar I make. His dick don't stay up too long."

"I know. That's the problem," I said. "I don't like wasting my pussy's time."

"Come on, Emerald, please. We probably get like twenty Gs outta this nigga."

Twenty Gs was a good lick, but my time was priceless. "I'll pass on the little dicks. Sorry!"

"A'ight."

Angel looked disappointed, but I was tired of these little-dick-ass niggas. Besides, I was spending time with John and I wanted to give all my attention to him.

I met John at his place. When I rang his doorbell, he was waiting for me. "You ready, beautiful?" he asked as he grabbed his car keys to leave.

"Yeah. Where we going?"

"It's a surprise. I have a surprise for you. Can you ride with me?"

Surprise…I hope dis nigga ain't waste his money on a wedding ring, cause I already told his ass five times I ain't getting married. We got into John's G-wagon Benz and he couldn't keep his eyes off me.

"You like what you see?" I asked.

"Yeah, I do. You're so beautiful, Emerald."

"I know I am." I listened to John go on and on about us. I knew John would make a good husband. But he couldn't eat pussy right, and his dick was cool, but just not big enough. He had too many minuses in areas I needed to make a marriage work. *I gots to get fucked good. I'm a nympho. I have to have it all the time. But on the other side, he's so sweet, got mad loot, and sexy. I ain't tryin' be locked down. I ain't even 22 yet. Damn, it's such a curse to have a mean-ass kitty kat like this. Everybody wants to lock her down after just one whiff.*

I drifted off to sleep because it was taking forever to get to where we were going. *"If you see a bad bitch, point her out…"* R Kelly sang in my ear, waking me outta my sleep. John looked over at me. I pressed my ignore button. *Stupid people who call me private must don't want to talk.* I never answered those calls.

After the tenth time the person called back, I got so irritated that I answered. "Who the fuck is this?" I said, all nasty.

"So, is he the reason you don't want to be with me?" a deep-toned voice asked me.

"What?" I yelled. "Who the hell is this?"

"Just answer me, Emerald. Is he?"

"Joseph?" I asked as I looked over at John's face.

"So you wanna be with him. Is that it? You playing me for a white guy. How could you, Emerald, after I gave you everything?"

My heart started beating. I took a look around to see if I saw his car.

"You okay, Emerald?" John asked me.

"Yeah, just trying to find where I'm at," I answered John, holding my phone to my ear.

"I can't have this. He can't have you!" Joseph cried.

"Didn't I tell yo' ass to leave me alone, crazy nigga?"

"Emerald, I've been very patient with you. I'm not playing games no more. Now you're gonna be mine. You understand me?"

"Nigga, get a life, you loser!" I hung up the phone on him. I couldn't believe the nerve of him, talking that shit. I was starting to think he was crazier than I thought. He must have been following me if he knew I was with John.

"You all right?" John asked me.

"Yeah, just this crazy stalker…he ain't on nothing, though."

"You sure."

"Yeah," I said, but I really wasn't. I wasn't gonna worry about it either. If he wanted to pull it, I'd make him feel the steal without any questions.

We finally made it to the place. We were somewhere off in the country. It was a strawberry farm and winery. I had never been to anything like that before.

"What we gonna do here?" I asked.

"Pick some strawberries and drink wine."

This was so sweet and different. That was one of the things I loved about John—he planned shit. *Niggas don't do shit like this. I guess I have to put a plus down for this one.*

When we got in, I picked out a picnic basket, and John and I went out into the garden. I love strawberries. The weather out there was nice and breezy. I felt so free. All my worries were gone.

After I picked me a basket full of big juicy red strawberries, John covered my eyes and I followed him further out into the woods. When I opened my eyes, he had a picnic set up for us.

I couldn't help but smile. *He's the sweetest guy I fuck wit.* "Thank you, John! I didn't know picking strawberries could be so much fun."

"Anything for you, sweetie."

I let John lay his head in my lap and fed him some strawberries and grapes. After a few glasses of wine, I got horny and I made John take his shirt off. His body was cut up harder than Vin Diesel's.

I took the whipped cream and sprayed it all over his six-pack. I licked him from his navel up to his lips. Even though I kept telling myself, "He ain't the one," something kept drawing me to him.

I sucked his fingers one by one and unbuckled his pants. I took off my shirt and rubbed whipped cream over my nipples. I loved getting my nipples sucked. John grabbed my breast and sucked it just the way I liked it. He licked me down to my navel, pulling off my shorts. Then he went down and kissed me on my pussy. I shivered. He tried his best to lick me good, but it just wasn't good enough. I pushed him to the ground and slid down on his rock-hard dick.

We both fell back to catch our breath after forty minutes of switching positions.

"Emerald, I want to be with you," he said. "I'm not trying to pressure you into marrying me. I just want to be with you."

Why he always got to blow a good fuck? Damn, let a bitch breathe. "John, I understand that and I think you a cool motherfucker, but I ain't ready to settle down yet. I'm sorry."

"I understand," he said like a sad kid.

I got up and put my clothes on. *He had to kill my moment. Can I help it if I'm a hot bitch and everybody wants to get with me?* "We cool?" I asked him because he was walking around stomping like a little kid that lost his damn bike.

"Yeah, sweetie, we cool."

When we made it back to where my car was parked, I gave John some head to relax his nerves before I got out. *I think he cool and all, but I don't feel like he the one. I can't sell myself short.* I sucked him good too. John knew his ass wasn't going nowhere. Where else was he gonna find a raw bitch like me? *I'm the baddest bitch in the Chi...probably the whole Midwest. Shit, it gets no iller than me.*

CHAPTER 19
JOSEPH

I WALKED UP to my car and there was a note stuck to my window. When I picked it up, the smell of cologne hit me. *I know that cheap-ass Cool Water from a mile away.* I opened the letter. It was from Joseph's stalking ass. He was starting to get on my left nerve.

Emerald,
  Why are you playing games with me when you know I love you? Is he the reason that you won't come with me? How could you tell me that you love me and then sleep with another man? I saw you with him giving him my kisses and my loving. Emerald, I will not tolerate these games any longer. You don't play with people's feelings like this. You leave me no choice, Emerald. I love you and I won't let anyone else have you.
P.S.
You can make things easier if you just come and be with me.

I balled up his little raggedy-ass note and jumped into my car. *Who this lame-ass nigga think he making threats to? He done lost all his fucking mind.* I called him up just to check his dumb ass. I don't like people making threats to me.

He answered and I blasted his ass. "Nigga, you must be smoking some serious crack if you think you goin' stalk or threaten me."

"Emerald, I love you," he cried like a little bitch.

"Nigga, get over me. Listen to some Bow Wow and get me outta your system. Ain't nothing popping off between me and you."

"But you said you loved me."

"I never said that shit, and stop lying on me. I said I loved your dick, not you. I never liked you like that. I was only fucking you to get out of them meetings. Other than that, you woulda never had a chance to holla at a dime bitch, partner."

"So you used me?" he asked as his voice cracked up.

"Well, if that's the way you take it. I call it helping. You helped me get out of them meetings and I fucked you good. Too damn good ya ass sprung out on this crack I got."

"So you never loved me?"

"Nigga, how many times I gotta tell you the same thing? No! I mean, really, you not even on my level. You broke as hell. What am I gonna do with you? Please." I laughed at his dumb ass.

"So you think you can get away with using people and playing with their feelings?"

"Joseph, stay the fuck away from me and get a life." I hung up the phone on his simple ass. *Sprung nigga! I don't give a fuck about his feelings. Nobody cared about hurting mines. Fuck 'em*

CHAPTER 20
SLIM

I THOUGHT ABOUT calling Joseph all night and apologizing to him. I wanted to tell him I was sorry for using him. *He didn't do nothing to me. I should apologize to him.*

I picked up the phone, and all my memories of being in jail and how Dollar hurt me flooded my mind. "Fuck that nigga," I said to myself. *He got free pussy and that was good enough. That's his own fault for getting sprung. It's all about me. I'm doing what the fuck I want to.*

When I slammed the phone down, Slim called me up and asked if he could come over and talk to me. I didn't mind. I wanted to see him. I wanted to fuck him, and if he had a big dick, I might give him a free pass. *But he's gots to whip it out and let me see it. Shit, I ain't got no time for the little dicks.* I showered and lotioned myself in my chocolate mousse lotion. It tasted good. I made sure my pussy was fresh and my ass was lickable. I threw on my La Perla boyshorts and a tank top—something real sweet and sexy.

I went to the kitchen to fix us a snack, and then I chose a movie. When he rang my doorbell, my pussy started throbbing. "Calm down," I told her. I opened up the door and he was standing there looking too sexy. He'd just gotten himself lined up and his big arms were sticking outta his tank top.

"Come in," I said.

When he walked in, I caught a whiff of his Kenneth Cole Black cologne. "Don't wear that cologne no more," I told him, because it reminded me of Dollar.

"Why?"

"Cause I don't like it," I said. But the truth was that I was flaming inside. He was all that and a bag of chips. I wanted to lay him down and show him what I got.

"A'ight," he said as he flopped down on my couch. "You fix me something to eat?" he asked, like I was his bitch or something.

"I did, but don't get beside yourself or you'll be hungry." He just laughed at me. I went in the kitchen and got the sub sandwiches I'd made and grabbed a bag of chips and juice.

"So what's up?" I asked.

"I can't seem to get you off my mind. I been thinking about you all the time."

"I know," I said all cocky, knowing my pussy stayed soaking wet thinking about him.

"No, serious," he said.

"Well, what you was thinking about?"

"I was thinking you should come down to the hall with me and read the Koran."

Dis nigga just blew the fuck outta me. "You want me to go to church?"

"Yeah."

What type of fucking drug dealer is this simple-ass nigga? Drug dealers don't go to fucking church! Dis nigga better get his mind right. "Look, Slim, I don't know what's your deal. Do you sell drugs or not? Because right now I think you's a wanksta."

"I ain't trying to sell them forever."

"Well, to be truthfully honest, you look broke, like you faking dis shit."

"Why, cause I ain't iced out?" he asked.

"Pretty much."

"Look, Emerald, I ain't been hustling long—just a little over a year. Guess how much money I got saved?"

"How much?" I asked. It really didn't matter to me. I was rich already.

"Over six hundred thousand dollars, and that's because I don't buy ice and all that unnecessary shit. I got a game plan, and selling drugs is only a two-year thing for me, sweetie."

"Then why you want to take over Dollar's turf if you getting outta the game?"

"More money to save up for my legit business."

"What you want to do?"

"Be a rapper and own my own record label," he said.

I just looked at him. *Every nigga in da hood want to be Lil Jeezy. But I ain't goin' shit on the man's dreams. All dem niggas was hugging da block before they made it.* "You nice?"

"Yeah, me and my boy, I got big dreams."

"Well, I'm happy for you," I said. "I hope ya make it. But how you gone be a rapping Muslim?"

"I haven't figured that out yet. I'm not a Muslim. I just study with them."

"Um," I said, cause I wasn't trying to hear nothing about it. I knew that shit wasn't for me. I wasn't walking around with my head wrapped up walking behind my man. Shit, I'm a boss bitch and I like to show my toes out in the summertime. "Well, what you want me to do?"

"Clean some of my money up."

Here we go wit that bullshit. I ain't trying to go to jail for nobody. Fuck dat. "Look, Slim, I ain't trying to go to jail for you."

"Believe me, Emerald, I don't want to put ya there. You seem like a smart girl. You got your own business. I'm just looking for a legal hustle and thought maybe you had some ideas."

It made me feel good that he called me smart. That made me dig him even more. "What about a barber shop? You know anybody who can cut hair?"

"Yeah, I have a few homies that can."

"Good," I said. "As long as they have a license, then that's where you start. And since you helping me, I'll front you the money, but you gotta give it back to me under the table." *Shit, cause I pays no nigga's way.* "So, I'll give you thirty grand and you give me cash. That way it looks like everything was done legal."

"That's what I'm talking about," Slim said. "I can't wait so I won't have to stress and look over my shoulder, ya know?"

"Yeah. So what about ya girl? She down for ya?"

"I don't have a girlfriend. I'm single."

"Yeah, right." *You know niggas be popping that shit. I don't give a fuck, because this mean pussy right here is a man-snatcher.*

"No, serious, I don't," he said.

"Nigga, stop lying. You tryin' to be a Muslim so you can have two wives."

"No I ain't. I'm looking for one bad chick so I can spoil her—somebody I can connect with on every level. These birds that's chasing me just want my paper."

I wanted to tell him that he was looking for me, but I ain't looking to be nobody's bitch. "Well, you'll find her," I said.

He started looking at me, and I know he wanted some of this pussy. I know he caught a whiff of this fat pussy when I uncrossed my legs.

He reached in and rubbed the side of my face so softly, I started trembling. I wanted Slim so bad, but it wasn't happening between us. "Look,

Slim, I've been hurt and I ain't looking to be nobody's bitch. And I don't fuck for free, so if you want a piece of my fat kat, you gots to run lil' momma some bread."

"I don't pay for pussy!"

"Well, suit yourself," I said as I cocked my legs open. "You see this fat pussy?" He just looked at me. I knew he wanted it. "Fucking wit dem low-rate bitches is worthless. Finding a piece of pussy this mean...now, that's priceless."

He looked at me, and I saw him moving his dick from one side to the other. "Don't deny yourself the best fuck of your life, cause after me, you won't try another, trust," I said.

"Emerald, I think you're gorgeous, and the pussy's definitely fat, but I don't pay for pussy."

"Well, let's keep it strictly business, then," I said. *Shit, his loss, not mine. I gets dick on a regular. He ain't goin' find a piece of pussy this mean.*

Slim got up and left out. Too bad for him, cause I was goin' give him some of my super head.

(HAPTER 21
IRRESISTIBLE

I COULDN'T GET my mind off Slim. He was the only man that ever turned me down. I wanted to see what he was working with. He was kind of mysterious. Every time I laid my head down, he was on my mind—holding me and touching me.

My doorbell rang and my heart started racing. He must have come to his senses. He changed his mind and wanted to get a piece of this mean kitty kat. "Who is it?" I asked through the door.

"It's me, Angel. I left my key."

Angel. Shit, I got all excited for nothing. She needs to hurry up and get her own place. She working my left nerve.

Angel came in, sat on the couch, and turned on the TV. Although she was barely ever there, I still wanted her to get her own place fast. "When you getting a place?" I asked. "I mean, you got a new car and all."

"I told you, it ain't ready yet."

"Um, what's taking so long?" *Shit, I don't like having roommates unless they got a dick hanging.*

"You know how long it takes. I'm moving in this building."

"What? You ain't tell me that shit!"

"I did," she said.

"Why you biting me?"

"I'm not getting a penthouse, just a two-bedroom. I'm not on the same floor as you."

One thing I hate is a swagger jacking bitch. This trick knows that. Next thing I know she gonna wanna walk a mile in my shoes too.

"I just wanted to be close to you."

"Why?" I asked. "We ain't sisters or friends…we just cool."

"Whatever, Emerald—Shiesty—whoever you are at this time."

"What the hell is that supposed to mean?"

"It means one minute you cool and the next minute you acting like a bitch."

"Watch you mouth before I slap you in it." Angel should have known better than to be running her mouth at me.

"I'm sorry. It's confusing me. One minute we cool as hell and the next I ain't shit to you."

"Don't nothing mean shit to me except money. That's all I care about, sweetcakes. And speaking of money, you ready to go see Mandingo?"

"Wait," Angel said. "I thought you said you was gonna teach me how to deep throat?"

"Damn, I'ma start charging ya ass." I went into my room, took out a dildo, and walked back to the front room. "You ready? Cause I don't have all day to show you how to suck dick."

"Yeah."

"Good. Now open your mouth." When she opened her mouth, I shoved that dildo down her throat. I didn't give her time to pull away. *You gots to get gangster wit it.* That was how Ginger did me—she just shoved that dick right down my throat.

Angel's gag reflex was going crazy and she was trying to throw up, so I gave her a towel. Tears were forming in her eyes, but she took it like a champ.

"Sit like that for twenty minutes," I told her as I walked off to finish getting dressed.

Angel was right about me. I was flipping out. One minute I was fine and the next I felt like "Fuck the world." It was like one half of me wanted to do good, but the other half was just evil. Shiesty took over me sometimes and I didn't give a fuck, but when I was myself, I didn't like hurting people.

Angel was still gagging, but she was holding up like a soldier. She didn't take the dildo out of her mouth. After ten minutes had passed, she stopped gagging and was more relaxed.

When I came and took the dick outta her mouth, she took in a deep breath. "Damn, bitch, you was tryin' to kill me!"

"No, just a crash course in dicksucking. Now act like you sucking the dick."

She did. She took it down her throat without any problems. Once she felt like she was getting good at it, she stopped and started to smile.

"I'm too glad," Angel said. "This nigga I'm talking to, name Black... he been lacing a bitch. I'm thinking about moving in wit him. I really like him."

I knew who Black was. He was making little moves in the hood. *She can be a fool if she wants to.* "You can be stupid and fall in love wit that nigga if you want," I said.

"But I know he really likes me, Emerald."

"And we thought that same shit about Dollar. Shit, I can't run ya life. I'm just saying, keep ya eyes wide open, cause these niggas ain't shit."

"I know that," she said as she took in a deep breath. "So what, we supposed to be out here tricking forever?"

"Bitch, I ain't no trick. I'm getting paid! I'm rich. I don't need a nigga's money for nothing."

"I think he's the one."

"Then go on and be wit his ass. But you know what all comes with dating a hood nigga? Hos and drama."

"Yeah, you right, Emerald."

I know I'm right. Fuck these simple-ass niggas. Angel sat there with a sad look on her face. *She must be really digging dis nigga.* "Look, Angel, if you like the nigga, fine, be wit his ass, but trust me, you better keep treating that nigga like shit. When you treat these niggas good, that's when they run over yo' ass. When you treat them like shit, that's when you have to pull them outta ya ass. Shit, niggas love to be treated like shit, so keep that in mind."

"Yeah, you right, Emerald. I think I'ma stop tricking around and be faithful to him."

I couldn't help but bust into a loud laugh. *Sprung bitch.* "Girl, you going too far with this love shit. If you think a street nigga gonna be faithful, you dumber than you look."

"I know that."

"Well, why you giving up yo' dick? You better keep a piece of dick on the low. It's the American way."

"I'm just getting tired and want to settle down and start a family—get married and be normal."

"Girl, please save that shit for Little House on the Prairie, cause ain't no such thing as white picket fences and shit in the hood," I said. Angel was completely gone in the head if she thought for one second a drug dealer was gonna make a good husband.

"Well, let me dream, then!" she said. "I know he's the one for me. Unlike you, I'm over Dollar stupid ass. All niggas ain't like him."

When she said that slick shit outta her mouth, she hit my nerve bad. "Bitch!" I yelled as I jumped into her face. "Don't you ever fix yo' mouth and talk down to me. I will slice ya ass up and send you packing. You hear me? I run this shit, me. Don't mention that nigga name ever again in my house. You understand?"

"Sorry, Emerald. I just know there's more to life than hurting."

"Girl, get a life. Life ain't shit but a big-ass game, and if you playing it, you better play to win, because it's cold and it ain't fair."

When we got into the car, I thought about what Angel said about being married. I mean, tricking ain't easy…but being married? I was too young for that shit. *Fuck that. I'm pimping for life! Shit, fuck a nigga. I ain't falling in love with none of they asses. Fuck you, nigga, pay me. That's my motto. I gots to get mine.*

I pulled up to Mandingo's house, and I was already nice and wet thinking about his big dick. That was one piece of dick that I always looked forward to.

When the housekeeper let us in, I went right to his big-ass bedroom. Mandingo was living phat, and this was just one of his spots. His wife and kid stayed at another place across town.

Mandingo was standing there with his body all oiled up, looking good enough to eat. He was built like a boxer and was packing something major below. His dark skin was smooth and pimple-free. His Jamaican accent got on my nerves. I couldn't understand half the shit he was saying.

"Baby girls, I been waiting for you," he said as his words slurred.

"Me too," I said as I started to take off all my clothes. I knew what time it was.

Mandingo ripped off my panties. I didn't even care that they were La Perla. I was just ready for his big dick. "Bloodclot, I want you to let little momma eat you out. I want to see it like that," he said. His accent was such a turnoff, but I was always down for getting some good head.

I lay back on his oversized plush bed and kicked my legs back. Angel crawled over to me and licked me from my inner thighs up to the lips of my pussy. I threw my head back and closed my eyes. She started licking me slowly as her free hand went in and out of my pussy at a rapid speed.

Mandingo came over to me and pushed his long dick into my mouth. I wanted this Marc Jacobs bag I'd seen, so I was giving him the super treatment so he could break me off extra. I sucked him with all my might, catching all the thrust he was giving me from his hips.

"Oh baby girl, you de best, I swear," he chanted over and over again.

He started to speed up. I knew he was about to explode, and so was I. Angel's tongue strokes were getting deeper and deeper until my body started shaking. Screaming was not an option because my mouth was full of Mandingo's dick.

"Oh, drink it down, baby girl," he moaned.

I normally don't swallow no nigga's nut. But for ten to twenty Gs, I felt it was only right to give the man what he paid for. Once I sucked him dry, he got up and kissed me on my mouth, and then Angel.

"I want you to turn around," he commanded me, and I jumped right to it. Getting hit from the back is my favorite position.

"I want you to lay down right there," he told Angel.

Angel lay down, and he ordered me to eat her out. I hesitated at first. I'd never put my mouth on Angel before, but I knew that if I wanted all my money, I needed to do it.

I licked Angel lightly at first. I didn't know what her pussy smelled or tasted like. But once my tongue hit her, she didn't taste half bad. Mandingo slid his long dick inside me, giving me long deep strokes. I gave Angel the best head I could. Shit, his dick was feeling so good to me, I kept losing focus.

After two hours of fucking, we all fell back on the bed. I was ready for a nap. *I swear, I'd fuck him still even if I got married. I don't think the dick gets better than Mandingo.*

"Look, baby girls, I need you to do something for me," he said, but I was halfway asleep.

"What?" Angel replied.

"I need you to carry something across town for me."

"Like what?" Angel asked, as if she didn't know already.

"It don't matter. Just a package. Me pay you sixty Gs to take that across town."

"Hell no!" I yelled. *I don't give a fuck how much he's paying. I ain't getting into that shit again.*

"Why you tripping, bloodclot? I thought you was down."

"Mandingo, ask your wife to haul that shit!" I yelled as I rolled my eyes.

"Me wife has nothing to do with this conversation."

I got up and started to put on my clothes. I wasn't fucking with him no more. I didn't need no extra drama in my life. If I got caught with drugs, I was gonna have to finish serving my sentence. Fuck that.

I got my jeans on and looked at Angel still sitting on the bed. She could be the fool and haul that shit. I'd leave her ass right there too.

"Give me my money!" I yelled with my hands out.

"I can't believe you tripping on me," Mandingo said in his slurred words.

"Nigga, I don't need your drug money, sweetheart. I sell pussy and that's it."

"Emerald!" Angel called my name, pulling me to the side.

"What?" I yelled.

"Why you tripping? You said get money by any means. Sixty Gs to go across town is a lot."

I looked at Angel's stupid ass. I coulda slapped the shit out of her. "Bitch, did you forget we just got out of jail nine months ago?"

"It's just one run, Emerald. I need the money."

"Well, I don't!"

"So you goin' leave me hanging? I thought Shiesty didn't give a fuck."

This bitch was tryin' to play with my emotions right now. "Well, right now I'm Emerald and I ain't getting into that shit. You can do what you want, but I ain't wit it. I ain't yo' fucking momma. You can do what you wanna do. But don't bring that shit around me, in my house, nothing. I don't want that shit in my life, period."

"Fine," Angel said as she got all jazzy. She forgot her ass rode here with me. *I'll make your ass walk back home if you wanna get smart at the mouth.*

"Well, I hope that nigga got a ride for you, cause I'm leaving. And I hope you don't get caught with that shit, cause sixty Gs ain't worth your life."

"Emerald, come on."

"Girl, you already know how the game go. One leads to two, and then your ass is in too deep." *Fuck that, I got cake in the bank!* My line had expanded faster than a speeding bullet. My net worth had tripled since I'd been out. I wasn't thirsty like that to carry some dope for a nigga. *Fuck that.* "And besides, you all in love wit a dope dealer. He ain't kicking you down like that?"

"He take care of me," she jumped bad.

"Well, tell him to pick ya ass up from here, then." I turned back to Mandingo. "Give me my money!" I yelled.

He handed me two stacks of money, and I grabbed my Gucci bag and left. This was the last time I was ever stepping foot back into this motherfucker. Yeah, the dick was the bomb and he paid good money for the pussy. Shit, I wasn't risking my freedom for nobody.

I ran out the door so fast. I didn't look back and didn't care how Angel was getting home. *Fuck her stupid ass.*

CHAPTER 22
MAGIC STICK

Two Weeks Later

DEAD IN THE middle of my sleep, my phone went off. I didn't know what the hell I was thinking putting ringtones on my phone. R. Kelly's "Your Body's Calling" was ringing, and that was Slim's ringtone. I looked at my clock. It was 10:30 at night.

"Hello," I said.

"Did I wake you?" He asked such a dumb question.

"Yeah, but it's cool. What's up?"

"Can I come see you?"

Nigga, this time of the night it's all about fucking. "Something wrong?" I asked.

"No, I just need to see you," he said.

"Cool."

I hung up the phone and jumped back into the shower to freshen up. I lotioned myself with my Lemon Ice. It tasted great. I made sure every inch of me was fresh. I got my pussy ready and prayed dis tall-ass nigga's dick wasn't small. I was going through withdrawal since I left Mandingo. I needed some dick. I put on my Agent Provocateur laced nightie and heels.

When my doorbell rang, my pussy started jumping for joy. I wanted Slim so bad. I opened the door and he was standing there looking too sexy. He had on a wifebeater and some creased up jeans. He was always so plain-looking, but his aura was so commanding. He smelled great, very lickable. "Come in," I said.

"I just wanted to bring you something."

"At this time of the night?"

"Yeah. Here," he said as he handed me a box. I took it and opened it. Inside was a tennis bracelet. I took a look at it. It was cool, but he wasn't fooling nobody. "You bringing me a gift you took back from one of yo' penguins?"

"No, sweetie, I just copped that. Look in the bag." I looked through the bag and found the receipt. He'd just bought it that day and he paid six thousand dollars for it.

I flashed on the light so I could take a good look at the bracelet. It sparkled like my gray eyes. It was real icy. I was surprised, because he said he didn't like ice. "I thought you don't buy things like this," I said.

"I don't, but when I saw it, I knew you'd love it," he said.

Damn right I love it. I'ma rock dis bitch tomorrow. "Thank you."

"Well, I'll see you later," Slim said as he turned around and walked away.

I don't know what type of game he was playing with me. "Slim! Wait, come back!" I yelled down the hall. He came back. "Where you going?" "Home."

"I want you to stay," I said.

"I don't want you to do something you don't want to do."

"I want to."

I pulled him back into my house and dropped my robe to the floor. My body was looking off glass. Slim's eyes got big as he searched it.

I pushed him to the door and tore his shirt open. His body looked so damn good to me. Slim had me so open right now. *I gotta show him how I throw this pussy. After I finish putting this pussy on his ass, he won't play hard to get with me no more.* I licked him from his navel up to his neck. Slim's trembling body let me know he wasn't used to getting it like this. I licked his arms from his shoulders blades down to his fingertips. I sucked each of his fingers one by one. I licked his hands all the way down to his underarms.

Once I made my way over to his nipples, he was moaning my name out loud. I sucked his nipples so gently, flicking them with my tongue. Slim rolled his eyes in the back of his head and ran his fingers through my hair. I ran my tongue across his bottom lip and sucked his top lip gently.

I backed off of him and told him to come over to the couch. Slim's dick was bulging outta his pants, and it looked big. *Oh God, please let him have a nice-sized dick.* I closed my eyes and unbuckled his pants, letting them fall to the floor.

When I opened my eyes, I got excited. His dick was huge, like Ms. Peaches's. *Jackpot.*

I rubbed my hand across his long dick and licked my lips. I looked up at him and smiled. I was too excited. I hoped he knew how to break backs like Mandingo, cause I needed that right now.

I licked the bottom of his shaft with my tongue. I knew I had to put my best foot forward. I pushed him down on my couch and pulled him down to the edge. I fell to my knees and started at the bottom of his feet. I licked him from his heels to his toes. I felt him shivering. I sucked all his toes one by one. I licked from the tops of his feet all the way up to his thighs.

"Oh shit, Emerald, what you doing to me?" he moaned as he wiggled around the couch. I licked the inner part of his thigh slowly, sucking soft hickeys on it. I made my way over to the other leg and did it the same way.

I hesitated at first to lick his ass, cause I didn't know what his reaction would be. Niggas be acting crazy sometimes when you play back there. I picked up one of his legs and threw it over my shoulder. I licked his ass cheeks first, and he flinched up. *Damn, niggas kill me with this shit, knowing they love their ass played with.* I slowly took my tongue and licked down the middle of his crack.

His moans told me to give him more. I teabagged his balls in and out of my mouth. "Damn, girl, what you doing to me?" he asked, shaking like a crackhead.

I licked up his shaft till I reached his pee hole and stuck my tongue in it, wiggling it around gently. Once I had him calling my name, I pushed his dick deep into my throat. He was way bigger than I was used to sucking, so I kinda gagged. But I'm a soldier. I was gonna get this dick all the way down my throat even if it killed me.

Once I passed my gag reflex, I was bobbing and weaving like no tomorrow. "Shit, Emerald!" Slim yelled out loud. *Yeah, nigga, I told you I'm tha baddest bitch.*

I pulled off him and licked the head of his dick. "Who tha baddest, nigga?" I demanded.

"Shit, girl, it's you."

"Damn right," I said as I made my mouth water and spit on his dick.

I took him down again. I had to show him what I could really do. I flexed my throat muscles around his dick so hard he couldn't take it.

"Shit, Emerald, I'm coming, baby!"

Yeah, that's right. Let's get dis first nut up out ya so I can see how strong ya fuck game is. Shit, my pussy had been going through withdrawal since I stopped fucking with Mandingo. I needed to be fucked good for at least two hours.

I swallowed him down some more, but his dick was too long for me to put his balls in my mouth. I cupped his balls with my hand and massaged them. I sucked him up and down until I felt his cum in my mouth. "You like that shit, daddy?"

"Baby, you the best. Shit, girl," he said, trying to catch his breath.

"Damn right," I said as I spit his nut back on his dick.

I stood up and Slim took a good look at me. My pussy was on fire. I wanted to feel that big dick. He got off the couch and came over and ran his hand across my face. His touch felt so good to me. He untied my nightie and it fell to the floor. I went for my shoes, but he told me to keep them on.

All right, I'm down for trying new shit, ya know. He took two steps back and sat on the couch. I don't know what his deal was. "Dance for me, baby?" he asked.

Oh, shit, I was getting more excited by the minute. I'd never done this shit before. I turned on my TP2 CD and had R. Kelly's "Strip 4 U" playing. I worked my ass like it was tip drill Fridays at The Lick. All I needed was a stripper pole and some strobe lights. I dropped it down low and brought it back up. Slim was just looking at me, rubbing on his long dick. I was so anxious to jump on his dick, my pussy was leaking all over my legs.

I turned my ass around and dropped it down low again and started rolling my hips. I got on the ground and crawled over to Slim. I licked up his leg and gave him a lap dance, grinding on his dick as hard as I could. I wanted him to slide his big dick in me, but he wouldn't let me slide down on it. "Not yet," he ordered.

Not yet, shit! I'm ready. I don't know about you, but my pussy is smoking. He took his hands and grabbed my breasts and licked my nipples just right. I'd never been touched like this by a man. I loved the way he touched me.

Slim laid me down on the floor and licked me from my ankles up to my thighs. He sucked my inner thighs so good I was shaking. *I need this shit. I haven't been licked like this since Ginger's ass.* He turned me over and licked me from my neck down to my back. He bit my ass cheeks so hard my body was trembling. He licked my round ass and buried his face in it. "Shit, Slim!"

I was totally out of control of the situation. Slim was taking care of his business, handling me like a real man should. He picked up one of my legs and began to lick my pussy from the back. When his tongue touched my bare pussy, it drove me crazy. I hadn't had nobody make my pussy feel good like this since Ginger. I was convinced that niggas couldn't eat pussy, but Slim was almost better than Ginger at this shit. "Oh yeah, baby, eat this shit," I moaned. Fuck, he had me going crazy.

He turned me over and picked my ass off the floor with his two hands. He started licking me from the front to the back. I was coming so hard my body began shaking. "Slim, baby, I'm coming!" I cried out.

He took one of his long fingers and stuck it in me. His finger was hitting my G-spot while he continued to suck my pearl tongue just right. "Baby, I'm—I'm—shit, boy!" I was speechless. I'd never come this hard in my life. I felt that shit gush outta me like period juice.

My body went limp, but Slim's hard dick was ready for some pussy. He pushed himself into me slowly while I cringed. He felt so good sliding in me. He bent my legs back and started pumping me as hard as he could. I was able to take all of him and he was feeling too good. I'd never screamed so loud while I was having sex before.

Slim was what I'd been missing. His dick was like that magic stick 50 Cent was talking about. He'd beat it up and then go down and eat it up. I was going crazy, and he loved it too, claiming my pussy. And I let him, too!

The way he was hitting it, he didn't have to spend no Gs to hit this shit. We switched positions to doggystyle and he was pounding me. I was throwing it right back at him, hard as I could. "Shit, Emerald, dis pussy so good," he moaned. "Baby, please tell me it's mine?"

"Yeah, Slim, it's yours," I told him. Shit, I usually don't let niggas claim the pussy, but the way he was hitting it, he could claim this pussy anytime he run up in it. *Shit, I'm gonna let him hit it whenever he wants to.* I was coming again, so I started throwing my hips back at him harder. "Hit it harder, Slim, I'm coming!" I commanded, and he did.

The more I yelled, "Harder!" the more he pounded me. The feeling of his thick long dick hitting my G-spot was unexplainable. "Slim!" I yelled, cause I was coming so hard my body started shaking. "Baby, don't stop. Hit it harder!" I begged. Slim grabbed me by the hair and banged me so hard I felt him in my chest.

"You like this shit?" he asked.

"I love yo' dick," I said.

Once I came for the sixth time, my body got weak. I wanted to lie down, but Slim's dick was still on rock. We'd been fucking for an hour and a half, and his dick was still rock-hard. *My pussy can't take another beatin'. I'm gonna have to suck dis nut outta him.*

I reached down and grabbed it with my hand so I could suck it, but he pulled away. "No, I want to fuck you in the ass," he said.

"What?"

"Yeah. You said you's da best. I want to try it."

Dis nigga done flipped on me. I don't know if a six-thousand-dollar bracelet worth getting hit in the ass.

"I ain't never done that," I said.

"What, you scared?"

I saw him trying to pull my ho card. I'm a gangster bitch; I don't run from the dick. "Nigga, hell naw. I'm wit it."

Slim turned me over and pushed my ass in the air. I was so scared. He licked the crack of my ass up and down so good he had me climbing the walls. My pussy started to come back alive. "Be easy back there," I scolded.

"Just relax. You got some Vaseline?"

"Yeah, in the bathroom."

Slim got up and went into the bathroom and got the Vaseline. I saw him take some of it and rub it on his dick. When he started to push it in me, I cringed up. "Relax," he said.

He gotta lot of nerve to tell me to relax. Nigga, let me stick a dick up your ass and see if you relax. I felt every inch he stuck in me. It was like a knife slicing my asshole open. When he got halfway in, I swore he couldn't push it in me anymore, but with a few more strokes, he was all the way in my ass and it hurt like hell.

I tried to hold back my tears and be gangsta with it. He was stroking me and I was screaming so loud. I just wanted him to hurry up and get it over with. He kept pushing himself deeper and deeper into me. I couldn't do nothing but scream. *This shit ain't for me at all. Please come.*

After another ten minutes, he finally bust. Once he took his dick outta me, I was able to breathe. *I ain't doing this shit no more.*

"Damn, girl, you right. This shit here is priceless," he said as his hand stroked my coochie up and down.

I just looked at him. Slim shocked the hell outta of me. He was so low-key, but he was a big freak. His dick was the best I ever had. I thought Mandingo's dick was the best, but Slim's, hands down, was the best dick I ever had. *I gots to claim that. That's my new piece.* I ran me some hot water so I could soak my sore asshole.

After a long hot bath, me and Slim got into my bed and we fucked three more times before we fell asleep. Now I know what R. Kelly meant when he wrote his song "The Greatest Sex." This was the greatest sex I ever had. I needed this in my life. Slim was my new dick. I wasn't letting him go. Even if I had to pay for it, I would. *I'll pay for that dick.*

(HAPTER 23
SURPRISE

Three Weeks Later

EVERY DAY I woke up feeling different about Dollar and Sissy. Part of me wanted to move on and the other half wanted to kill them both. This day, I was in my "fuck the world" mood. I wanted to get anybody and everybody that had something to do with my downfall.

Slim tried to get me to come to the hall with him, but I wasn't going to church. I'd been splitting my time between Slim and John, and I barely had time to think. I knew Slim was no good for me, but the dick made me think otherwise. John had everything a woman would want in a husband except a big dick. I didn't want to settle down with nobody anyways.

I needed to go to my store on the westside to take care of some business. I usually didn't go to this store. All Dollar's hood rats shopped on that side of town, so I stayed clear away from the westside, but I had no choice today. It was time to go over inventory and balance out the books. We had to do all twelve stores today, and Ms. Peaches couldn't handle that alone.

Besides, I hadn't seen Ms. Peaches since I moved out. I knew he was feeling all lonely without me. I couldn't wait to shoot the shit with him. I needed to talk to him about this getting fucked in the ass shit. It had been three weeks, and my ass still felt funny.

"What's up, Peaches?" I said.

"Hey, bitch, you finally made time for a bitch."

"Naw, I've been chilling. You know I can't be up in the store."

"Girl, I thought you was moving on from that…forgiving and forgetting?"

I looked at him. "Some days I feel like moving on, and others I feel like going to find them and blow they ass up."

"Well, keep praying about it. I think you doing the right thing. The Bible says, revenge shall be mine, said the Lord," Ms. Peaches said.

"Don't start that." Ms. Peaches was right, but I didn't want to hear it.

"What's up with Angel? Where she at?" he asked me as he snapped his finger to Beyoncé's new hit "Get Me Bodied."

"I don't know. I ain't her babysitter! I saw her last night. I let her use my car cause she's getting something fixed on her car. I don't keep up with her. She got her own place now."

"I know. It's fly."

"Please, Ms. Peaches, it ain't flyer than mines! She biting my style anyways." Angel's place was cool, but my shit was much better. "I was over there last night."

"You always think somebody tryin' to be like your ass."

"Cause it's the truth. Everybody wants to be me. I'm just like Mike."

"Please, child," said Peaches.

"Stop hating. Anyway, Peaches, I got fucked in my ass a couple of weeks ago and I don't like it."

He turned and looked at me. "You gots to get used to it."

"How could you get used to that?"

"After a few more times, it will start feeling good to you," Ms. Peaches said.

"Shit, I don't know. My shit was all loose. I ain't feeling it."

"Trust me, you'll enjoy it after a few more tries. Then you can start doing tricks like me."

"What kind?"

"We'll be here all day, child. Make sure you douche back there to keep it clean."

Douche? "For what?"

"Let's say you get hit from the back and then the nigga want his dick sucked."

"After he been in your ass? That's nasty."

"If you douche before, it won't be nothing on his dick," he said. "Trust me, honey, I'm a professional."

Shit, I guess you learn something new every day.

After three hours of sorting, tagging, and logging inventory, I got tired and hungry. "Let's get something to eat," I said as I sat down and took off my Prada heels.

"It's almost time for the store to open. Go get some IHOP and bring it back."

"IHOP? What you want?"

"Steak and eggs and some pancakes."

"All right." I hadn't eaten IHOP in a minute, and I had a taste for their strawberry pancakes.

It was cold as hell outside today. I ran to my car and turned the heat up. "Shit!" I screamed, trying to shake the cold off me. After my car warmed up, I popped in my T.I. CD and pulled off.

I looked around the area. It had been so long since I'd been this way. It all looked different.

When I stopped at the light, I saw that chick I made eat my pussy, looking raggedy as hell. "Stupid bitch," I laughed. *Still ain't getting shit outta Dollar.* I sped up so I could make it through the yellow light before it turned red. Shit, I was hungry as hell and I was ready to get to IHOP. "Watch what you say to me," I sang to T.I.'s latest tune.

"Pull over!" I heard, cutting through my radio. When I looked up, I saw flashing lights behind me. "Damn!" I yelled. *I don't need no fucking ticket.*

As the male officer approached me, I thought about letting him know I'd suck him off if he didn't give me a ticket. But when he got closer, he was fat and ugly, so I said fuck it. I'd rather pay the ticket. I was done with them lame niggas. I ain't have no time for no more niggas to get pussy-whipped.

"License and registration, please?" he asked me, all country.

I took out my license and gave it to him. "May I ask why you pulled me over?"

"Ma'am, I'll be the one asking the questions. I need your insurance card as well, Ms. Jones."

I reached over to the glove box and took out my car guide, where I kept all my insurance information. Two bags filled with white stuff dropped out of my glove box.

"Don't move, ma'am!" the officer yelled as he drew his gun.

What the fuck? My heart started racing. *That can't be what I think it is.*

The officer radioed in for a woman officer to come on the scene. He walked over to the passenger side of the vehicle and opened the door. He reached in, picked up the bags, and looked at them.

"Ma'am, do you know what this happens to be?"

"I don't know where that came from," I said. "I swear."

"Um-hmm," he smirked. "Ma'am, I need for you to step slowly out the vehicle."

I did as I was told. I knew arguing or getting loud wasn't gonna help me out of this situation. I tried to give him my "I'll let you fuck me" face, but he wasn't having it. "Put your hands behind your back!" he yelled.

When he came to handcuff me, I knew it was now or never. I needed to

99

try to use what I got to get out of this situation. When he turned me around, I looked at him with my gray eyes. "Officer, I really don't know where those came from. I swear. But I'll do anything you want me to if we can make this go away."

"Really, anything?" he asked, like he was with it.

"Anything," I said, sexy and seductively.

"Well, ma'am, you're barking up the wrong tree. I like men. So I'll make sure to add bribery to your file."

Damn, I shoulda known he was gay. Wouldn't no real woman want his ugly ass. "Please!" I yelled. "I don't know where that came from!" I started yelling and crying like I was crazy.

"Ma'am, if you don't calm down, I'm going to taze you."

Fuck, how did drugs get into my car? This is not good. The judge said if he saw me back, I would have to finish my sentence. I couldn't stop crying. *Why me? Here I am, trying to do the right thing in life, and look what's happening to me.* When the next police car pulled up, my stomach started hurting real bad.

"I need you to search her and take her down to the station," the officer said.

"What do we have here?" a familiar female voice said.

"Two bags of heroin," he replied.

When I looked up, it was a face I'd been dodging since I'd been out of jail. She bent down and whispered in my ear, "Look at what you got yourself into, Emmy."

I just looked up at her. I knew she wasn't gonna make this easy for me.

"Well, well, well. You back smoking rocks again, Emmy?" She laughed.

"Bitch, don't play with me."

"Name-calling, are we, Emmy? Long time no hear. Now I got you right in the flesh." I had been dodging Linda since I'd been out. I wasn't finna be licking up in her pussy for nothing.

"Linda, can you help me?" I asked.

"Help? Now you want me to help you? After you played me?"

"Come on, Linda." What were the odds that this bitch would be the one to show up?

"What you doing smoking drugs anyway?" she asked. Like I was a fucking crackhead.

"Bitch, I ain't never smoked no damn drugs."

"All right, I see you're a little angry. Maybe I'll tell him to book you."

She turned to walk away from me. I knew I had to swallow my pride. I needed her ass again. Damn, how could this happen?

"Linda," I yelled, "I'm sorry. I'm just upset because somebody put that in my car. I ain't never smoked drugs, and I ain't tryin' to get locked back up."

"Look, Emerald, there's not much I can do, because this is not my arrest," she said. "I'll book you and give you an I-bond and see what else I can do. But my hands are kind of tied now."

"Okay, anything would help."

"Yeah, but…"

I knew it was coming, and I knew what she wanted. She didn't have to ask me. I knew it. "I'll do you for a month," I said.

"Two."

"A month and a half."

"Fine." Linda picked me up and pushed me into the back of the police car. My head was spinning. The last time I'd been in a police car, I was on my way to jail to do a bid.

"You know, Emmy, I really missed you."

"I know," I replied. I just wanted her to shut the hell up talking to me.

"Hey, Emmy, I thought about telling Dollar about you being out, and then I thought, what would I get out the deal ratting on you?"

"So, you set me up?"

"No, that's not my style. Whoever set you up knows where you stay and had access to your car. I don't know where you live."

When she said that, my only thought was Angel. *Dirty bitch tried to set me up so she could take the top spot from me. I knew she would get jealous and start some shit. She had my car yesterday, and she was probably doing those runs for Mandingo. I knew she wanted to walk a mile in my shoes. I shoulda got rid of that bitch a long time ago. That's why she moved into the same building as me. She thought she was goin' take away my kingdom that I built.* I couldn't wait to get outta jail, because I was gonna kick her ass.

Linda let me get my one phone call as soon as I got to the station. I called up John so he could call the lawyer to see what he could do. I got fingerprinted again. I couldn't believe I was right back where I left almost a year ago. *Damn, I'ma kill this bitch.*

I saw Linda walk over my way. I was so irritated. All because of Angel, I had to lick up in the bitch's steel pussy for six weeks. *Damn.* "All right, Emmy, I got you an I-bond," she said as she handed me some papers to

101

sign. "Since it was only two dime bags, you can say you was smoking it and the judge will put you back into them rehab classes."

"Fuck, man!" I yelled.

"Well, that's the best I can do. I'll check the report and try to minimize all that I can so it won't hurt your probation. The worst thing that can happen is a fine of three thousand, and since this is your first offense, it won't be that much."

"Thanks, Linda," I said as I grabbed my Marc Jacobs bag.

"I'll see you tonight at my place." She smiled at me, making my skin crawl.

"Fine," I muttered. I didn't want to go two steps backwards. But what could I do? She had the upper hand right now.

CHAPTER 24
TRYIN' TO BE ME

AS I PULLED my new Benz CLK into my parking spot, I felt a bolt of rage come through my body. "She a dead bitch!" I yelled to myself. Angel was on my shit list, and I was finna teach this bitch what happens to hos who wanna try to take my spot. *You'd think this bitch woulda learned from me, but no. She goin' try to play me and put me back in the cage.*

I'd been so nice to her ass, helping her get money and shit. I'd let the bitch live with me for months, but now since she got her own shit, she thought she could step on my toes.

Once the elevator hit the twentieth floor, my heart started racing. I walked as fast as I could to get to Angel's door.

BAM...BAM...BAM! I kicked at her front door as hard as I could.

"Who the fuck kicking the damn door?" I heard her nickel-and-diming-ass boyfriend yell.

"It's me, nigga!" I yelled back. Black swung open the door and looked at me.

I pushed him right out my way and looked around for Angel's ass. "Angel!" I screamed like a madwoman.

"In the kitchen," she yelled. When I entered the kitchen, Angel was there cutting up bell peppers.

"Emerald, what's the matter with you?" she asked, concerned.

Before she could close her mouth all the way good, I took my backhand and slapped her across her kitchen table. "Bitch!" I yelled as I punched her in her face like I was Layla Ali. I punched Angel until blood was all over my fist.

"Emerald, please stop." Angel's eyes were so swollen, she couldn't fight back.

"Black, help me!" she screamed to him. He was trying to pull me off her, but my grip was too tight.

"Bitch, you trying to set me up?" I yelled.

"Emerald, please, I don't know what you're talking about."

Once Black pulled me off her, Angel got up and ran into the corner. Black pushed me down to the floor. "Calm down, bitch!" he yelled.

"Bitch! I got yo' bitch." I grabbed a pair of scissors off the table. It was the first sharp object that I'd seen, and I swung it at him.

"Emerald, please," Angel cried. "I didn't do nothing."

"You a liar," I said as I walked over to her and grabbed her by her long pretty hair. "Bitch, you want to be like me…set me up and put drugs in my car."

"Drugs?" Angel yelled.

"Yeah, bitch, don't act brand new now."

"I didn't put anything in your car. I would never do that."

"Liar!" I yelled as I chopped off her ponytail with the scissors.

"My hair!" she cried as tears fell from her eyes. Angel managed to get up and run from me.

"Bitch, stay the fuck outta my life. You're dead to me!" I yelled.

"My hair, my face…Emerald, why?" she cried like a little-ass baby. *That's what happen to bitches who want to play like they was me. There's only goin' be one me, and I don't play that shit.*

"Emerald, look at my face!"

"Bitch, I ain't Emerald, so save yo' little tears, cause Shiesty don't give a fuck about you crying. You lucky you still breathing. I shoulda rocked yo ass."

"Emerald, I didn't do it. I swear."

"Say that one more time and I'ma finish yo' ass. You used them drugs that Mandingo gave you to drop off."

"I didn't do it. Ask him. I haven't touched no drugs in years."

"Fuck you, bitch," I said. "Get a life and stop trying to live mines."

I walked outta Angel's house. My adrenaline was pumping so hard I could hardly see. I got into the elevator and went to my house to clean myself up.

When I went into the bathroom and looked in the mirror, I saw a face that I didn't know. "Fuck!" I yelled. I could have killed Angel. Shiesty was taking control of me too much. I was doing things that were beyond bad. I still had Angel's hair in my hand. I took it and put in the drawer.

I let the hot water from the shower run down my body and wash all Angel's blood off me. All I could think about was her telling me that she didn't do it and that she did not run that dope for Mandingo. "She's lying," I said to myself. It had to be her. There was nobody else who could have done it. She got what she deserved. *Fuck it and fuck her. The bitch is dead to me.*

When I made it over to Linda's place, I was more pissed off. This was something I didn't have to do.

I made it to her door and rang the doorbell. An older gentleman answered. He was handsome and had a cut-up body. He looked to be in his late 40s, early 50s. He was a sexy old man. I was digging him. "Come in," he said as he waved me in.

"Is Linda home?"

"She's on her way back from the store. I'm her father, Lieutenant David Smith."

"So all you guys are police officers?"

"Well, I've been on the force for thirty years now. That's why I'm a lieutenant," he said.

"Lieutenant," that sounded kind of hot, and he was looking all fine and shit standing there with his shirt off. I needed some dick. I was so stressed out. Slim was out of town and John was not around. *I should whip dis pussy on him.*

I didn't give a fuck about Linda. She wasn't my bitch. I could fuck 'em both if I wanted. I'd get his ass sprung, so that way, what she wouldn't do, I bet I could make him do it. It was a win-win situation for me.

"Well," I said as I switched my big ass around Linda's house. I saw his eyes glued to my body and I wanted him to look at me. "How long is she gonna be gone?" I asked him in a tone to let him know I was down for fucking now or later.

"Um, I don't know. She been gone for thirty minutes. You want me to call her?"

"If you could?"

He walked to the back to call Linda and I started to make my move on him. I got me some water and waited for him to come back.

"She said she'll be back in thirty minutes," he said.

Good, just enough time to get me some of his dick. I took the cup of water off the counter and fumbled it, wasting it all over my dress. "Damn, can you get me a towel?" I asked.

He rushed off to get me a towel, and when he came back, I was standing there in my bra and thong. I took the towel from him, wiping the water out. "Does she have a dryer?"

His eyes stayed glued to me as I stood before him. He didn't say a word.

"Does Linda have a dryer?" I repeated.

"Yeah, I'm sorry," he said, snapping outta his daze.

"Don't be," I said. "I know it's hard not to look at me."

He took my dress and put it in the dryer and came back with a towel. There was no more time to waste. I had thirty minutes to make a nigga fall in love.

"I don't need a towel, but my bra's wet too," I said as I unsnapped it. My nipples were poking out. My firm breasts were looking more than lickable. Mr. Smith couldn't take his eyes off me. "You like?" I asked him.

He just looked up at me. I took his hand and placed it on my breast. At first he pulled back, but when I put his hand there the second time, he grabbed it and started licking my nipples. He sucked my breast as if he was a baby getting some milk. It felt good to me. I needed it to take my mind off the bullshit with Angel. He moved to the other breast, licking it the same way.

I knew we didn't have much time, so I pushed him back off of me and onto the counter. I unbuckled his pants and his dick was already on rock. His dick was a nice size, too—way bigger than Mike's waste-a-bitch-time dick.

I needed to put in my best work yet. I needed him to be willing to do anything for dis mean head. I licked him up his shaft slowly, and he was already shivering. *His old lady must don't wax his joint.* I pushed him into my mouth, making sure it was nice and wet.

I was going at him at rapid speed. I needed him to bust as quick as possible. I stuck my tongue in his pee hole and started playing with it. After a few more sucks, he was coming. I pulled him out my mouth and let his cum run on my hand. He was trying to catch his breath, and Linda was gonna be back in less than ten minutes.

I climbed on top of the counter and let my ass hang off so he could fuck me real fast. He slid into me. "Oh, your pussy is so tight," he moaned.

"I know. Hurry up," I said, because I ain't feel like hearing him telling me shit I already knew. He was banging me right at my G-spot and it was feeling too good. I made a memo to myself to try this with Slim later on. Slim's dick was the biggest. I knew this shit would feel off the chain with him.

After a few more strokes, he came and I got up. I went and put my bra back on and got my dress out the dryer. I fixed myself back up.

David wanted to get my number, but when I reached for my phone, it wasn't there. *I must have left it at home. I need to go back and get that.* I took his number down and he took mine.

When David heard the doorknob turn, he got scared. I wasn't. I didn't give a fuck. I'd do both of them right there if I wanted to, cause I'm just that bad. Luckily, my pussy didn't stink, so the house didn't smell like sex. David grabbed his things and headed out while Linda was coming in.

"Dad, you leaving?" she asked him.

"Yeah. I have to go to work, sweetheart. I'll call you."

I couldn't believe this shit. I was right back licking this bitch's pussy. "What you want from me?" I asked.

"I thought we could see each other."

"Bitch, please. I ain't looking to recruit no bitches right now. Check back with me."

"Please, Emmy?"

"Bitch, you call me Emmy one more time and I'ma backhand your ass. Listen, Linda, I'll break you off once a week for a month and a half. Then that's it."

"Please, I need more," she said. "What you want me to do? I'll do anything."

Dis bitch all in love and shit. I ain't got time for this shit. "Look, bitch, be easy wit that love shit," I said. "I ain't tryin' to be your bitch, but when I need you, I'll get at you."

"What if I pay you?"

Boy, it gots to be a sin to be dis damn good. "Pay me, bitch? Bye. You ain't clocking that kind of paper."

"I got money," she lied. The bitch started running around like a chicken with her head cut off, looking for something to give me for dis head.

"Look, I ain't got all day. Lay back so I can get you right and leave. If you want more, you gotta pay for more."

"Okay. I need some tomorrow too. What about this Spy bag?" she asked. "I just got it yesterday."

I took it and looked it over to see if it was real. These Chicago bitches was known for going to New York and buying that bootleg shit. I'd seen this same bag when I went and got my Fendi bag. It cost ten grand, so I couldn't see how she could afford it. "Bitch, give me the receipt."

She went into her room and got the bag and gave me the receipt. "How could you afford this, working at the jail?" I asked her.

"My daddy's rich."

Oh yeah, no more free head for him. "Look, bitch, I ain't got all day," I said. She jumped on top of her kitchen counter and spread her legs open. I dropped to my knees and gave that bitch what she was feenin' for—dis boss head.

(HAPTER 25
NO MORE MS. NICE BITCH

One Week Later
Courthouse

I WAS SO pissed off this morning. All because of Angel's ass, I might be going back to jail. Every time I thought about it, I wanted to go and fuck her up again. *She lucky I got a little bit of Jesus in me, or she would be six feet deep.*

She went crying to Peaches about how she didn't do it and how she didn't touch no drugs. *Lying bitch.* I was there when she told that nigga she was running that shit for him. She made sure to stay clear outta my way, because I told her and Peaches, if I see her again, her ass getting fucked up. I was sick of these hos trying to be me.

I finna reclaim my crown and let these hos know who still runs the Chi. I'm still the baddest bitch in the Chi, and these hos about to feel my wrath.

I let two bitches cross me. The third bitch that try it is gonna be laid in a casket. So whoever ain't down for the new and improved me, fuck 'em. Ain't no more Ms. Nice Bitch. I'm Shiesty. I'ma do whatever I have to, use whoever I have to, to get what I want. This is a vow. I ain't letting nobody else fuck me.

Ain't no more bullshitting around, going back and forth being nice to no good-for-nothing people. It's me against the world and I ain't going out without a fight.

That night I was gonna take care of business, and that included getting Sissy and Dollar back. Revenge was gonna be mine. I already wasted a year being nice.

I made sure I was looking nice and presentable in an older-lady two-piece Banana Republic pantsuit that I wouldn't want to be buried in. *But image is everything.* I needed the judge to think I was a good girl, ha.

When I made it to the courthouse, my lawyer was waiting for me. I crossed my fingers as we walked in, took a seat, and waited for the judge.

"Please rise," the bailiff said.

My knees started to get weak, but I knew that it was just Emerald try-ing to come back out of me. Shiesty wasn't worried about the outcome, because if I went back in, Angel would get it worse this time than last time.

My lawyer approached the stand with all his ducks in a row. I couldn't believe it myself. He had all my drug tests from my once-a-month visits to the doctor, and he stated that the vehicle was my old car and the drugs had been in there and overlooked. He said I would be willing to submit to six months of drug testing and pay a fine.

I was hoping the judge wouldn't order me drug rehab, because I wasn't in the mood to be bothered with Joseph's crazy ass. When the judge hand-ed down his sentence, he gave me a three-thousand-dollar fine and three months of drug testing.

I was so happy that I didn't get any meetings. I gave my lawyer a smile as he saluted me. I handed him a check and left on my mission.

I'd peeped Sissy's whole routine for months now, and she was biting my style hard. She was just an imitation of me. She was never goin' be me. She could try as hard as she wanted, but that bitch would never be able to compare to me.

I'd been slipping, trying to forgive and forget what they did to me. But I was back now, better than ever, and it was time to put my plans in motion.

Sissy and Dollar had a big house two doors down from R. Kelly. *Ain't that some shit!* They put me in jail while they were out living like some ghetto superstars. I mean, they had a guard at the gate, acres of land—they living it up real big. *I should burn this motherfucker down. I'm the one who paid for this shit. I was the one running dope back and forth. Now the next bitch living good off my hard work.*

I was looking like Sissy's twin. I had the same hair color and cut. I even went to Sissy's beautician once and he thought I was her.

I made my way to their estate. I knew Sissy left for school at ten, and she would make it back home by one.

I saw that she had on a DKNY tracksuit and her hair pulled back into a ponytail. So I went and copped the same tracksuit from Macy's, went to the hotel room I rented, and changed. I pulled my hair into a ponytail like Sissy's and put on my Gucci shades. She was carrying a Spy bag, which

I already had.

I went and parked my car a block away and walked to the house. I was praying my plan would work, but I didn't know if I could fool the guards.

When I walked to the gate, my stomach was turning. "Mrs. Miller, why are you walking?" the guard asked.

I looked at him. "Cause I want you to mind ya business."

He opened the gate for me and I exhaled. I walked to the door and the gardener was out. "Senorita Miller, how are you today?" I just looked at him, because they all were pissing me off calling her Mrs. Miller. *What, this bitch done married this nigga or something?*

When I stepped into their crib, I was blown back. The house looked like paradise. It made where me and Dollar was living look like a project. My house wasn't shit compared to this place. They had a big-ass Tiffany chandelier hanging in the hallway and the spiral staircase leading upstairs was made of marble.

I shot a look at the maid. "Senorita Miller, you're home early," she said to me.

Can you believe that? A maid! After I cooked every day of my life for that nigga, Sissy gets a maid. When I made it up the stairs, there was a picture of Dollar, Sissy, and his bastard-ass son. The ten-carat princess-cut diamond on her ring finger confirmed that they were married. When I took a closer look, I saw that it was the same ring Dollar gave me.

I opened the French doors to the master bedroom and saw the posh lifestyle they were living. I was here for a reason and I was getting sick to my stomach, so I needed to leave. I reached in my purse and pulled out a picture of me and Sissy that we took at my birthday party. I found Sissy's dresser and put the 8x10 picture of us on top. Then I heard footsteps coming, so I hid in the closet.

When I looked around, I realized it was Sissy's closet. I was impressed. *Pretty nice.* I peeped out and saw Dollar standing there with a towel wrapped around him. He was still built and looked sexy as hell. He looked over at my picture, then took it off the dresser and threw it in the garbage.

He walked out of the room, and I ran out and took the picture out of the garbage and put it back in the same place. I shot back into the closet and looked out. *I didn't know he was gonna be here.*

Even though I shouldn't have felt this way about him, my pussy was wet just looking at him. I was having hot flashes, thinking about how I used to put this pussy on him. *I know Sissy ain't throwing her pussy like me. She just a knockoff version of me. I know Dollar miss this pussy. Shit, I just fucked a nigga into love just yesterday.*

Dollar went to Sissy's dresser, saw the picture was out of the trash, and looked around. "Sissy, are you home?"

He stared at the picture and rubbed his hand across my face. "Damn, Emerald, it seems like you here." He put the picture back into the garbage. "Sissy, baby, you here?" Dollar took his towel off and his dick was just hanging there, looking all tempting.

I looked around Sissy's closet for some scarves and I found some. I pulled out two, got Sissy's eye mask, and snuck behind Dollar.

I placed the eye mask over his eyes so he wouldn't see me and I pushed him down on the bed. I tied his arms over his head, licked his chest, and sucked on his nipples.

"Damn, Sissy, you trying something new for ya man?"

I knew that bitch wasn't throwing her pussy like me! I licked him in all his favorite spots. "Shit, Sissy," he moaned. I got tired of him calling me Sissy, so I slapped the fuck outta him. *This ain't Sissy, nigga. I'ma show you whose pussy this is in one minute.* My mind went into a place where I should beat his ass like ol' girl did in *Diary of a Mad Black Woman*, but I decided not to bother. Dollar was going to get what was coming to him in due time.

I got undressed, took my panties off, and stuffed them into his mouth. I didn't want to hear him call me Sissy again. *Sissy ain't gonna fuck you like this.* I sucked on Dollar's neck right behind his ear—that was his favorite spot. I licked every inch of him.

When it was time, when I knew I had him feenin' for me to suck his dick, I shoved his dick down my throat to let him feel it for old times' sake. I sucked the life outta Dollar's dick. I was making sure I was getting him good. When it was time for him to bust, I slurped his balls into my mouth, flexed my throat muscle around him, and gave one powerful suck. The loud screams coming outta his mouth told me he was loving it. Shit, I knew he was. *I am the baddest.*

I climbed on top of Dollar and slid down on his dick. I rode him like a stallion. *Shit, I'm a PDR, and for you slow bitches, that means Professional Dick Rider.* I bounced on top of him like no tomorrow. I was coming hard. I had to admit, Dollar's dick did feel good to me, but I didn't miss it. Slim's dick was much bigger and better.

After I busted, I got off him with his dick still standing at attention. I whispered in his ear, "She ain't goin' never be able to fuck you like me." I licked the side of his face and kissed him on his lips for the last time in my life.

I got dressed, took my picture back out of the garbage, and put it on the dresser. As I made my way outta his bedroom, I told the maid that Dollar needed some help in his room. She rushed off to see what he wanted; then I heard her scream, "Mr. Miller, you're naked!" I laughed.

I saw Sissy coming up the stairs, and she was right on time. I hid behind the column in the stairway. I heard her calling out to Dollar. She was gonna be surprised when she got into her bedroom.

Sissy busted into the room, and all I heard was "bitch" this, "bitch" that as she yelled at Dollar for cheating with the maid.

My time was done here. There was so much yelling going on that the guards left their stations to see what was wrong. On my way out, I stopped at the security desk, pulled the tape out, and left unnoticed.

I was so happy with the outcome. I got off easy at court and wound up getting a bonus. I got to bust a good nut—my day went well. I wasn't worried about Dollar thinking it was me. He had so many freaks that he wouldn't know who it was.

The next time I come back, it's gonna be hell to pay. Sissy's gonna pay the piper soon.

CHAPTER 26
HOOKED

I COULDN'T FIGURE out a plan to get Dollar and Sissy back. I didn't know how and what I wanted to do to them. I couldn't get caught because I didn't want to go back to jail. Slim didn't have no ideas, Ms. Peaches called himself having a attitude with me, and I didn't fuck with Angel. So I was on my own. I had to figure something out and soon.

My phone was ringing off the hook from a private number. If they knew like I knew, they would call back with their number showing. *I don't answer private calls.*

They kept calling back. When they called back for the tenth time, I had to answer. "Who the hell is this?" I yelled.

"It's John. I've been trying to reach you."

"Calling me private? I don't answer those calls."

"I left you a few voicemails."

"I don't check those either. What's up? Something wrong?"

"I wanted to see you and take you to an art gallery."

I'd been laying low from John. He was sweating a bitch too hard. Besides that, Slim's dick was so good, I really was hopping on it every other day. John had his hands too deep into my money for me to piss him off. If I got on his bad side, he could wipe me clean. I didn't think he'd do that, but I didn't trust no-fucking-body at this point in my life. He was pissed that I told his ass that I wasn't tryin' to be his bitch and I ain't bout to marry nobody.

"I'm kind of busy right now," I told him. "You know, with expanding the stores, it's been hard finding free time. And I'm getting the Secret Garden Collection together, and it has been a task. I'll be free at the end of the month."

"End of the month it is."

I hung up. John was a good man—probably the one I needed to marry and get my life right with God. But I was a freak, and he just couldn't handle this pussy like Slim. Shit, Slim knew how to rock the boat and work the middle. He wanted me to be his bitch, too, but I ain't tryin' to marry his ass either. All these niggas wanted me to upgrade their ass, but I was kicking it single, sexy, and free.

I flopped down on my couch to watch *The Wire*. This year, it had been off the chain. My doorbell rang. I wasn't expecting no company, and I knew Angel's ass wasn't at my door unless she was smoking some good crack and grew some balls.

"Who is it?" I yelled.

"It's Slim." I almost didn't buzz his ass in. *He think he can drop by my crib without calling now?* When I swung open my door to give Slim a piece of my mind, I saw that he was covered in blood. "Slim, what happened?" I yelled as I pulled him into my house.

"I got into it with yo' nigga."

"My nigga?" I asked as I ran to the kitchen for a rag and some ice. "I don't have a nigga."

"That faggot-ass Dollar. He ran up on me when I was alone and I left my strap in the car."

"Why he run up on you?"

"Cause he know I'm taking over his spot, so he wanna go to war. He just on some hating shit," he said as he pulled away from me. I went to the bathroom and got some peroxide and started to clean up his busted lip. Dollar had kicked Slim's ass good.

"So what we goin' do, baby?" I asked him.

"Something fast," he said. "That nigga gotta pay. If it wasn't for my Koran sitting on my car seat, I would have went back and blasted his ass."

When I looked at Slim upset and hurting, my feelings started going crazy. I didn't know if it was the dick or him. I was feeling him too much. I felt myself liking him more than what I needed to.

He a nigga just like everybody else. Don't fall for his ass, I told myself.

"I'm glad you didn't," I said. "I don't want you to go to jail."

He just looked at me and reached his hand out and rubbed my face gently. "Emerald, you figure out what you want to do?"

"Not yet. I'm trying to figure something out, but I don't know. Everything needs to be right, you know?"

"Yeah. I got a personal question, Emerald."

"What?"

"Are you fucking other guys?"

Damn. Why he had to go there? What the fuck am I goin' say? Dollar must have knocked something loose in his head. "Are you fucking other bitches?" I asked.

"I got a few."

When those words flew outta his mouth, I got mad and turned red. Just the thought of him fucking dem bitches like he give to me had me ready to ring the alarm on his ass. "Good for you," I said as I slammed the peroxide down on my table so hard it spilled out. I started pacing the floor like a madwoman. *Why am I so mad? Emerald, pull yourself together. Remember, niggas ain't shit.* "I mean, it's cool, I got a few too."

Slim got off my couch and grabbed me close to him. He smelled so good. "Do they touch you like this?" he asked as he ran his fingers down my body.

I was shaking. I wanted Slim to give it to me hard from the back. "They ain't goin' treat you like me," he said as he took off my shirt. My body was trembling. He fell to his knees and kissed my nipples with his bruised lips. "I want you, Emerald. I don't want to share you."

I wanted him too. I wanted him to touch me like this every day. I wanted him to make me feel this good every day. He licked me down to my navel, took off my boyshorts, and buried his face into my pussy. Even though I knew his lips were sore from Dollar punching him, he ate my pussy so good, I could swear he was the next best thing. When he picked me off the ground and slid his big dick in me, I melted in his arms. It didn't take Slim long to learn all my spots, and he was hitting them all. "Say you'll be mine," he moaned in my ear.

I couldn't bring myself to tell him a lie. I just wasn't ready to be all his. He was hitting it so right, I knew the next door neighbors heard me screaming.

We were wrapped up into each other making love for hours. A part of me wanted to tell Slim I'd be with him and the other part of me wanted to be free. But whatever I felt for him, there's one thing that was for sure: Slim had me hooked.

(HAPTER 27
LONG TIME NO SEE

THE END OF the month came quicker than I expected. I had so much shit going on at one time. Linda and her father were just a plain headache. I couldn't wait until next week, when I was gonna be done with Linda. On the other hand, her father was a big spender that I could hit from time to time. I really needed some help with my Secret Garden line, but I refused to ask anybody. Ms. Peaches called himself still upset with me over that bitch, Angel.

I had plans with John tonight, so I needed to get home to get myself ready. I'd been ducking and dodging him too long. He ain't never done nothing to me. I knew I needed to lighten up on him. He was a good man and a good person.

When I got on the elevator, my eyes grew big. A sudden rage shot through my body. Angel was standing there looking scared as hell.

"I'll get off and walk," she said.

"If that's what you want. I ain't goin' do nothing to you."

Angel had a short do like Kelis. The color was real pretty on her. I had to admit it, cause I wasn't no hating bitch like her.

"Emerald," she whispered, but I pretended not to hear her.

When the elevator stopped at her floor, she turned and looked at me as she was getting off. "Look, Emerald, I would have never done anything to hurt you. You was like a sister to me. If you don't believe me, you can call Mandingo and he can tell you. I left right after you did. I thought about what you said, and I knew it wasn't worth losing my freedom. Now, I don't know how those drugs got in your car, but I swear I didn't do it."

I looked at her lying through her fucking yellow-ass teeth. "Bitch, I ain't got words for you, and you better step off, or I'ma kick yo' ass worse this time, you lying ho."

Angel let the elevator door close, and I was glad. I was sick of looking at her lying face.

When I made it back to my place, I jumped into the shower and got ready to go out on the town with John. I was meeting Slim later, so I was happy that I could have a nice date and get broke off too.

My doorbell rang as I got dressed. I knew John was coming at seven, but it was only six. "Who is it?"

"It's John," he said. I buzzed him up. I was ass-naked. When I opened the door, he was standing there looking all sexy.

"You're an hour early," I said.

"I know. I wanted to bring you something."

"What?"

"This," he said as he handed me a painting.

"It's gorgeous." The painting was fly. It matched my living room to a T. The sticker said $25,000.00. *It's fly, but damn.* "You paid all this money for this picture?"

"Yes. It's an original—a housewarming gift for you."

"Thank you," I told him as I gave him a kiss.

John had mad paper. His family was Italian and they owned the bank he worked at. They also had five car lots and a host of other businesses.

John started staring me up and down. "You want something you see?" I asked, cause closed mouths don't get fed with me.

"Yeah," he said. "I want you."

"We goin' be late."

"I can live with that," he said as he grabbed me by the waist and started kissing me on my body. He kissed me everywhere and made another attempt at eating my pussy, but he just couldn't compare to Slim. He was a three and Slim was off the charts. Once he got finished playing games with my pussy, I freshened up and got dressed.

John took me to a gallery opening his friend was having. The crowd was uppity, but I fit right in with everyone. His friend's work impressed me. The paintings were very rich in color. I'd never been into a fine art gallery. I'd been missing out on a lot of things.

I saw one piece that caught my attention. I walked over to it and stared at the beautifully painted woman. It reminded me of my mother. Her piercing eyes were looking at me like she knew what I was thinking.

"It's gorgeous, isn't it?" a deep-toned gentleman whispered in my ear. "Yeah."

"I appreciate beautiful things and hate to let them go. You know, this picture is perfect. It won't let you down or use you. What you see is what you get—no phoniness, no one leading you on. Just a beautiful picture to brighten your room." The gentleman ran his hand up the arch of my back. "You're beautiful," he whispered.

"Excuse me," I said, pulling my back away from him. I didn't want to cause a scene, so I tried to keep my voice down. "Don't touch me," I said as I turned around.

"Oh, you used to like it when I touched you like that."

My heart started racing. "You following me now?"

"Why? This is a big city."

"Stay away from me, you clown."

"Emerald, it's been a while. How are you?"

I started to walk off, but Joseph pulled me back to him and kissed me on my cheek. "You can't run from me. I know where you live. I know what you do. I know everything about you."

"Fuck you, you crazy bastard. I'ma call the police on you."

"Go ahead. They're not my favorite people right now, anyways. You must have a hell of a lawyer."

"I do, and he'll slap a harassment suit against you so fast your head will be spinning."

Joseph gripped my arm tighter as he pulled me closer to him. "Well, he might have got you off this time, but he can't stop me."

"Let go of me!" I yelled as I struggled to pull away from him.

"I want you to get rid of the white boy, Emerald, and I'm not playing with you. I let you have your way too long now. It's my way now."

"Let go of me," I yelled again, fighting him off me.

"I'm not playing with you. I'll kill him if I have to."

"Joseph, please, stop this," I pleaded with him. He was scaring me. I thought he was deranged by the look in his eyes.

"It's too late now. You do as I say. I'm not playing any more games with you. Get rid of him, or I will, and if you think your lawyer can waltz into court and keep getting you a slap on the wrist, think again. If you don't start playing by my rules, next time I'ma make sure you won't see the light of day."

I pulled away again, but harder this time, and managed to get loose of his grip. I spotted John and yelled his name as I waved him down. I took off running to get away from this fool, but Joseph's stupid ass followed me. I didn't know what else to do. I wanted to get the hell outta there.

"Emerald, I've been looking all over for you," John said. "I wanted you to meet some of my business partners." *Oh God.*

"Hello, Emerald, I'm Isabel," the older lady said to me as she shook my hand. "I've heard so many wonderful things about your line."

"Thank you." I smiled, shaking in my boots.

"John, you didn't tell me she was so gorgeous," the other gentleman said.

"Isn't she?" Joseph interrupted, smiling. "She can suck a mean dick too," he said sarcastically.

I was so embarrassed; everybody turned and looked at me.

John's face turned red. "Excuse me, sir, who are you?" he asked.

"Emerald, you didn't tell your friend how I used to blow your back out so you wouldn't have to go to your drug addiction meetings?"

I felt like balling up in a corner. All of John's family was there, including his mother. I'd never been so embarrassed in my life. I couldn't see or think. John looked at me like I was a ho, which hurt me the most.

I knew I had to do something and do it fast. "Excuse me," I said to John's friend who owned the gallery. "Do you have security? This man has been harassing me for over six months. I want to call the police on him."

"No problem," he said as he called for security. When they got him to leave, I made up a bogus lie that I didn't know him, I had only met him once at the gym, and he'd been stalking me. I apologized to them all. They seemed to have bought it, as John agreed with my story as well. I knew I had embarrassed the hell outta John tonight.

When it was time to leave, I was more than ready to go. John had been giving me the cold shoulder all night. "John, I have to pee," I told him. He waved his hand up at me and kept walking out the door.

I ran to the washroom. I knew it was gonna be a long ride home. My mind was all over the place. *Why can't this crazy nigga leave me alone?* I flushed the toilet with my feet, pulled down my dress, and went to wash my hands. I bent over and closed my eyes to splash my face with some water to calm my nerves down.

"You know that's my favorite position with you, Emerald? You can take all my dick good and hard from the back."

"What the fuck?" I yelled as I turned around and backed into the corner. "What the fuck do you want from me?"

"I told you already. If I can't have you, then nobody can."

I grabbed my purse and pulled out my stun gun. He was lucky the first time. I left it with the coat check. *But this nigga about to get fried.* I fired my gun up, letting him see the sparks fly. "Nigga, I will fry your ass. You better leave me the fuck alone."

"Emerald, I'm not playing with you. Get rid of him."

"Fuck you," I said. "I'ma fuck him and suck his dick real good tonight just for you. Get a life. You can't control mines, and if you come around me again, I'ma get you arrested."

"Emerald, I'm warning you, this will get ugly."

"Fuck off." I laughed as I started to walk out the door.

"Emerald, you really shouldn't leave your car door open. You never know who's been in there,' he said. "Nice car, by the way. I never been in a CLK before. I like the custom seats with your logo. It's hot."

My stomach turned. I ran out the door as fast as I could. I couldn't believe it. All I kept thinking about was him telling me I got off easy at court. *Was Joseph the one who put the drugs in my car?* I was confused and dazed. *I don't understand why he won't leave me alone.*

John was waiting for me in the car. When I got in, I looked spaced out.

"You okay?" John asked me.

I turned and looked at him. "Yeah, I guess."

John stared at me. I knew he was still pissed off about earlier, and if I was him, I'd have been pissed too. "Look, John, I had no idea that he would be here. I know you were embarrassed. I'm so, so sorry, John. I swear, it's been months since I even talked to him."

"Look, Emerald, I really care for you and love you, but embarrassing my family is out of the question."

"I know that. I feel terrible right now. I don't want to hurt you."

"That guy seems crazy. You probably should call the police on him."

"Yeah, you're right, John." I felt so stupid. I'd never felt so low in my life. I didn't like feeling like a ho, even though I slept around. It wasn't fair for John to judge me. I reached over and placed my hand in his lap. I wanted to try to get him to forget the whole incident.

"Please, Emerald, not tonight," he said as he moved my hand.

I felt so little right then. "Okay," I said.

When John dropped me off back at my place, he didn't even kiss me. He pulled off. John had never treated me this way, and I didn't like the feeling. Joseph kind of scared me, so I called Slim up and asked him to come over. *I don't want to be alone tonight.*

CHAPTER 28
I SHOULDA LISTENED

SLIM'S STRONG HANDS stroked my firm breasts while he kissed them softly. This was what I needed to get my mind off things. His soft wet kisses planted on the small of my back made me shiver. "Slim, I need you," I moaned in his ear.

Slim commanded me to bend over, and I did. I arched my back as high as I could get it. When his thick, long, hard dick entered me from behind, my body shook. Slim knew just how I liked it from the back. He had my juices streaming outta me like a flowing river.

"This my pussy!" Slim yelled as he pushed deeper and deeper into my wetness.

"Yes, daddy, it's all yours, baby." I couldn't shake my feelings for Slim. I needed him in my life, but I needed John too. I wished I could make them one.

As Slim pushed himself into me as hard and deep as he could, I threw my hips back at him, making him scream my name uncontrollably. I loved when he screamed my name in his bitch tone. It made me feel like I was the baddest bitch in the world. "Oh, daddy, your dick is so big," I moaned to him. I started arching my back up and down, which made him pick up the pace of his thrusts.

Slim slapped me on my ass and pulled my hair back, turning me on even more. I didn't think I could leave him alone. I knew I didn't need another street nigga in my life, but shit, the dick was so good, I couldn't leave 'em alone. If he tried to leave me, I'd be on his ass like a stalker.

My body started clinching up as I reached the point of no return. "Slim!" I yelled at the top of my lungs. Once I busted hard all over him, Slim came right after me. He was the only man I'd been with that knew how to control his nut, and I was glad.

We fell back on my bed to catch our breath, and I laid my head on Slim's ripped chest. Slim ran his fingers through my hair until I fell asleep in his arms.

Ring...Ring...Ring...

My house phone went off at three in the morning. I looked at the caller

ID and it said Chicago Police Department. "This ain't nobody but Linda and her father. I don't know how this bitch got my house number," I told myself. I ignored it and turned over and put my arms back around Slim's waist.

They called back again, and I answered so I could cuss me somebody out. "Hello!" I screamed.

"Is this Emerald Jones?"

"Who wants to know?"

"Hi, Ms. Jones, I'm Detective Reynolds and I'm sorry to have to wake you. Your store was set on fire tonight, and I need you to come down here."

"Excuse me?" I yelled, because I couldn't believe what I was hearing. "How long do you think it will be before you get here?"

"Listen, I have four stores in Chicago," I said. "Which one? Are you sure?"

"Your store on Madison. You are the owner?"

I dropped the phone on the floor and jumped outta the bed. How could something like this happen? I'd been in that store for four years and nothing ever happened.

"Slim," I yelled to him. "Look, my store burned down. I need to go."

"What?" Slim said as he sat up.

"Listen, I need to go. I'll be back."

"Well, I'm coming too," he said as he got up and threw on his pants. I was glad he was coming. I really didn't want to go by myself, just in case Joseph's ass showed up.

We made it downstairs to my car, and I got nervous. "Fuck that," I told myself trying to get gangster. I ain't finna be scared of him. When I got to my car, I saw a single rose lying under my windshield wiper.

I took it out and looked around. Slim looked at me and rolled his eyes. "So you got secret admirers now?" he said smartly.

I threw the rose down on the ground and smiled at him. I was a little scared. *Did Joseph put that there? How in the hell does he know where I stay?*

When I got down to my store, it was burned to a crisp. Ms. Peaches was there with Angel. I jumped out of my car and ran to them. "What happened?"

"Girl, I don't know what the hell is going on. It looks like somebody threw a cocktail through the window."

"Oh my God." My stomach went sour. All the hours I'd spent working on my Secret Garden Collection were gone down the drain. "Why would someone do this to me? Is somebody trying to ruin me?"

Once the police finished questioning me, I sat down on the curve and looked at my store burned down to the ground with nothing left but ashes.

"Sorry, Emerald," Angel said in a soft voice. I couldn't even be mad at her. I was so distracted I couldn't think straight.

"Baby, let's go home," Slim said to me.

I picked myself up off the ground, trying to stand up straight without my knees giving out on me. When I made it back to the car, another flower and a note were stuck on my window. I rushed to the car so I could grab them before Slim saw them. I stuffed the note and flower into my purse and asked Slim to drive me.

I was so dizzy when I got home. I didn't want to eat or talk; I just wanted to lie down. Slim climbed into the bed with me and rubbed his strong hands down my back. I fell asleep in his arms as he held me so tight that I heard his heartbeat.

"Emerald," Slim whispered in my ear.

I turned over and opened my eyes. My vision was still blurry because I was still sleepy.

"I need to make some runs and I'll be back later."

"Okay," I said like a little lost schoolgirl. I didn't want him to go, but I understood.

After he left, I got up and fixed me something to eat and checked the messages on my answering machine. John had called me nine times already. I didn't feel like talking to nobody. I knew he was handling all the insurance papers. He was always on top of things like that. I reached into my purse to check my cell phone, and the note that had been left on my car fell out. I picked it up and opened it.

Emerald,

Do you like me doing these things to you? I see you're such a fucking whore. You're sleeping with that white boy and that nigga you was with earlier. You fucking whore, you used me and I'm going to make you pay. I hate whores. Emerald, I tried to give you the good life. I wanted to make you my wife and be your all. But you'd rather be a whore, and whores must be punished.

Since the drugs I put in your car didn't put you back in jail, I found another way to hurt you. I hope you like barbecue, because I'm just getting started, you fucking tramp whore. I won't stop until I ruin you. You hear me? You whore. I'm going to make you hurt like you did me. I'm not letting

124

anyone else have you. You're mines, you fucking no-good whore. And if I can't have you, no one can.
Love you,
Used and Abused.

I dropped the letter to the floor. *What have I gotten myself into? Joseph is crazy.* I couldn't believe this. I'd beaten Angel half to death for nothing. She was telling me the truth the whole time. I cut off all her hair. I couldn't believe I did this to her.

I got up, threw on something, and went to Angel's place. I needed to tell her how sorry I was. *Why is everything going wrong now? I don't need this shit.*

When I made it to her door, my knees where shaking. I was so embarrassed to have to apologize to Angel, but I had to. I was wrong and I wouldn't blame her for not wanting to be my friend again.

I rang her doorbell twice before she answered the door in an apron. "Emerald, what are you doing here?"

"I need to talk to you."

"Look, I did not have anything to do with your store burning down, okay?" she yelled to me as she rolled her eyes, shutting the door in my face.

"Angel, wait," I said as I put my foot in the door to stop her from closing it. "I need to talk about something else, not that."

Angel opened the door up wider, placed her hands on her hips, and looked at me. "I'm listening."

"Can I come in?" I asked her.

"No," she said smartly.

"I understand. Look, Angel, I was wrong. I found out who put the drugs in my car, and I wanted to tell you how sorry I am for not trusting you. I put my hands on you, and I know that was over the line. I don't know how I can take it back or make it up to you."

"Umm." Angel looked at me and rolled her head. "Emerald, I never done nothing but try to be your friend. We both came from the same place, and I just wanted us to be friends. I still honored and respected your wishes of not wanting to be my friend and stayed loyal to you. We done been through a lot and seen a lot together. You didn't even hear me out. You cut all my damn good hair off. I can never forgive you. I was pregnant and you made me lose my baby. I'm not even mad about that. I'm hurt that you didn't trust me. I don't need nobody in my life who don't trust me."

My heart fell to the floor. *I made Angel lose her baby.* Tears started flowing down my face. "Angel, I'm so sorry I made you lose your baby."

Angel looked around the hallway and pulled me inside. "Look, Emerald, Black don't know about that. I wasn't for sure if it was his anyways. You have too many personalities. One minute you're cool, and the next minute, you're like fuck-a-bitch. You Emerald, then Shiesty, and I can't deal with Shiesty."

I understood why she didn't want to be my friend anymore. I had to man up and deal with it. "Well, I'm a woman, and I was wrong, and I needed to tell you I'm sorry. I will pay for you to get some good hair if you want."

"I'm cool. Black likes my new cut. I'm getting used to it."

"Yeah, it's cute on you. For what it's worth, I know that I missed out on having a good friend, because we all need somebody, right?"

"Well," Angel said as she stood up and escorted me to the door.

When I walked out, I felt so lost—like I needed her. The feeling was weird. "Well, if you want your job back, it's yours," I said.

"I'll think on it. I've been trying to get my restaurant thing going. Besides, I'm having fun sitting in and playing wifey." Angel giggled. "See ya around." She closed the door on me.

I couldn't believe it. I had totally flipped out on Ms. Peaches, Angel, and John, being zoned into my own world. I wished I could talk to my dad, but I hadn't heard from him yet.

When I made it back to my place, I sat down on the couch and flicked on the TV. After flipping through the channels, there was nothing on that I wanted to watch. I went to call John back on my cell phone and I couldn't find it. I called down to Angel's house and she told me I'd left it there, but that she and Black were leaving in a little while and she would drop it to me.

I needed to relax my mind. I turned the shower water up as hot as I could take it. I sat down on my bench and cried my eyes out. I couldn't believe all this was happening to me. I'd lost my store and my best friend. Dollar and Sissy had my head all fucked up. I couldn't trust anybody. I needed some help. I couldn't keep going on like this.

After sitting in the shower for thirty minutes, I got out and dried myself off. I needed to lie down again. Slim said he was coming back later, but I needed him now. I would have asked John, but we'd been distant from each other since that little thing at the art gallery. I knew he still felt salty at me for making his family look bad. *Damn that fucking crazy-ass Joseph.*

I turned down my TV. It was loud as hell. I didn't even remember turning it on. I walked inside my closet to get me something to wear.

I dropped my towel and grabbed my La Perla shirt off the rack. "Leave it off," a voice whispered to me.

My heart started beating. I knew that voice all too well. I turned around and tried to make a run for the door.

"Bitch, get over here," he yelled as he caught me by my long ponytail.

"Please, leave me alone!" I cried as I tried to get loose from him.

"You whore, you thought I was going to let you leave me?"

"Why you doing this to me?"

"I love you, Emerald. I thought if I gave you time, you'd see how much I love you. But no, you'd rather be a whore."

I had never been this scared in my life. Even when I got sentenced to jail, I wasn't as scared as I was then. I didn't know what he was going to do to me. Joseph didn't even look the same. He was crazy and deranged.

"Joseph, maybe we can work this out," I said to him so he would let me go.

"Bitch, do I look stupid to you?" he asked.

"Joseph, come on. I ain't worth you spending the rest of your life in jail."

"Nothing matters to me no more. How could you use me, Emerald? I loved you."

In my twenty-one years of life, I'd never imagined that I would be in this situation. "Joseph, what do you want from me?"

Joseph dragged me by the hair into my bedroom. "Emerald, I have to punish you. You need to learn a lesson about using people." It scared me even more to see him being so calm and know that he was going to hurt me.

He pulled down his pants and pushed his dick inside me as hard as he could. My body cringed up. I mean, I'd never been one to turn down some dick, but I felt violated. As he humped on top of me, moaning my name like he was crazy, tears fell out of my eyes a mile a minute. I needed someone to help me. I tried to pull away from him, but his large frame was just too heavy for me to get away.

Joseph finished and yanked me out of the bed by my hair, down to the floor. "You see, Emerald, it didn't have to be this way. All I wanted to do was love you. Why wouldn't you let me love you?"

"You can love me," I yelled to him, trying to get him to loosen the grip he had on me. I was praying to God that Slim came back and rescued me.

"Bitch," Joseph yelled as he slapped me so hard I saw stars. "You're a whore and I don't want a whore for a wife. And I can't have you running around free. That's the price you pay for disobeying me. I asked you countless number of times to marry me. You said you loved me. I heard you." Tears started to flow from his eyes, and I got scared. "Emerald, how could you sleep with me and make me feel like this and then turn your back on me? I helped you when you asked me to, and you were just using me the whole time. You never cared about me."

"Joseph, please, we can work this out. I can be your everything." I knew I was lying through my teeth, but I had to get him to let go of me so I could grab my .22. I was gonna blast his cake ass.

"It's too late for us, Emerald." Joseph picked me up and slammed me onto the floor. I'd never felt so much pain in my life.

"Please, don't hurt me," I cried.

"Bitch, I'ma kill you." Joseph planted one foot dead in the middle of my back. He stomped me harder and harder as his tears fell. "I loved you, Emerald." The more he said he loved m,e the deeper and harder his Timb boot went into my back.

My vision started to fade. I felt my life slipping away from me. There was nowhere for me to run. My whole life flashed before my eyes. All I kept hearing was Ms. Peaches telling me that when you used people, it could come back to haunt you. I thought about how I'd alienated Angel from my life and how I needed her right now. I kept hearing Ms. Peaches saying that the one person you be nasty to is the one person you're gonna need.

Joseph stomped his Timb boot into my face. My nose started bleeding all over my rug. I couldn't see anything. All I could hear was a voice calling out my name. I didn't know if I was hallucinating. I lifted my head and tried to open my eyes, but I couldn't see anything. My body was too weak.

I heard somebody screaming my name. I was praying to God it was Angel, but I wasn't sure. I felt one last kick, and then it stopped. My body was so weak, I couldn't even roll over or move. I just lay still and blacked out.

CHAPTER 29
RECOVERY

TWO WEEKS LATER

MY BODY WAS so sore I could barely move. I tried opening my eyes, but they seemed to be glued together. The harder I pulled, the more I couldn't see anything. "Am I blind?" I asked myself. I started fighting myself to open my eyes.

"Emerald," a soft voice said.

"Help me," I cried out. I needed somebody to help wake me up. I tossed and turned. "Help me," I cried out again.

"Open your eyes slowly," a male voice said to me.

I opened my eyes as slowly as I could. The room was bright and hurting my eyes. "That's it, Emerald. Open them as wide as you can."

When I looked around the room, I was in a hospital bed and Angel was standing next to me rubbing my hair.

"How many fingers am I holding up?" the doctor asked me, like I was a retard.

I moved his hands out of my face. "Why you asking me dumb questions?"

"She's back!" Angel laughed.

I tried to get out of the bed, but my body was so sore, I fell back down. "Careful, Ms. Jones, you have two broken ribs that need to heal. Do you remember what happened to you?"

I looked at Angel. "No. I mean, I got into a fight, right?" I replied.

Angel rubbed her fingers through my hair. "You were attacked by Joseph. He was trying to kill you."

When she said that, everything that happened went through my mind—how Joseph almost killed me. "Where is he? What happened?

"Well, I came down to bring you your phone and you wouldn't answer the door. I was gonna leave your phone on your table, because I didn't know where you had gone. I still had my spare key and opened the door. I called out your name and walked into your room and found him stomping you in the back with his boot. I called for Black and he knocked him out.

I couldn't get you to wake up, so I called the ambulance to come and get you."

Tears started to pour down my face. Angel had saved my life, yet again. "Thank you for helping me, even though I was so mean and nasty to you and I cut off all your hair. Thank you for saving my life."

"Emerald, I would do it again. I never wanted us to fight each other or be mean. I would never in a million years do anything to hurt you. I've already lost one friend for being stupid for Dollar. When we became friends, I thought I would have that kind of friendship again. I thought many nights about throwing that key out and writing you off. But I knew in my heart you never hated me. You're just confused and fighting with getting yourself to trust again. I mean, Dollar hurt me, but you had bad blood and I took that into account. If my sister would have done me dirty like Sissy, I probably couldn't trust another female too. But I'm not trying to hurt you or take your spot. I'm happy with my life. I made some bad choices and my share of mistakes. I've paid for them all. I'm just moving on with my life, keeping it pushing. I'm happy with Black, and at the end of the day, that's what life's all about...being happy."

I'd never cried so hard. I couldn't believe how mean I'd been to Angel. She could have left me there to die. I'd done and said a lot of things to her, and she still helped me. Ms. Peaches was right—you never know when you gonna need somebody in your corner.

"Angel, I hope we can be friends again, and not just business partners. I mean true friends." I wouldn't have blamed her for saying no, especially after all the wrong I'd done her.

"Oh, of course we can, but I ain't hoing around no more. I'm being faithful to Black," she said.

I looked at her and almost said something negative, but I kept my comment to myself. If she wanted to love him, that was her choice. "Well, I'm happy for you guys. When is the wedding?"

"I don't know. Speaking of holding out on a bitch, who is this fine tall chocolate brother that keeps coming up here? He said his name is John."

John? I only know one John. "I don't know a John besides white John."

"White John been here to see you every day almost. But I'm telling you, it's been this tall fine-ass nigga that will not leave your side. He said he been kicking it with you for a year now. I ain't never met him, and he cute. Why you was holding out? We could have did him. Now, I done turned my life over to the Lord and all."

The only person she could be talking about was Slim, and I wasn't sharing that dick with no other bitch, period. "You have to be talking about Slim, and I ain't want to have to cut you, cause I'll slice a bitch over that dick."

"Tell me about it…a year, girl. So y'all serious?"

"Naw, we just fucking. I ain't falling in love with nobody."

"Well, he's fine, honey."

"Have him and John crossed paths?" They really didn't know about each other. And how ironic that they had the same damn name.

"No, not yet, but here he is now."

Slim walked through the door with a fresh haircut. His low-cut Caesar made him look so sexy. He was clean from head to toe. He had on a fresh Coogi outfit. I'd never seen Slim look this way. He always stayed low-key. Although he only had on a watch, his Rolex was serious. He must have just left his bitch. It pissed me off thinking about him being with another woman.

"Emerald," he said, smiling as he stretched his long arms around me and hugged me close to him. He smelled so damn good that I didn't mind the pain that I was in. "Oh God, I was so worried about you. I thought you wasn't gonna wake up and I would have to kill me a nigga."

"Please," I smacked my teeth. "You roll up in here looking so fresh and so clean. You sure are stepping out for yo' bitch…all I get is some jogging pants and a white tee."

"I'ma go and leave you two alone," Angel said as she grabbed a fly-ass Marc Jacobs bag.

"Damn, that's a hot bag," I said. "Where you get that?"

"Black bought it for me. My birthday had passed."

"Damn, I forgot. I'm so sorry, Angel."

"No, don't be. We'll have plenty more to celebrate together."

Angel gave me a hug and waved goodbye to us, even though I had my lips poked out at Slim. I was glad Slim was here. I needed him. He was looking too fine, and despite all the pain, my pussy was getting wet.

"Hey," Slim said as he kissed me on my lips.

"Don't hey me. Where you just coming from?"

"Home."

"Don't play games with me. Why you dressed like that in that fake-ass New York Coogi outfit?" I knew if he bought it, he would get offended by it. But I knew Slim wasn't dropping no two hundred dollars on no jeans, period.

"This real," he said.

"Where you get it from?"

"It was a gift," he said as he took a seat in the chair next to my bed. If my arms weren't sore, I would've reached over there and slapped his ass.

"So yo' bitch is cheap, huh? Can't even buy you real shit."

"This came from Fresh Wear." He smiled.

I got so angry I turned red. *I know he fucking her. Damn!* The bitch was trying to stay cool with him so she could keep getting some of his dick. This was a problem. *I know we not official and all, but I don't want him doing them bitches like he do me.* He could just give them hos the tip. I knew he went in deep in this bitch. That's why she buying clothes and shit.

"What you tripping for?" he said. "I'm here, ain't I? She don't mean shit to me."

"Shut up!" I screamed at him. I was so angry I couldn't control my emotions. I took in a deep breath and let it go slowly, because I needed to calm down. I wasn't finna worry about that bitch, but if I saw her, she was goin' get slapped the fuck up. *That's my dick.*

"Emerald, you're up?" a voice creeped at me. When I looked at the door, it was John standing there with some red roses for me.

"John." I smiled harder than normal to make Slim jealous.

"Oh God, I'm so glad you're awake. I've been so worried about you." John came closer to my bed and sat on the edge and rubbed his fingers through my hair.

Slim threw him an ice grill. "I'm sorry," John said as he stood up. "I'm John." He held out his hand to Slim for a shake. Slim just looked at him and gave him a mean mug.

I thought this was perfect timing. That was what his ass got, rolling through here with an outfit on that a bitch bought. "John, this is…"

"John," Slim said as he rolled his eyes at him like a little girl.

"You two have the same name." I laughed.

"What a coincidence?" John smiled.

"Whatever," Slim moaned.

"Thanks for the flowers. How is the store?" I asked.

"Everything is fine, baby girl." John planted a kiss on my forehead and Slim's blood pressure went up a few notches; I heard it. "I'll come back tomorrow and we can talk."

"Okay." I blushed like a little schoolgirl.

"Nice meeting you," John told Slim, but Slim turned up the TV like he wasn't talking to him. I laughed to myself. Y*eah, two can play that game.*

"Who was that nigga?" Slim asked me all nasty.

"Don't trip. He ain't nobody."

Slim just looked at me and frowned his face up. "You hungry?" he yelled.

"Yep." *Yeah, be jealous.*

CHAPTER 30
BACK TO THE REAL WORLD

BEING STUCK IN the house sucked. I'd been home from the hospital for two weeks. I was ready to go outside and kick it.

The trial for Joseph was open and shut. He pleaded temporary insanity. They sent him to the mental institution for two years. I didn't really care. I just wanted him away from me. Two years was enough time to move away and get on with my life. My body had healed up, and I was going out. I needed to go by Big Momma's house, get the mail, and stop and see the new store.

Joseph didn't admit to burning down the store, even though we all knew he did it. It worked out for the best. The insurance check was three times the amount I paid for the place, and I'd gained more money than I put in, so I thanked his pussy-whipped ass. *You can't stop my hustle, nigga.*

I got dressed and headed out the door to hit the streets. It had been a year and I still wasn't sure what to do to Sissy and Dollar, or even if I wanted to do something. I had lost so much and gained so much in this last year. I didn't know if it was even worth it. Life was too short, and I'd almost died. I didn't know if I wanted to go through that again.

When I made it to Big Momma's place, it looked different. I hadn't been there in months, but something wasn't the same. I got out of my car and checked the mail. There was nothing. I headed up the stairs and a woman opened the door.

"Sissy," she said, smiling. I couldn't place my finger on it but she looked so damn familiar to me. I looked at her and gave her a smile, hoping she wouldn't notice that I wasn't Sissy.

"I'm glad I caught you," she continued. "I'm on my way out of the country for six weeks. I won't be back for a month and a half, so you can't reach me by phone or e-mail. I thought I was gonna have to come all the way to your place. Now I can leave earlier than planned." She handed me some papers. "I know you and Dollar have been trying to get rid of this shack, so there's the check for you, and I also was able to put your sister's check in your name, since you got a certified letter from her saying she didn't want anything to do with the property." She laughed like it was a joke.

I looked at her and tried not to frown my face up. I was so angry that I could've spit in her face. *Dirty bitch!* I yelled to myself. I smiled at her while I opened up the envelope; there were two checks for one hundred and fifty thousand apiece, made out to Sissy Jones. "Wow, you got this much?"

"Yeah, minus my fee. You know what I mean. Sorry it took so long, but I had to convince the financing company to put the checks in your name. Smart move, having it stamped from the jailhouse…that was the icing on the cake. They couldn't do nothing but honor it."

"Where's the mail?" I said as I rolled my eyes, fighting myself.

"Here," she said, handing me the mail. "Get the mail forwarded to a new address."

"Okay."

"Well, you know, when ya dead, everybody knows you ain't paying them no more. Anyway, Sissy, I will talk to you when I get back into the country. Y'all won't be able to reach me, so I hope you guys don't have a problem with the checks. If you do, you have to wait until I get back. Dollar told me he needed the money to buy up some work, so I got it as fast as I could. You running it for him?"

I wanted to know what move she was talking about. I didn't want to sound like I didn't know. "Nope, I don't want to," I replied to get her to talk more.

"Girl, don't be scared. It's in and out. I do it all the time. That's where I'm headed now."

I didn't know if she was talking about drugs or what, but I knew I needed to play my cards right. "I ain't trying to be where Emerald is at," I said.

She looked at me. "Please, Sissy, you know Dollar ain't playing you, real talk. The first day I met Emerald, I knew she was going to be gullible. Dollar told me right away that he was playing her. Then when he started to bring you around, he said you was the real deal. I was shocked my damn self. Me and my brother made lots of money running this scam." *Sister.* I bucked my eyes. She did look just like Dollar, and I'd seen her many times before. She was the one who did all my real estate deals.

"Dollar married you, not your sister," she went on. "He's not looking to hurt you. And I'm not just saying that cause he my brother. I'm saying that cause it's the truth. Nobody ever knew who I was when they met me.

They thought I was his real estate agent. I got all their Social Security numbers, and I knew all their business. I got credit cards and all types of shit in them dumb hos' names, and they didn't have a clue. Dollar hasn't put you in one position to hurt you, period. So don't worry about him playing you. He could have been done that. He loves you. I never seen him so mushy over any woman, to be truthful, girl. He ready to stop and be a husband, and I never thought I would live to see the day."

"Yeah," I said as my voice cracked.

"Girl, stop looking sad. Don't worry about your dumb-ass sister. By the time she leaves jail, we'll all be in Paris, if this drop goes right."

"All right," I said as she leaned in to hug me, making me almost throw up.

I stepped back and took a good look at her. Every bone in my body was aching to slap the hell out of this ho. She walked off and jumped into her 2008 CLK.

I went to my car and turned up my radio. I needed to hear something that was gonna make me feel better. I couldn't hold back my tears. I didn't know if it hurt more that Sissy was with him or that he'd been playing me all along. Deep inside, I wanted to believe that he really loved me and just wanted the money. But knowing that this was a scam and that he never loved me made my stomach turn.

"How could he?" I cried as I drove to my store.

I'd never felt so hurt. I felt more hurt now than I did finding out that Sissy played me. He made a fool of me, and all along he never loved me like he said he did.

I walked into the store and went to the back. I didn't bother to take a look at the place. I didn't care. I was lost at the moment.

"Girl, what's the matter with you?" Ms. Peaches asked me.

I looked up at him and busted out crying. He just looked at me and placed his hands on his hips. "Girl, you stop taking your medicine or something?" he asked.

"No." I laughed at him. He always had a way of making me laugh when I needed to the most.

"Then what's up?"

"I just left Big Momma's house and Sissy sold it," I said to him handing him the checks.

"That little bitch! She didn't put one red cent on the funeral. Bitch."

"I know. It gets better. The lady thought I was Sissy, and she ran her mouth off to me. I thought I knew her from somewhere. She was the same lady who did my real estate deals, and she's Dollar's sister."

"Sister?" he yelled. "He got a sister?"

"Yeah, and she ran her mouth off about how they be running scams on girls like me, and he loves Sissy and wouldn't do her like that, blah, blah, blah."

"You need to call the police on his ass and his momma and put them in jail."

"Ms. Peaches, you and I both know Dollar ain't going to jail that easy. I gotta figure out a way, a street way, cause I ain't got no evidence or proof, and he'll just beat the case."

"You right, but you gotta do something. He can't keep getting away with murder."

"He won't. He fucked with the wrong bitch's feelings! Him and Sissy are both marked for death."

I sat down in my office and made a shit list with everybody's name that I was coming for. I had tried to let bygones be bygones, but somebody had to pay. Dollar, his momma, his sister, Ginger, S.L., and Sissy would all feel my wrath. I only had six weeks before that bitch got back and ran her mouth. I had to get a game plan together fast.

(HAPTER 31
GOT IT

One Week Later

I WRECKED MY brains for a whole week trying to figure out a plan. It wasn't as easy as I thought it would be. I had to cover all my tracks. I already had all my people that was gonna help me in line. I did the right thing and asked them instead of using them. I easily got Linda and her nasty father to help with the power of the P. Everybody else I had to pay, but it was gonna be money well spent.

I lay back on my couch and flipped on my plasma to watch *The Wire*. The show was filthy. They was doing some dirty shit on there. It was the season finale, and I couldn't miss it. *Damn, that was dirty,* I thought once the show went off. *Omar and them is some dirty niggas.* My eyes were so heavy I couldn't stay up another minute. I went to my room and crawled into bed.

When I closed my eyes, a sudden thought crossed my mind. I jumped up and put on my clothes. I needed to go see Slim. I needed to talk to him face to face.

I jumped in my Range and made it over to Slim's crib. It was jumping over there. I walked in and bitches and niggas were everywhere. I got pissed. Slim was having a house party and didn't invite me?

"Where's Slim?" I asked his friend.

"In the back."

I walked back into the kitchen and spotted Slim in the corner with some stank bitch up in his lap. She was rubbing all over him, and I was ready to draw blood. *That's my dick. These bitches don't know shit about me. Once I claim something, it's mine.* Just the thought of him doing that bitch like he did me made me crazy. I didn't want him, but I wanted his dick and I wasn't letting it go. This probably the bitch that bought him that phony-ass Coogi outfit.

I went over there and pulled that bitch outta his lap. "So you settling for second-rate bitches now?"

"Emerald," he said, surprised to see me.

"You need to step, bitch," I told her.

"You don't own Slim," she said, not knowing I slap bitches over my dick.

"I do own him, and if you know what's best for you, you'll step."

"We can share him," she said.

I almost sliced her throat. "Bitch, I don't share shit wit second-rate bitches." I gave her that look for her not to say nothing else to me. "So that's one of your few? You throwing parties and have the nerve not to call me."

"Naw, Emerald, why you tripping?" said Slim. "You know you don't like coming over here."

"Tripping?" He got me fucked up. "Well, you can have that bitch and I ain't fucking wit ya ass no more." I was so angry I could have ripped Slim's head off. Yeah, I didn't like to come over there, but he could have asked. I knew his ass was just like Dollar. *Motherfucker. I should stab his ass for playing with my emotions.*

"What kind of games you playing?" Slim said, looking at me confused.

I looked at him. I was totally tripping right then. I wasn't trying to get like this again over no dick. I was letting my feelings for him grow too deep. I had to get my shit together. "Look, my bad. I stepped outta line. We cool, right?"

He just looked at me, crazy. "Look, Emerald, you the one that wanted it this way. Beside the fact, you fucking ol' boy."

I looked at him and saw the jealousy all over his face. "You're right. Do you and I'ma do me."

Slim jumped outta his seat. "Yeah, so you fucking that nigga?"

I thought twice about my answer, because he looked upset. "Look, I didn't come over here for this."

Slim looked at me and frowned his face up. I knew he was pissed. Niggas always get mad when they think or know you fucking somebody else, especially when you got a mean pussy like I do. "Good. What's up?" He smacked his lips.

"Look, let's go to your room, cause it's too many ears in here."

Slim took my hand and took me up to his room. I did hate coming over there. He was living like a typical hood nigga. No bedroom set—just a box spring and mattress and a big-screen TV. "Damn, you still sleeping on the floor? One of your bitches ain't bought you a bed rail yet?" I laughed

"Believe me, I can get one if you want me to, by tomorrow," he said smartly. Slim knew his dick was the bomb, and I was ready to take my backhand to his ass for being smart.

"Whatever," I said as I sat down on his bed. Slim was looking extra fine today. He'd gotten a fresh haircut and smelled so damn good it made me wet. He always looked good when he got his hair faded and his beard trimmed.

I wanted him so bad. Slim turned me on in every way. I couldn't control my feelings for him. I knew I shouldn't have been digging him so tuff. I knew I needed to be with John; he was the better man for me. But I couldn't deny how deep my feelings were for Slim. I didn't know if it was him or the dick that I was so in love with. He was just a street nigga like Dollar that loved money and pussy. He had big dreams about being the next 50 Cent and his barber shop was gonna open up in a little while. The fact was, he was still a street nigga. I needed to be with John. He was the best choice: smart, rich, and handsome. *But, damn, he got a little dick. And Slim lays that dick on me until I can't take it.* I was confused.

"So what's up?" Slim asked me while he took off his shirt.

Slim's body was cut up harder than normal. The gym was doing his body right. With his sagging jeans on, Slim showed all his new cuts and I wanted to lick all of them. "Why you take off your shirt?"

"Cause it's hot in here."

My mind went blank. I forgot why I drove all the way over here. I wanted some of my dick. His bulge that was coming out of his pants was making my mouth water. I wanted to wrap my lips around it and suck it until he promised me he wouldn't see any more girls but me.

I knew I was being selfish cause I was fucking with John, but he really didn't even count. I'd stop sleeping around with the other guys I was tricking with. He should at least give me a little credit. I knew I was giving him some, no questions asked.

I needed all them ten inches deep inside of me, right now. "Slim, come and fuck me," I told him, straight and to the point.

He came over and pulled off my shirt and unsnapped my bra. He grabbed me just the right way. My pussy was leaking. He took my pants off and buried his face into my pussy. He was licking me so good. I was going crazy. "Yeah, baby," I moaned.

Slim was a freak with a capital F. He licked me everywhere on my body—spots that I didn't know could be licked. When he got naked, he told me to stand up, and I did. I always did as I was ordered. I bent over and waited for him to enter me. When he pushed himself inside of me, my whole body cringed. "I don't want you to do nobody else like this!" I cried out to him.

"I won't. This yo' dick," he said as he went deep into my guts.

After Slim put his pound game on me for an hour, I couldn't take any more. I climbed under his covers, which I never did because they always looked so dirty. I didn't care at the moment. My body was weak. I needed to lie down and get some energy.

I laid my head on Slim's chest and we talked until the wee hours of the morning about the plan I'd come up with. Once we both agreed on what we were gonna do, I went to sleep in his strong arms.

I knew I had to control my feelings for him. I felt myself falling in love with him. I already knew he was no good for me. After this whole thing was over, I was goin' fall back from him and spend more time with John. I knew he was the best choice for me. I didn't need another street nigga in my life.

I couldn't stop comparing Slim to Dollar. I would never be able to trust him all the way because of the hurt. It would never work between us, and I'd be damned if I let anyone come in and hurt me like Dollar did.

I was going to focus on my shit list. I needed to finish what I set out to do a year ago. When I finished with Dollar and Sissy, maybe I could forgive myself, love again, and fully move on with my life. It was time for them to pay the piper.

CHAPTER 32
SLIPPIN'

Two Days Later
October 31, 2009

EVEN THOUGH IT was only fall, it was cold as hell outside. The weather in the Chi was crazy. It could be snowing in June. The brisk breeze outside was blowing so hard you needed a winter coat. The light chill that roamed the air instantly put your nipples on hard. It felt like it was wintertime again.

"Shit!" Sissy ran for her truck. "Dollar!" she yelled as she turned up her radio. "I'm bossy, I'm tha first bitch to scream on the track," Sissy sang as she popped her fingers to Kelis's hit.

"What's up, baby?"

"Damn, it's cold outside today. You know, fall and winter are here and I need some money to shop."

"Sissy, money tight. I need to find somebody to do this drop for me and then we'll be straight."

"How come Me-Me can't do it?"

"I don't trust her carrying ten million dollars of my money back," Dollar said. "She might flip out about Emerald slicing up her face and run off."

"Dat's true. Look, Dollar, I'm in med school. If I get caught, then I ain't gonna finish my degree."

"I know, Sissy, I feel ya and I ain't tryin' to make you do it neither. You know that's what we always talked about—you finishing school and starting your own practice. Then I ain't got to hustle no more, but funds are low and I need this drop done so I can get out the game."

"What happened to all that money Emerald was running?"

"Shit, look where we staying. Dis a three-million-dollar house and it's paid for. All them clothes, the maid, the cook, and your school—all that shit costs money. Plus, I had to pay back my connections. I wasn't getting all the money. Then, I saved enough for dis last sell. I used all my own money. So once the drop was made, that money will be ours to keep. I ain't got to split that with nobody. Then we'll be set."

"I'll think about it, Dollar," she said. "I got two weeks."

"All right, baby. See you later."

Sissy turned her music back up and pulled outta the driveway. She stopped at the local Dunkin' Donuts and grabbed a latté and a donut. The wind outside blew Sissy's freshly blow-dried hair all over her head.

When she got back into the truck, she pulled down the mirror, fixed her hair back, and took out her MAC Oh Baby! lip gloss to retouch her lips. "I'm da baddest bitch in tha land," Sissy said to herself as she licked down her baby hair in the mirror.

"No, bitch, I'm the baddest," I said as I sat up in her back seat.

Sissy looked in her rearview mirror and saw me waving to her. She froze up and turned pale. She closed her eyes and reopened them, looking into her mirror to make sure I was there. "Emerald?"

"It's me, bitch. You know, you coulda tried to get your own style. You biting the shit outta me."

"Emerald?"

"That's my name. So what's been up, sis? It's been a while."

Sissy was speechless. I saw her trying to reach into her purse, so I took out my strap. "Bitch, try it and I'll blow your head off and won't think twice. Nobody knows I'm here. I'd get away with it, you dirty bitch."

"Emerald, what you goin' do to me?"

"I haven't decided yet," I said.

Sissy's face turned into stone as the driver's side door opened. "Damn, Emerald, y'all do look like twins," Slim said.

"I told you that. Put that bitch in the back seat of your car."

Slim grabbed Sissy and tied her arms together. "You can go peacefully or the hard way," he told her.

I knew we had to be careful because were out in these white folks' neighborhood. Slim parked his car close to Sissy's truck. I took Sissy's latté back in and raised a fit about how I'd asked for something else. I wanted them to be distracted. Once the lady got me a hot chocolate, I saw Slim's car was gone, so I jumped into Sissy's truck and went to our hideout.

When I planned this, I had to get Sissy's routine down to a T. Every move she made, I studied. For the last year, I knew everything she did. Sissy did the same thing every day. She was very predictable. I scoped their house out for several months. The guard always left at three o'clock in the morning to go to the local Dunkin' Donuts. The whole house was asleep at that time, and that was when I made my move. Sissy left her truck door unlocked. People always do that when they don't live in the hood. I knew Sissy would end up at this Dunkin' Donuts because she went there every morning. It might have taken me a year to do it, but I remembered what my father told me. I had to move swiftly.

When I made it to our hideout spot, Sissy was there crying. "Emerald, please don't kill me."

"Bitch, you think I'm finna go back to jail for you?" I asked.

"Please, Emerald, I'm sorry."

"Bitch, you ain't sorry," I said as I slapped her across the face with my backhand. "You and Dollar got big plans to get out the game and live happily ever after."

"Emerald, it ain't like that."

"Tape dis bitch mouth up before I choke her to death for lying to me," I ordered Slim. Sissy made me want to slice her face up. "Don't be crying me a river now," I said as I picked up my heel and kicked her in the back. I took off all the clothes she was wearing and put mine on her. I was going to be Sissy for the next two weeks. I got her cell phone and locked her ass in the basement tied to a chair.

"Emerald, what's the plan again? You goin' be living wit Dollar?" Slim asked. I looked at him pacing the floor. He knew what we planned to do.

"We already talked about this and we both agreed to this."

"Yeah, so that mean you got to fuck him?"

I knew it! His pussy-whipped ass tryin' to act tuff when he know he wants me. If he had any common sense, he wouldn't be asking me such a dumb question, but the power of the P will cloud the truth any day. I had no choice but to fuck Dollar to make the plan work. And besides, I already knew Sissy wasn't gangster like me. She wasn't taking ass shots. "What does that got to do with anything?"

"What if this don't work?" he said as he paced the floor faster. "Why you got to sleep wit him?"

"I don't," I lied, just to make his ass be easy. I didn't need his ass flipping out on me.

"So what if he want to?"

"I'ma tell him I'm on my period."

"What if he say he don't care? You know niggas be hitting the pussy when you on your period."

"Relax, Slim, dis pussy is yours. I ain't going nowhere."

"But…" he said.

"Look, man up, shit," I said. "We down to the last quarter. I don't need your ass flipping out on me now. Chill out."

Slim took a seat on the couch. I knew I needed to suck his dick to calm his ass down. "Momma still gonna bring dis pussy over here to you," I said as I got on my knees and unbuckled his pants.

I started sucking on him to take his mind off me and Dollar, but it only made him act more crazy. "Emerald, please don't do him like this," he begged. Once I made him come, I promised him I wouldn't suck Dollar's dick. *He can be the fool to believe that. I ain't his bitch, anyway. My pussy belongs to me, and I can share it wit who I want. He got his bald-headed bitch that be sucking him for love, so oh well.*

When I got into Sissy's car, I looked through Sissy's phone to see whose numbers she had. Ginger's number was nowhere to be found, so that told me Sissy ain't dykin' with her. Because the way that bitch ate pussy, she woulda been on my speed-dial.

CHAPTER 33
FALL IN LINE

I NEEDED TO make sure I had all my plans in order and everybody with me fell in line. I wasn't about Linda. My mean-ass tongue game kept her doing what I wanted her to do. On the other hand, her father was a problem. Even though he said he was in, I knew he would back down with the quickness. I knew I had to get him cornered where he had no choice but to help me. It was kind of wrong, but fuck it. It was all or nothing right now. I was playing to win.

Linda's father was a freak in a nasty way. He had me doing all kinds of shit to him. You would think he wouldn't give me a problem, but some people won't admit to nothing unless it's dead in their face. This day. he wanted the works, so I called in for reinforcements.

"Damn, bitch, you was supposed to be ready already," I scolded because I was on a tight schedule. I still needed to go see Mandingo.

"Don't get me started, bitch," said Ms. Peaches. "I'm doing you a favor."

We got into my Range and I headed full-speed over to David's crib.

"I don't know if this is gonna work," he said.

"Don't be scared now. You bring the camera?"

"Yeah. You got me out here hoing."

"You getting paid, ain't you?"

"All money ain't good money."

"Yeah you might be right, but money makes the world go around," I said.

"Yeah, and it's the root of all evil."

"I'd rather have it than be broke."

"I thought you learned your lesson, Emerald," Ms. Peaches said.

"I did. I still love money ,though."

Once I pulled up to David's house, I parked and made my way into his house.

"Hey, Big Daddy," I said. "You ready for what I got for you?"

"Yeah." he grinned. "All this for me? "

"Yeah, baby, it's all for you. You got my money?"

"Here," he said as he handed me the money.

"Good, Sugar Daddy, you finna get fucked like never before." I pushed David down on the couch and took off his shirt. I took off his pants and rubbed his dick. He was rock-hard.

Then I went, sat down, grabbed the camera from my purse, and turned it on. *Lights-camera-action*. Ms. Peaches was fucking him in the ass as hard as he could. David was moaning and screaming. This shit was so nasty to me.

"Yes, Big Daddy, hit this shit!" David yelled out. I was trying not to throw up, because this shit was too gross. Ms. Peaches was wearing that ass out. He had him screaming louder than Slim had me. After Ms. Peaches came, David went down on him and sucked his dick. I was so totally grossed out. I couldn't believe I'd sucked dis nigga's dick and fucked him. *Fucking faggot.*

"You enjoy yourself, Big Daddy?" I asked him when he was done.

"Yeah, I did."

"Good. Let's go over the plans one last time."

"Yeah, Emerald, I don't think I can go through with this. I can't lose my job for you."

"I knew you would try some shit like this," I said as I got the camera and put it in playback mode. "I think they would love this down at the police station. And your wife would love to know she's sleeping with a DL man. What you think? I can have this all over the Internet in a matter of minutes."

"You wouldn't," he said.

"Try me. I'll call you when I need you."

We left. I got into the car and my mind wandered off. I'd been living a dangerous lifestyle. I needed to get tested for HIV and all kinds of shit. I was deep in thought when Ms. Peaches broke my concentration.

"What you thinking about, Emerald?"

"A lot. I been living kind of reckless, like, that shit was mindblowing, ya know? It's AIDS and everything out here, and he swore that's the first time he done something like that."

"He a lie, girl," said Ms. Peaches. "His asshole was a loosey-goosey. Honey, he been getting hit back there by somebody."

"I know, but it's hard for me to trust again."

"Girl, in life you live and learn, sweetie. Don't let Dollar take that away from you."

"Yeah. Something gotta give. I refuse to go back to selling my body.

It's just plain stupid. I'm sorry for acting like a bitch to you. I do thank you for always being in my corner and loving me and telling me the truth even when I didn't want to hear it."

"No problem, Emerald. I love you. We'll always be friends."

I gave Peaches a hug. I needed him in my life. "Man, I wish I could find my dad," I told Peaches. "Having him around would be good for me."

"I'm sure he'll get into contact with you some kind of way."

I dropped Ms. Peaches off and continued over to Mandingo's house. We had to take care of some business. And I would be lying if I said I wasn't going to fuck him, cause I was. Just this last time. *He got some good dick. I'll hit it for old times' sake. After this one, I'll be done.*

(HAPTER 34
LET THE TRUTH BE TOLD

I TOOK A long ride out to Dollar and Sissy's crib. My heart started beating fast as I pulled into the gate. I didn't know if I could fool Dollar. I mean, what was I thinking? *This might not work out.* When I walked into the house, my knees started to shake.

I instantly got pissed when I saw Me-Me sitting in the kitchen. I took a good look at her face. She didn't look that bad. But she did have makeup on, so I really couldn't tell.

"Hey, Sissy," she said.

"Hey," I said trying not to frown my face at her ass. I wanted to slap her ass outta that chair she was sitting in. But I had a plan for that bitch.

I went upstairs to Dollar's room. Before I went in, I said a prayer to the good Lord to make sure this was gonna work.

"Hey, baby," Dollar said as he kissed me on the lips.

"Hey, boo," I said as I gave him a kiss and rubbed him behind his ears. That was one of his favorite spots. "I was thinking about something."

"What?"

"Let's have a threesome. Me, you, and Me-Me." I wanted to make that backstabbing bitch lick my pussy

"Where's this coming from?"

"I don't know. I want to try something new. I saw it on Cinemax last night."

"Wow, Sissy, you sure?" he asked.

"Yeah, you scared or something?"

"No, I ain't scared." I knew Dollar would go for it. At the end of the day, he was a freak.

"What, you think she ain't goin' do it?"

"If I ask her to."

"Well, go and ask her, and I'ma freshen up," I said.

I took a good look around their room. They were living extra-large. The bathroom floors were heated and they even had a gold toilet. *Too bad they ain't goin' have all this shit for long.*

I jumped into the shower and freshened up. *I shoulda let her lick my pussy just like it is.* When I got out, I dried off and came out naked. I lay down in their oversized bed and waited for Dollar and Me-Me.

When they came up the stairs, I took a good look at Dollar. *His ass ain't really all that. I don't know what I was thinking. Slim looks much better, and his dick is bigger and better.*

"You ready, baby?" I asked.

"Yeah," Dollar said as he sat down on the bed. "Sissy, you sure you want to do this?"

"Yeah, what's the difference? You fucking the both of us anyway." Dollar just looked at me and smiled. *Yeah, nigga, Sissy coming outta her shell, ain't she?*

I took off Dollar's shirt. His body was cut up like I last remembered. I motioned for Me-Me to come over and get in the bed. Dollar took my breasts and licked my nipples softly. He licked me all over my body, but he wasn't hittin' on shit. Slim was much better. Me-Me removed all her clothes and Dollar sucked her breasts while I was licking his back. I whispered in his ear, "Make her eat my pussy, baby."

"Me-Me, lick Sissy's pussy," Dollar ordered her. I lay back and cocked my legs back as fast as I could. She looked at Dollar but didn't speak. I guess she knew better than to backtalk him.

She crawled over to me and sniffed my pussy as if it stank or something. "Bitch, it's clean!" I said.

Me-Me licked me softly, first sucking on my clit. Once she seen it tasted good, that bitch went to work on me. She licked me so good. I had to give it to her, she could eat a mean pussy. I was moaning, going crazy. Dollar was sitting on the edge of the bed rubbing his dick. He was trying to hit Me-Me first, but I wasn't having it. I don't do seconds.

After that bitch made me come, I jumped on his dick and rode his ass. Me-Me lay back like I was fin to lick up in her cat. *Sorry, bitch, you gots me twisted. I ain't licking ya puss.* I rode Dollar silly, and then I jumped off of him and told him to handle Me-Me, cause I wasn't licking her pussy. He went down and licked her ass. *I bet she ain't feel as good as me. Dollar can't eat pussy, unless he done stepped his head game up.* After he banged Me-Me from the back, I told her ass to get her shit and be gone.

I jumped back into the shower and washed up and got ready for bed. I was tired. I'd had a rough day. I was glad I had Dollar fooled. This would make everything so much easier. I went through Sissy's sleeping clothes and found something cute to sleep in.

Dollar was already lying in the bed, waiting on me. *Ain't that shit cute.*

150

When I got in the bed, Dollar started rubbing my back. His hands touching me felt good, but I didn't love him no more. My feelings were gone.

"You shocked me today, Sissy," he said.

"Why, cause I got gangster wit you?"

"Yeah."

"You like it?"

"It was cool, but I don't know…it feels funny at the same time."

Spare me the drama, nigga. What I got in store for you goin' blow yo' mind. "Dollar, I've been thinking about doing the drop, but I'm not for sure. I'm scared that you'll do me the same way like you did Emerald."

Dollar raised up out of the bed and turned on his light. I got scared. My heart started racing. *Did I rat myself out? Does he think something's up?* He looked at me and kissed me on my forehead. "Sissy, you know when I met you, you were different than your sister? That's what drew me to you—when we used to have those long conversations about us and our plans to get outta this lifestyle. That made me fall in love wit you. Emerald didn't want nothing for herself. She had no goals in life. She only wanted to spend my money. You made me see that she wasn't goin' be about shit but the hood."

I sat up in the bed. I was furious. *First thing in the morning, I'm going to go and kick Sissy's ass.*

"Sissy, we both agreed that was the best way to get Emerald outta our lives," he went on. "Yeah, I done played a lot of chickens, but you're different. You made me see that there was things to do besides hustling. You made me believe in a better way. Emerald never once came at me about stop hustling—let's get this and that with the money. You even said it yourself that she ain't even finish high school. How far was she gonna take me? All Emerald wanted to do was be a hood bitch."

My emotions were going crazy. While he was talking, I wanted to slice up his face. "So, just like that, you turned on Emerald because of what I said?" I asked him.

"Well, you had me see that she wasn't going nowhere in life. My momma said the same thing too, that she wasn't no good for me. I knew I needed to get somebody to do the runs and shit, so I just said, 'Fuck it.' It was a lot of reasons why I did what I did to Emerald. When you said you were pregnant, I was too happy. I wanted you to keep it. No matter if it was a girl or a boy, I wanted us to be a family. I ain't tryin' to do you like that, put you in jail. I'll make the drop myself if you feel like that, just to show you how true I am about you."

Pregnant? Sissy went and got pregnant by my dick and then convinced him not to be with me. I wanted to cry so bad. I felt my heart break. "Dollar, I hear you," I said. "Did you ever love Emerald? And tell me the truth, I can take it. I'm a big girl. I'm the one who has you."

Dollar took in a deep breath and stared deep into space. I could tell he was thinking about what he was going to say. "Sissy, I can't lie to you. I did love Emerald once upon a time."

"Well, you loved her and did her dirty. How I know you won't do me the same way?" Dollar just looked at me. I didn't want to pressure him, but I wanted to know the truth. "Dollar, look, I ain't tryin' to stress you. I just want to know."

"I know, Sissy. We never really talked about this, and I knew one day this conversation was gonna come up." I looked at him with all ears. "Look, Sissy, when you told me you were pregnant, I knew Emerald was gonna do something to you, because that's just the way she is. I couldn't see you get hurt when I was in the wrong." *You damn right. She still getting that ass stomped tomorrow!* "At first, when I met her, I really did like her. I never ran into no girl like Emerald. She kind of made me relax and be easy, but business is business. In the beginning, I was like, maybe I'll keep her and not play her, but…"

"But what?" I commanded him to tell me.

"I met you and you were like a breath of fresh air. I never seen two sisters look so much alike but be so different. Once you started coming around more, I started to feel like everything that I needed was in you. My momma liked you, and my sister. They couldn't stand Emerald. So I just gave up on her and did what was needed to secure our future, and that meant playing her. No bullshit, that's real talk. Emerald didn't know nothing about us or about my family and how we made our money, and I kept it that way."

My chest started hurting. *How can somebody be so cruel not to even care about slapping somebody in jail?* "So you played her for me?"

"Yeah and no. I knew I needed to play somebody, and it was gonna be her or Me-Me, and unfortunately Me-Me got pregnant with my son, so that left me with no choice. I did what was best for me, my family, and us. I knew once she was gone, we could be together, and I never even cared for Me-Me. I was just using her ass."

Dollar wrapped his arms around me and I wanted to throw up. My whole body was numb lying next to him. "So you did love her, but not as much as me?" I asked to clarify.

"Yeah, I loved Emerald, but I was in love with you the whole time. I cried when you lost our baby. I was gonna leave her then and I told you that. But you said no. You told me to wait until we got all the money and put her in jail. I was gonna bounce and take all that I had and leave just like that. I knew you and I would have a much better future than me and Emerald. And I was so tired of hustling. I was ready to leave. Emerald only wanted to be a gangsta bitch. I just wanted to move on and make the best choice for us."

"So, just like that, putting her in jail was the best choice?"

"I mean…it was hard for me to hurt Emerald. She never gave me a reason to. But we all agreed, and I've been doing it so long, it didn't even faze me anymore. It was like, 'Okay, next.'"

I just looked at Dollar. A tear formed in my eye and I tried to hold it in. I didn't want to cry in front of him. How could somebody be so cold-hearted? "Fine, Dollar, I'll do it," I said.

"Are you sure?"

"Yeah, baby, I'm sure. We forever, right?"

He looked at me in a funny way. I used to tell him that all the time. Then Dollar kissed me on my forehead and lay down for bed.

I couldn't sleep; my heart was hurting. *How could my own sister do me like this?* I wanted to talk to Slim. I needed him to hold me and tell me it was okay. I lay awake wanting somebody to love me like Dollar loved Sissy. *That bitch! I'ma kick her ass. I might kill her ass tomorrow. Why would she be so jealous of me? I woulda done anything for her. How that bitch goin' say I ain't goin' be nothing cause I didn't finish high school? Bitch, I'm rich and I am somebody. I don't need your approval!*

I just turned from Dollar. I couldn't stand to look at him, not after he made me kill my baby and had Sissy and Me-Me keep theirs. I cried all night long on the inside. I cried for me and my unborn child. How could somebody be so dirty? *I hate Sissy. I hate her.*

CHAPTER 35
SLIM

I WENT TO Slim's house when I got up. I needed to talk to him. I rang his doorbell three times and he didn't answer. I called his cell phone, and still nothing. "Where the hell are you, Slim?" I said to myself. I paced back and forward on his porch like a mad lady.

Finally, his friend answered the door after fifteen minutes of standing in the cold. "Damn, nigga, I been standing out here in the cold," I said.

"That doorbell don't work, girl."

"Where Slim at?" I yelled at him, cause I was in the mood for slapping motherfuckers.

"He upstairs," he yelled as he lay back down on the couch.

I went upstairs to Slim's room and opened his door. There he was, stretched out over the bed, and some bald-headed bitch was lying next to him, ass-naked. Before I knew it, I took his cell phone and cracked him over the head with it.

"Emerald!" he said, jumping up.

"So you goin' leave me outside for this bitch?"

"I didn't know you was outside."

I just looked at him. I was so pissed. *Dis nigga a liar, just like the rest of them.* "Fuck you, Slim," I said as I ran outta his room with tears in my eyes.

Slim ran behind me and grabbed me when I made it to the bottom of the stairs. "Let me go!" I yelled as I tried to pull away from him. But he was holding me too tight.

"Emerald, please talk to me."

I coughed up a gob of spit and spit in his face. Then I started punching on him and crying. He wouldn't let me go. He took my blows like a soldier. "I hate you, Slim. Let me go," I cried.

"Emerald, please, baby, talk to me."

"Just let me go," I cried. "You don't care about me."

"I do, Emerald. You the one that wanted us to see other people."

"You're a liar, just like him! You want to hurt me just like he did!" My emotions were all outta control. I fell down to the floor and cried. I'd never cried like this in front of him before. I was hurt because I fell for him when I knew he was just like Dollar's ass.

Slim bent down and tried to comfort me. "Please, Slim, you're a liar, you don't care for me, nobody cares for me!" I cried. "I hate everybody."

"What's the matter, Emerald?"

"I'm just sick of everything and everybody tryin' to use me."

"I'm not trying to use you, Emerald," he said. "I tried to be with you from the first time I saw you. You kept turning me away, saying you wanted to be single, and do you and I'ma do me. This is not what I wanted. That bitch don't mean nothing to me."

"You're a liar. You just want to hurt me. You left me out in the cold for that bitch," I said as I got off the ground. "You played me, Slim."

"I swear on my momma's dead grave, I did not hear no phone ring." Slim reached in to touch my face but I pulled away.

His friend was sitting on the couch watching us like this was an episode of *One Life to Live*. "Girl, didn't I just tell you the doorbell ain't working?" he said. "I saw you pacing the porch. That's why I got up, or ya ass woulda still been out there."

"Fuck you, nigga," I said.

"Whatever. Slim, take this shit up the stairs and put some clothes on ya ass. Nobody want to look at yo wrinkled balls," he said.

Even though I was pissed, I couldn't help but laugh at his stupid ass.

"Emerald." Slim reached out for me. "Please come upstairs and talk to me?"

"What, you, me, and she?"

"Naw," he said as he went up the stairs and told that bald-headed bitch to bounce. I wanted to turn around and walk out the door, but my feet wouldn't move. *Slim ain't the one for me. This the same shit, but a different day. I've already dealt with this shit with Dollar's ass. I ain't dealing wit it no more. Never again will I be a nigga's fool.*

When that bitch came down the stairs, it was the same bitch that I told to step off my dick weeks ago. When she brought her bald-headed ass down the stairs, I spit in her face and dared that bitch to get froggy with me cause I was ready to kick some ass.

Slim grabbed my hand and took me up the stairs and looked at me. "Nigga, I ain't sitting on them same sheets you just fucked that bitch on," I said.

He took the sheets off the bed and threw them in the closet. "Baby, tell me what's wrong with you."

I just looked at him. *You niggas is what's wrong with me. Y'all ain't shit.*

"It's everything, Slim. How could you go and make a big deal about me fucking Dollar and than turn right behind my back and fuck another bitch?"

"Man, I was lonely and I couldn't call you cause you was with that nigga. I lay down and started thinking about what you was doing to him, how you was touching him. Was you making him feel as good as you make me feel? My mind started fucking wit me. So I just called her over cause I wanted to take my mind off you."

"Please!" I yelled. *That raggedy bitch can't even compare to me.*

"Emerald, I asked you so many times for us to be together, and you keep saying no. I can't take the thought of you having sex with other people; it drives me mad. I felt like a fucking sucker for loving you like I do, knowing you sleeping with that white boy—probably sucking on his dick," Slim yelled. I could tell he was serious from the look in his eyes and how he kept slamming his hand on his dresser.

He came over to me and got on his knees. "I want you to be my wife, Emerald. I want us to be together forever."

"Please, run that line on another bitch, cause I heard that one before."

"I'm serious. We can go right now."

"Please, Slim, you don't care for me. If you did, you wouldn't be cheating on me."

"Cheating? When did you tell me you was my woman? Cause our last talk, you said do you and I'ma do me."

"You know what I mean."

"I don't know what you mean, but there's something else wrong with you. What's bothering you?"

I couldn't hold it in any more. I had to tell him. "It's my sister," I said as the tears started back pouring down my face. "She played me. She got pregnant by Dollar and she told him to leave me cause I wasn't gonna be nothing in life."

"Baby, come here," he said as he held me close.

"She put me in jail. Slim, she knew all about it. She told him to do me that way so she could be with him." I was crying so hard and Slim just held me tighter and tighter. "I want to kill her. I want to kill her, Slim."

"Baby, I know."

"Why would she do me like that?"

"Jealousy will make people do almost anything," he said.

"I'm gonna hurt her!" I yelled. "Slim, I'm gonna hurt her. She took everything that I had. I want to kill her and make her pay for what she did."

"Baby, sometimes you can kill a person even more by proving them wrong. Look at you, baby; you got a lot going on for yourself. Don't let her break you, baby. She goin' pay in the end. Don't let them break down everything you built."

"It hurt so bad," I cried as I put my face in his chest. "It hurts so bad."

"I know, sweetheart. It's gonna be okay. And you don't have to question my motives. I want to be with you. I put that mother's grave. I only want you."

I wanted to believe Slim so bad. I wanted him to love me. Slim held me close to him for hours as I cried on his chest. He comforted me, and my feelings for him grew much deeper as he held me. I just couldn't leave him alone.

CHAPTER 36
SISSY

I WAITED A few days before I went to see Sissy. I had to clear my mind. I knew if I woulda seen her, pissed like I was, I woulda killed her ass. She'd been locked in this basement for four days with no food or nothing, just water. When I unlocked the door, she jumped up and tried to make a run for it, but I slapped that bitch down to the ground.

"Emerald, please, let me go."

"Bitch, since I'm nothing, not smart enough to be nothing but a hood bitch, you should already know I ain't letting you go."

"What you talking about?"

"Bitch!" I yelled as I pulled her up by the hair. "You got pregnant by Dollar and told him to leave me!"

"That's a lie, Emerald, I promise!"

Before I knew it, I slapped her so hard she blacked out. When she came back, I was still waiting on her ass. "Emerald, please don't hurt me, I'm your sister and I'm the only family you got."

"Bitch, you ain't my family! You sent me to jail. Family wouldn't do that. Why, Sissy? I paid for your school. I made sure you had all the flyest shit. Why would you stab me in my back?"

"You didn't pay for nothing. You used Dollar's money, so really, he paid for my school."

"Bitch, is that what you think? You think I ain't got shit and I wasn't gonna be shit but Dollar's bitch? I have my own money. Dollar ain't paid for shit. Those clothes I was sending you was mine. I own that clothing line. I got millions in the bank, bitch. You see, that's the difference between being street-smart and book-smart. I'm a self-made millionaire. I took Dollar's ten thousand and flipped it into millions. You, on the other hand, take his money and give it to a school, hoping to make some money when you finish."

Sissy just looked up at me. "Everybody thought Emerald wasn't gonna be shit cause I ain't finish high school," I went on. "Everybody thought I was gonna die in jail. But everybody was wrong and everybody gonna pay."

"Emerald, please forgive me," she said. "Can't we just start over… just me and you, like our mother would have wanted us to? You know she wouldn't want us fighting each other. She probably turning over in her grave. Please, let's be a family again. I know Big Momma wouldn't want this for us."

"Bitch, don't you even mention Big Momma name. You had her rotting to death in that cheap-ass hospital. Then you sell her house and keep the money. You didn't put one dime on her funeral or have the nerve to show up. You ain't nothing but a lowlife bitch," I said as I back hand her in the mouth. "You think you're so smart. You thought you was gonna get away with hurting me, bitch? I'm so stupid, right? But we will see who's the stupid one."

"We can work this out, Emerald. Just untie me. We family."

"Bitch, you ain't my family. My family is dead, rest their souls, just like you gonna be. You're gonna pay, you scandalous-ass bitch."

"Can I at least have something to eat?"

I looked at her and took a pack of crackers outta my purse. "You better eat slow, cause I don't know when I'm coming back, bitch."

I got ready to leave, but I felt like I'd let her off too easy. I thought back to when I called her in jail and how she was flipping off at the mouth. *Her ass ain't a bit of sorry.* I went back while she was eating on her crackers and slapped her outta the chair again. I kicked that bitch's ass good. "Bitch, you think I was gonna let you get away easy?"

"Please, Emerald," she begged.

I grabbed my Spy bag and left that bitch lying on the ground. *That ho better thank God I found Jesus, cause I really want to take out a knife and slice her ass up.*

John and I had a date planned. We really hadn't been on good terms since the gallery. I understood why. I embarrassed him and his family's name. So I wanted to give him time to get over it, because I knew how he felt about it. I did miss him, though. There was a part of me that needed him in my life, but a part of me needed Slim as well. It was just too confusing.

I met John at The Steak House. I hadn't had a good steak in a while. When I walked in, John was sitting at the table with the chef, waiting on me. "Hey baby," I said as I gave John a kiss on the cheek. He was looking so good. He smelled like Perry Ellis cologne. It smelled so good on him.

"Emerald, you're looking fabulous as usual."

"Thanks," I said and smiled. After John and I ordered our New York strip steaks, we loaded up on drinks. I knocked back three martinis in a matter of minutes. John's dimples were turning me on. It had been a while since we made love to each other. I needed his touch for some reason.

"So, John, did everything pan out with the insurance?" I asked. I knew we got the check, but I didn't know if they was gonna drop me.

"Yeah, no worries. Did you see the place?"

"Yeah, I glanced at it. It's a big upgrade."

"Yeah, I got some more proposals in. It's just amazing how you kept climbing up the ladder. I'm so proud of you."

"Thanks. I wouldn't be here if it wasn't for you." I smiled as I planted a kiss on his lips.

After we ate, I went back over to John's house for a little D&R—dick and relaxation. I set my alarm on my phone so I wouldn't oversleep. I still needed to get back to Dollar's stupid ass.

I took off John's shirt and licked his rock-hard chest. I kissed my way up to his ear and whispered, "I'm sorry for what happened at the gallery."

John pulled away and looked at me. "Don't worry about it."

I remembered something. "Oh, yeah, I need a favor. When you ran my credit report, did I have credit cards on my report?" I had never owned a credit card except my black card.

"Yeah, like five, all not paid. But I got them removed because you were underage."

"Is there a way to pull up the person's info who got those cards? I never had one, so I want to find out who got them."

"Yes, if you need me to."

"I need you to," I said as I pushed him down on the floor and showed him how sorry I was for our whole little incident.

CHAPTER 37
GAME TIME

I WOKE UP lying next to Dollar. He made me feel sick as hell. I couldn't sleep. I didn't want him to touch me, but he couldn't seem to keep his hands to himself. I just had to hold out for a few more days, and then all of this would be over.

"Dollar, can you give me Ginger's number?" I asked him.

He looked at me with a confused look on his face. "You want Ginger's number?"

"Yeah. I wanted to ask her where she got one of her bags from." I thought it was a good enough lie. Ginger was always rocking some hot shit.

Dollar gave me the number without thinking twice. I was so glad. I'd been feenin' to see this bitch. *I want her to eat this pussy up for old times' sake.*

When I left, I called Ms. Price. I wanted to see my old mother-in-law and take her out to eat.

"Hello," she said.

"Hi, Ms. Price, this is Sissy. I was wondering what you were doing today?"

"Hey, baby. I didn't have nothing planned."

"Good. I'm taking you out for a mother-daughter day at the spa. Meet me downtown at Joe's Crab Shack in two hours."

"You sure, baby? What about school?"

"I'm out today, so it's me and you today," I said.

When I made it to Joe's Crab Shack, Ms. Price had already gotten a table for us. This was perfect timing. It was early and nobody was there but us. I wasn't worried about fooling her; it didn't matter at this point. When I approached her, my stomach turned. I felt the hate that was boiling through my blood.

She was sitting there smiling like she just won millions. "Sissy, baby, I'm glad you called me. We need to do this more often," she said as she kissed me on the cheek. *I could slice her ass right now and get it over with.*

"We do," I said as I took a seat. "You order yet?"

"No, I was waiting on you."

I waved my hand for the waitress to come over and take our order.

"May I help you?" the waitress asked.

"Yes. I want the steak and shrimp special, well done, please."

Ms. Price thumbed through the menu. "I want blackened chicken with some dirty rice," she said.

"Anything to drink?"

"Water for me," I said.

"Me too."

"So, Ms. Price, what's new?" I asked.

"Nothing, baby, glad you called."

"I just wanted to spend some mother-daughter time. I saw Kenzy before she left. Who was she going to scam?"

"Girl, who knows? She always scamming somebody. I think she shopping with somebody's credit card," she said.

"She better stop while she ahead."

"I told Kenzy that, but a hard head makes a soft ass. She said this was her last time. Once Dollar makes this money, we all gonna give our life over to the Lord." She laughed.

I just looked at her. *You dirty bitch. I should take this fork and jam it in your eye.* "Emerald didn't know that Kenzy was your daughter?"

"I ain't like that bitch. I never cared for her. I met Emerald before she met me. She was a gutter lil' nappy head. I read her that day, and once Dollar asked me what I think, I was like, 'Hell no, she ain't the one.'"

"So you got the juice?" I asked.

"Yup, I tell Dollar what I want and he does just that. That's my baby boy."

"What made you not like her?" I was trying to laugh and be playful with her so she couldn't pick up on anything. *But nappy head—this bitch? Your bald-headed ass know I got white folks hair, hatin' bitch.*

"Emerald was uneducated. She spoke with terrible language. She didn't have any class about herself, always acting all loud and ghetto. You think I would have let my son be with that fool? Please." *I'm a fool, bitch? I got ya fool.*

The waitress was coming back with our food and water. "Yeah, she was a little ghetto."

"Honey, little wasn't the word. She was a dumb bitch, and she's where she belongs, and the rest of them too. Them little girls wanted the street

162

life, and now they have it."

"I understand."

"Don't you worry about that. Dollar cares for you and he wouldn't do you like that," said Ms. Price.

She was talking so freely to me. *So you and Sissy cool like that?* I tried my best not to let my facial expression change. "I feel ya," I said, doing everything in my power not to snap her fucking neck. The nerve of this lady to call anybody ghetto, with her phony-ass blue contacts and tacky weave. *Bald-headed bitch!* "So that's what y'all did, take people's Social Security numbers and get credit cards in their names and charge it up?"

"Yeah, pretty much. Also property too, and we resell it and keep the money."

"Man, how many people y'all did this to?"

"Shit, I lost count after twenty. Don't know…all of them weren't his girlfriends. Some of them that came into the office, we would use theirs too."

"At the real estate company?"

"Yeah, but don't you worry about that. Dollar married you, and he would never do anything to hurt his wife."

My legs were shaking. I couldn't control my anger. I needed to do something with my hands quick before I slipped up and snapped Ms. Price's neck. I reached for the salt and knocked her water over on her dress by mistake. "I'm sorry, Ms. Price," I said as I got a napkin to wipe away the water.

"No problem, baby. Let me go to the bathroom and use that hand dryer."

Ms. Price got up from the table, left her purse, and ran off. When she came back, she was waving her shirt.

"Did it dry up?"

"Yeah, baby, don't worry about it."

Ms. Price sat down and took a bite of her chicken and then her rice. "This food is great," she said.

"Yeah, it's real good." I smirked.

After her tenth spoonful of rice, she dropped her spoon and grabbed her neck.

"Is there something wrong, Ms. Price?"

"I can't breathe!" She was gasping for air. Her throat started swelling up like a cartoon.

"Ms. Price, what's the matter?" I asked.

She reached in her purse for her inhaler. "My inhaler," she muttered. She poured all her things on the table.

I looked around. The place was still empty, just me and her. She needed some help fast. She was black as fuck, but turning redder by the minute. "Are you looking for this?" I said as I held up her inhaler. She reached for it and I pulled it back. "No, no, no," I hissed.

She looked at me, holding her neck. "Sissy, please give it to me," she managed to find enough air to say.

I just looked at her and smiled. "It's Emerald, bitch!" Her eyes grew bigger and she started shaking. "All a setup, bitch…fifty thousand dollars was never missing. My, my, my, look at you now. You can't even breathe." I reached in and pulled her by her weave. "Bitch, I hope you die, you dirty motherfucker. I wasn't goin' even get you! But no, you gotta keep on bringing the devil out a bitch, Ms. Price, you and your fucked-up son. Your son ain't getting away with all the games y'all played. It's time to get back what y'all put in. You and Dollar setting up innocent people."

The more I talked, the more she tugged at my shirt. "Ms. Price, please spare me. I don't care about you not breathing, child. But what you and Dollar didn't know is y'all fucked wit the wrong bitch."

I took her inhaler, wiped my fingerprints off of it, and threw it in front of her. She picked it up right away to try to spray it in her mouth, but I had sprayed it all out. "Too bad," I said as I got into her face.

I took out my tape recorder and played it back. Ms. Price bucked her eyes wide open and tried to get the tape from me. "You tried to fuck me, so fuck you, bitch. Die slow. Who's the dumb bitch now?" I paused. "What you say?" I said as I put my ear to her mouth. "I guess I got ya speechless."

Once she started foaming at the mouth and shaking, I knew she was either going to be dead or in a coma. *When you cross Shiesty, ya goin' get dealt with, bitch!* I started to let her die, but that woulda been the easy way out. I wanted her ass to suffer like she made me.

"Somebody help!" I yelled, acting like I was scared. The workers all rushed back to see what happened. "I don't know. She can't breathe. Help her!"

"Is she allergic to anything?" the worker asked me.

"Yes, nuts, she's allergic to nuts."

Ms. Price's eyes were in the back of her head by the time the ambulance got there. She blacked out into a coma. I didn't know or care if she was gonna make it or not. *Fuck her.*

I knew getting in contact with Dollar was going to be impossible. Before I left, Dollar had told me he had to run Me-Me somewhere, but that was a cover up for "I'ma be knee-deep into her pussy this morning." I called his phone and he didn't answer. I just left him a message to tell him that his momma was in the hospital, that I had to make an important stop, and that I wasn't going up there until later.

I got into Sissy's car and scratched Ms. Price's name off my list. *I hope the bitch die. They'll never have proof that I put shit in her rice.* If she lived, she would have to suffer some more, but right now, she had been erased.

CHAPTER 38
GINGER

GINGER WAS SO excited to hear from me. *I bet she is.* She wanted to turn Sissy out, and I'd been wanting her to lick my pussy since I'd been out.

When I made it to Ginger's house, she still looked flawless. I had to admit, Ginger was a bad bitch. She was a perfect ten in my book. Too bad she crossed me, because she could have been my bitch on the side.

"Hey, Sissy," she said to me as I walked into her house.

"Hey, Ginger, what's up?"

"Nothing. Happy you called me. I always wanted us to be friends, you know."

"I know," I said as I looked around her house looking for the drawer Angel told me she kept her drugs in.

I felt Ginger's eyes sizing me up. I'd made sure I was looking good enough to eat, but frankly, I had other shit to do. "Ginger, can I get a drink?" I asked. I knew that if Angel was right, she was gonna try to drug me, or maybe not. It was a 50-50 chance, but I was hoping so, cause I wanted her bad.

I fumbled through their CD collection, pretending not to pay her no mind. But I followed her every move. She walked over to her bar and I saw her reach into the top drawer.

"I'm going to the ladies' room if you don't mind?" I asked.

"No problem," she said. I knew Ginger like the back of my hand. When she wanted something, she went after it. Even if Dollar was keeping Sissy around, Ginger always wanted something she couldn't have. She liked to know she had some type of control over you. Turning Sissy out would satisfy Ginger's ego—that she was still the baddest bitch. She never wasted any time making her moves. Her motto was, "You only have one shot, so why blow it?" I knew she'd fall right into the palms of my hands.

I know she was mixing that drink while I was in the bathroom. If only she knew she ain't gotta drug me to lick my pussy. I was flaming for her to put her mouth on me.

When I thought she was done, I came out of the bathroom and took a seat on the couch. "So what's been up with you?" I asked, trying to make small talk.

"Nothing, getting ready to do some upgrades to my place, that's it." Ginger sat next to me and handed me my glass. She smelled so good. I looked at my glass. Even though she gave me brown liquor, I still saw the pill dissolving in the glass.

I don't condone drugs or do them personally, but I had to do this to make the plan work out. I knocked my drink back in one sip and started to set things in motion. I knew I needed to work fast before the pill kicked in.

I got up off the couch ,making small talk with her as I walked over to her bar. I walked behind the bar and went into her top drawer and took her pills out and slipped them into my pocket. I poured me another drink and went back to the couch. She was cheesing so hard. I know she was thinking, "I got yo' ass."

I gulped down my second glass of Hennessy and Coke, sat it down, and went back over next to Ginger. I started to feel lightheaded and knew that this was how it all started the first time. This was how she turned me out. *Damn, this bitch is dirty.* "Sissy, you okay?" she asked me as she stroked her fingers through my long hair over and over. I just looked up at her because I was out of control at the moment. The drugs had me spaced out.

I lay back and I didn't mind what she was about to do to me. I'd been waiting so long for this moment, and I needed it.

I felt her hand rubbing up and down my body while she removed my clothes. "It's okay, Sissy, I'ma take real good care of you," she whispered softly in my ear. My pussy was flaming and I was in another world.

She unbuckled my bra and licked me from the neck down. My nipples were rock-hard, screaming for her to suck them. Ginger licked her tongue across my nipples, flicking them slowly. She sucked on them just right—not too hard, not too soft. She licked me down my spine, gently biting me, making me shiver. Ginger sucked my toes one by one. She was putting in her best work yet.

"You like this?" she asked me.

"Yeah, I love it." Shit, she didn't even know the half of it.

Ginger licked me up my legs, making her way to my inner thighs. She sucked me so good that I didn't give a damn if she put hickeys on my light skin. Ginger licked my bare pussy lips slowly. My heart was racing. I wanted her so bad. She buried her face into me, licking me like her life depended on it. "Yeah, do that shit," I moaned to her.

Ginger had me going crazy. *Damn, why she had to cross me? We could have been down wit each other.* Ginger was licking me in spots that Slim ain't never hit—and he was a good pussy-licker, too.

Ginger turned me over and I got on my knees doggystyle. She licked her tongue up and down the crack of my ass. She buried her face in me, tossing my salad so good. She had me trying to climb the walls. *Ain't no nigga fucking wit this bitch. She the best.* "You want me to stop?" she asked me.

"No, hell no!" Shit, I felt myself coming like a river. Ginger was eating my pussy from the back so right. She was fucking me with her two fingers and licking me at the same time. "Fuck!" I couldn't take it. She had me gone in the head.

I think I can forgive her. I shouldn't let a talent like this go to waste. She don't even know she eating this shit so good. She making me want to forgive her ass. I wonder how good she'll eat it if I told her man. I can just imagine. "Ginger, I'm fin to come, baby!" She went at me at full speed. The two fingers she was fucking me with was hitting me right at my G-spot. She started sucking on my clit harder until my body tensed up and I started screaming out of control.

Once I busted, I fell to the floor. I had to catch my breath. I just looked at her. Ginger was a dime plus ninety-nine. We coulda made some things happen. I coulda got married and let her lick my pussy on the low. It wouldn't be considered cheating, you know.

But she crossed me. Dis bitch head game was mean as hell—I done had a few bitches in my time and Ginger was hands down the best—but the fact is, when you cross Shiesty, you got to get dealt with. I reached over and gave Ginger a kiss on the mouth. I had feelings for her, but she fucked up.

I got dressed. "I'm having a party on Friday at our place," I said. "Make sure you tell S.L."

"All right."

As I put my coat on to leave, I took one last look at Ginger. *Damn, if only you wouldn't have fucked up with me.*

CHAPTER 39
PARTY TIME

GIVING A FAKE party took more work than I thought. Slim needed me, and I really missed him. I hadn't been with him since I started living as Sissy. I saw John a couple of times, but I didn't think he felt the same way about me anymore. Or maybe he did and I was just dick-dumb for Slim.

Slim had finally found a place for his barber shop. He promised me that once he went legit, he would leave all that mess behind him. I really wanted to believe him, but it was hard for me to trust him.

I left out early before Dollar's ugly ass got up. I needed to go to the bank. I wanted to get there before John got in, because I didn't want his nose in my business. I already knew that with him and Slim having the same name, he would know from the cashier's check that I was taking money out for Slim. *I don't want him questioning me.*

The party I was planning for Dollar was costing him a pretty penny. I started to take the thirty grand I was giving Slim out of Dollar's money, but I wanted everything to look legit, so I changed my mind. I had so much to do. I had to meet Slim at one. After I left the bank, I got my hair and nails done and headed back to Dollar's house.

When I made it home, Dollar had left me a message saying that he was on his way home from the hospital. He had been trying to get me to go, but I knew the Lord was looking over her, because I couldn't make myself go up there. I knew me, and pulling the plug on her would be the first thing on my mind.

I jumped into the tub and soaked in Carol's Daughter mango body gel, trying to release my stress. I was so scared about tonight. I hoped everything would pan out the way I want it to. *It's always a chance things can go bad. I'm not going to worry about it.* I put my cucumbers over my eyes and lay back.

I heard some heavy footsteps coming my way. I knew it was Dollar. When he entered the bathroom, I saw that he had heavy bags underneath his eyes and he needed a shave and a haircut badly. "What's the matter with you?" I asked him.

"It's Momma. She ain't doing too good."

"Really?" *Good for that trick-ass bitch.* I just looked at him, looking all sad and stressed. His ass was smiling when he locked me away.

"Yeah, I'm worried she goin' die."

"She gonna make it," I said, trying to sound concerned. Really, I hoped she did.

"I'ma sue that restaurant," he said.

"Baby, if yo' momma didn't tell them not to put nuts in her food, how would they know?"

He just looked at me like I was taking their side. I needed to calm his ass down. "Baby, take your clothes off and get into the tub wit me."

He followed orders, got undressed, and got in the tub. I massaged his feet, trying to relax him. Once I washed his feet up, I began to suck his toes, one by one. I could tell Sissy ain't never done him like this before. He was moaning for dear life. *Yeah, nigga, ya ass lost one! All this pussy could have been yours, but you wanted to play a bitch.* I licked the bottoms of Dollar's feet, sucking on his heels.

"Oh, Sissy, I need this, baby," he moaned, irritating the shit outta me. I licked up his legs to his thighs. He was searching for the right words to say.

He know Sissy pussy game ain't mean like mine. She ain't no freak like me. Yeah, I'm that bitch. Niggas know they need a freak to keep they ass at home. A good girl only good for show. When it comes to laying it down, niggas want to be fucked like no tomorrow's coming.

"Shit, what you doing to me, girl?" Dollar moaned, but he ain't seen nothing yet. I made Dollar push his legs back in their oversized Jacuzzi tub. I held my breath, pushed my head under the water, and licked the crack of Dollar's ass so good. I could only hold my breath a minute at a time, but I was getting too gangsta with his ass. I fucked up my brand new hairdo, but I didn't give a fuck. *I aim to please, always.*

I had him screaming like a bitch. I got up and slid his rock-hard dick in my mouth. I wanted to get his first nut up outta him, cause I was fin to lay this pussy on him. I sucked him like never before. Once I got him to come, I looked up at him while I was holding his cum in my mouth. "Oh, you taste so good, Big Daddy. You like the way I sucked it?"

"Yeah, baby, I love it."

I wanted to do something that was gonna totally blow his mind. "Good," I purred, and spit all the cum I had in my mouth dead in the middle of his face.

Dollar bucked his eyes wide open. He was so shocked I did that. He just looked at me and wiped off his face. I knew I just blew his mind.

I went to kiss him on the mouth, sucking on his tongue. He kissed me so passionately. He was so excited. I couldn't do nothing but laugh. He was probably thinking, "Yeah, my baby getting gangster." *Please, that bitch ain't me and she'll never be.*

I licked Dollar from his lips down to his neck, sucking a big hickey on his dark skin. I licked his chest, sucking on his nipples one by one. When I slid my tongue down to his navel, I noticed his dick was back on rock. I slid down his dick backwards. *I have a surprise for Big Daddy today.* I bounced on his dick froggystyle. Dollar wrapped his hands around my tiny waist, trying to keep up with me.

I jumped off his dick and went down and gave him some more head. He was tugging me by the hair, saying all kinds of dumb shit.

When I got up again, I slid Dollar's dick into my ass. His dick was much smaller than Slim's, so this would be easy. I pushed my legs to the side of me and started bouncing on him like no tomorrow's coming. I wished I was Ms. Cleo right then, cause I sure wanted to know what he was thinking.

"Fuck!" he kept screaming. "Damn, baby, what you doing? Dis shit feel so good!"

"I know," I replied. *Damn right, this shit the best, nigga.* I started jerking and bouncing even faster, and Dollar started screaming so loud. It was funny. "I'm coming, baby!"

"That's right, Big Daddy, I want you to bust inside of me." A few more pumps and Dollar let out a loud scream in a high-pitched bitch tone.

I wasn't finished with his ass. I jumped off his dick, went down, and licked up all of his cum. Dollar's ass looked spaced out. I know his ass was wondering where the hell Sissy learned all this shit from.

I climbed on top of him and gave him a kiss on the mouth. I wrapped my arms around his neck and nibbled on his ear. I whispered to him, "You like that shit?"

Dollar just looked at me. He kissed me on my lips. "I love you," he said. I could tell his mind was wandering—pussy-whipped ass.

I washed up and got out of the tub. My hair was soaking wet, and I needed to meet Slim in less than two hours. "Baby, be ready tonight at eight. You know the guests will be arriving by nine," I said to Dollar.

Dollar sat on the edge of the bed, staring at me getting dressed. He was off in La-La Land. "Dollar!" I yelled, trying to snap him outta his daze.

"Yeah, baby, I'm sorry, what you say?"

"Be ready by eight."

"All right. Where you fin to go now?"

That nigga head was all over the place. I done fucked his ass senseless. "Going to get my hair done over. Look at it."

"That's it?" he asked. "You ain't going nowhere else?"

"What is this, Twenty Questions?"

"No. I just wanna know, that's all. You need some money?"

"Yup." *Why spend mines? Pay me, nigga.*

Dollar reached into his pocket and gave me five hundred dollars. I gave him a kiss on the lips. "Peace!" I yelled as I left the room.

Dollar ran out in the hall behind me. "Sissy!" he yelled.

"Yes?"

"Call me when you make it to the beauty shop. I don't want to be worried about you."

I just bet. "Cool," I said.

That nigga's upstairs with his stomach hurting. Just the thought of his bitch giving her pussy to another nigga makes him sick.

I had things to do and people to do. I ran back to Mena's and got my hair blow-dried and curled. I left and made my way over to the hood where Slim wanted to buy his shop. *I'm glad I went to the bank earlier.*

When I pulled up, I couldn't believe the location Slim had picked to open his shop. *I wouldn't even ride down the street at night in this area.*

I walked into the shop and Slim was waiting on me. "Hey, baby," I said as I kissed him on the lips.

"Hey, cutie. You look hot."

"Thanks. Where's the guy?" *I don't have no time to waste.*

"He went down the street," Slim said. "He'll be right back."

Slim found his shop in the heart of the ghetto, right in Englewood. He wanted it, so hey. *He a nigga. He the one that has to deal with the drama.* I missed Slim. I needed to be with him. I hadn't gave him no pussy since I found that trick in his bed.

I sat down in his lap and kissed him on his lips. "I miss you, Big Daddy." I felt his dick coming alive. "I miss you too," I said as I ran my hand across Slim's dick.

"We've missed you too, baby. When you goin' take care of us? It's been a while."

"I know, baby. Lock the door and I can take care of you two now."

"The guy goin' be right back, baby."

"Whatever, scaredy-cat."

172

Slim just looked at me and hit me on my ass. I got up and took a good look at this dump. It was going to take a serious makeover to get this joint to look like something.

I walked to the back. It was just filthy in this place. It smelled like an old crack house. The scent was making me sick to my stomach. Merry Maids was gonna have to clean this place up. I'd be damned if I even tried to.

I heard Slim talking to somebody, so I walked back up front. Slim was talking to the realtor, so I came in and introduced myself, "Hi. My name is Emerald Jones," I said. He just looked at me, confused.

"This my girl," Slim said. "She goin' help me fix up this place."

I took a look at Slim. *Your girl? When did we establish that I was your bitch?* I didn't want to front him in front of him, so I went along with him. "It's nice to meet you."

Once Slim finished his transaction and the realtor was gone, I locked the door and got down to business with him. I had to make sure my main dick was taken care of too.

CHAPTER 40
S.L.

WHEN I MADE it back home, Dollar was on edge. "Why you ain't call me?" he yelled.

"I forgot."

"Why was your phone off, then?"

"It's off?" I said as I pulled Sissy's phone outta my purse. "I didn't know that. It must have shut off itself. You ready and excited?" I said, paying him no never mind.

He just looked at me. I know his head was all fucked up. I ran up the stairs, took a quick shower, and slipped on my outfit. When I came down the stairs, Dollar just looked at me.

"Big Daddy, you goin' sit around looking sad all night?"

He looked at me and smiled. "You look beautiful."

"Thank you."

I made sure that I invited everybody that I could and stocked the liquor cabinet. We all know when too many black folks get together, it starts trouble. I kind of liked the way I put this little party together. Everything looked nice.

S.L. arrived first, without Ginger. I was so glad they drove separate cars. This was better for me.

"Hey, S.L." I smiled as I batted my long eyelashes at him.

"'Zup," he said as he threw his head back. I hadn't seen S.L. in a while; he was looking good. I was gonna have to get me some of that before the night was over.

Once the guests started showing up and the DJ started playing all the cuts, the party got real live. Ginger finally showed up. She was looking dangerous, but nobody was dumb enough to holler at her. They didn't want no trouble.

Ginger came over to my table, sat next to me, and ran her hand up the inner part of my thigh. If I didn't have work to do, I would have taken her up the stairs and let her get what she wanted.

I got up and fixed Dollar a plate of food at his request. I started to say, "Get yo' own shit," but I knew I had to relax. When I came back, I set his plate down and he reached up and rubbed the side of my face so gently. "I love you, Sissy," he said as he pulled me close to him.

At that moment, I felt the love that he had for Sissy. I felt myself getting pissed off, so I shook it off. *Whatever. Love her ass, nigga. I don't give a fuck.*

The doorbell rang, and it was exactly 11:05 PM. It was time to turn this party out. I ran to the door and answered it. "Hey, come in."

"You got the key?"

"Yeah," I said as I handed her the car key.

"Good, I'll be back within fifteen minutes."

"Good, I'll leave this door cracked." I said as I walked off.

I kept S.L.'s glass filled to the rim all night. "You want to dance?" I asked him.

I took a good look at all the hood niggas at the party. I did all that fucking saying I was Sissy and none of them niggas knew Dollar. It was all just a waste of time, really, except Mandingo; he paid well and his dick was the business.

S.L. came and danced with me. His ass was gone off that shit. I started grinding my body so hard on him and touching him in all his hot spots. I could tell he wanted me, and I wanted some of that big dick. "I want you," I whispered softly in his ear. I didn't even give a fuck about Dollar. He was so far gone over Sissy, he wasn't thinking she was on something.

S.L. took two steps back and looked at me. I batted my eyelashes at him seductively. He pulled me close to him like we were dancing, but he was feeling me out. "What about Dollar?" he asked in my ear.

"What about him? He ain't got to know about us. Plus, my friend by the door," I said as I pointed to Angel. "We both want to do you right now."

S.L. took a look at Angel. She was real low-key and had on a wig, but she was looking real sexy. "So you coming or what?"

S.L. looked around the room. Ginger was nowhere to be found, and Dollar was shooting pool. "Meet me at my car in ten minutes," he said.

I gave Angel the signal and walked over to Dollar. "Hey, baby, I'm going to run to the gas station. We ran out of ice, and I want the help to stay here and start cleaning this place up. It looks a mess."

"Okay," he said trying to stay focused on his shot. Dollar had always been a real serious pool player. I knew he was going to be wrapped up into his game for at least an hour. I searched the room for Ginger and she seemed to have disappeared. I also noticed Danny was gone. If I had to bet my money on it, I would have bet him and Ginger were having a serious

175

talk somewhere.

I met up with Angel and S.L. by his car. He kept on staring at Angel, but I knew, loaded with booze and drugs, he couldn't recognize her. "You look high as hell. I'ma drive us up to the park. Get in on the passenger side," I said.

We made it to the park and I looked over at S.L. "So, Big Daddy, you ready for me?" I moaned as I ran my hand across his chest.

"Yeah, I been ready," he said, smiling.

I looked at the clock. It said 11:45 PM. I had fifteen minutes to have some fun. "Do you like my friend?" I asked him.

He looked back at Angel and she pulled off her wig. He squinted his eyes, trying to focus in on her. "Hey, papi, long time no see," she said.

I reached in and licked S.L. on the side of his neck, and Angel ran her hands up and down his chest. S.L. was so out of it, he didn't even speak. He just closed his eyes.

I unbuckled his pants and his dick was already hard. "Look, Angel, I know you faithful, but I can't turn down a long hard dick."

"I thought you said we wasn't gonna fuck him?"

"You don't want to?" I asked her. I really hated to let a big hard dick go to waste.

"I mean, I'm trying to be faithful to Black."

"Yeah, but he ain't goin' know. Besides, he don't even count. This is old dick."

"Right, it does look good. It won't hurt for ol' times' sake."

LL Cool J popped into my mind. "S.L. got a big ol' dick," I sang, "I know I told you I'll be true, but S.L. got a big ol' dick, so I cheated on you." We both busted out laughing.

"Okay, it's 11:48 PM. We only have ten minutes," Angel said.

I slapped S.L. outta his sleep. I needed him to beat up my pussy like he did Angel. I knew he was too drunk, but a good five minutes hard from the back would do.

I bent over and pulled my dress up and S.L. slid into me. He wasn't pumping as hard as I wanted him to, but once I started bouncing back on him hard, he started picking up his speed. "Oh, S.L., harder. I'm about to come!" I yelled.

"Hurry up so I can get my turn," Angel demanded.

"You said you want to be faithful. I can help you with that. Just say no to the dick." Shit, I didn't want him to stop. He was hitting it right, much better than he did last time.

176

Angel got out of the back seat and opened the door, "Bitch, move. This was my dick first." I looked up at her. She was lucky I busted, cause I wasn't moving until I did.

I got out of the car and fixed my clothes and let them do their thing in private.

When I saw the flashing light coming from the police car, I knocked on the window and yelled at her so she could put her clothes on. "The po-po is here!."

"Ma'am, can I get your license and registration?" one officer asked me as they approached the car.

"This not my car. I got a ride up here."

The police shone their lights inside the car and tapped on the window. Angel rolled it down.

"Ma'am, I need for you and the gentleman to slowly step out of the vehicle."

"For what?" Angel yelled.

"Is this your vehicle?" the officer asked Angel.

"No, this his car, but why we gotta step outside?"

"May I see your license?"

"Why? I ain't driving. He is."

"Ma'am, please step outta the vehicle now, and I want to see some ID on the both of you now," he ordered me and Angel.

Me and Angel handed the female officer our IDs, and the male officer went to the passenger side of the car to talk to S.L.

"Sir, is this your vehicle?" S.L. looked up at him spaced out and leaned back in his seat.

"Sir, I need you to step out of the vehicle, please."

S.L. reached into his glove box and the officer drew his gun. "Freeze! Don't move. Put your hands in the air."

I knew S.L. was stoned and not thinking clearly. The officer opened the passenger door slowly and advised S.L. to step out of the car slowly.

S.L. stepped outta the car, almost falling over. "Sir, please put your hands on the vehicle where I can see them."

"Why y'all messing wit us?" Angel yelled.

"Ma'am, please be quiet!" the officer yelled at her as he searched S.L.'s pockets. "What's this?" the officer asked the other as he pulled a glass capsule outta S.L.'s pocket.

"It looks like ecstasy pills," the lady officer replied.

"So y'all came down here to get high?"

"Hell no!" I yelled. "We was just fucking. That's it. I don't even know him like that."

"Search them," the officer ordered. The female officer searched me and Angel's bodies and purses.

"I don't do drugs," I told the officer again.

"Run their names in the system. If they come back clean, we will let you ladies go, but I'm taking him down for possession of drugs."

I wasn't worried. I knew our names was gonna come back clean. "How y'all know we were here?"

"We search this park every day at eight PM and midnight."

The officer put S.L. in the back seat of his car and told him that he was going to search his vehicle. The officer looked inside and out of his BMW 745 for some more drugs.

It had been thirty minutes already. I was ready to go. I wished our names would come back clean already. I was for sure Dollar was looking for me. The officer popped S.L.'s trunk open and pulled out a black duffel bag. He unzipped the bag and there were so many small glass tubes of ecstasy in there, S.L. was gonna go down.

The officer radioed in for backup and a tow truck.

"Damn, somebody's in trouble," I said to Angel.

"Hell yeah," she laughed.

The officer asked S.L. about the drugs. Of course, he was so high he didn't know if he was coming or going.

"They came back clean," the female officer told her partner.

"Good, can we go?" I asked. I was ready to leave ASAP. I didn't want no part of this.

More officers arrived on the scene, and it reminded me of when I got arrested. I needed to go. One of the officers agreed to drop us off, but before I left, I wanted to see if S.L. was gonna be okay.

Me and Angel got into the back of the police car to speak to him. "S.L., you cool?"

"No, man, call Dollar and tell him to come and get me."

I looked at him and smiled. "You want me to get Dollar to come bail you out?"

"Yeah, man, tell Ginger to get me some money. She knows where I keep my money. I don't know where those drugs came from. Sissy, I need you to get at Dollar for me. Tell them to come and get me."

I smiled again and then busted out laughing. "Oh, you want me to help you, S.L.? Do you remember this pretty young thing you used to run up in before me?"

"S.L., papi, you forget about your chica, our long nights, and how you used to fuck me for hours before Ginger came back home," Angel said. "At first we would sneak around, then at your place. All the lies about how you loved me and how you wanted to be with me. It's me, Big Daddy, Angel."

S.L. looked at her like she rose up from the dead. "Angel," he said like he got sober real quick.

He looked at me. "It's Emerald," I said. "I'm disappointed in you. How come you ain't beat my pussy up until I fainted like Angel?"

"That's not possible," he said.

"Oh, it's me. How you doing?"

"Wait," he yelled, trying to get one of the officers' attention.

"Hey, papi, don't trip," said Angel. "You just getting a taste of your own medicine. What goes around comes around."

S.L. was yelling like he lost his mind, but no one paid him any mind. Angel and I got into the police car, and they pulled off.

I scratched S.L.'s name off my list. We pulled over at the gas station and Linda's partner got into the car.

"Where's my money?" he said to me.

"There's half," I said as I handed him a brown envelope.

"Half?" he yelled.

"Yeah, half. You will get your other half once I know he didn't get any phone calls. I need him locked away for three days, no phone calls or nothing, understood?"

"All right. Linda, I want my fucking money or I'll kill you and this bitch," he advised.

"Nigga, ain't nobody scared of you. Take your money and get the fuck out!" I yelled.

Linda dropped us back off at the house. "Here's your cut, Linda," I said, handing her a brown paper bag.

"You know I want to see you."

"Bye!" I yelled as I got out of the car. I was through with selling my body for favors.

When I made it back in the house, Dollar was still playing pool for money. I slipped back into the party and no one noticed. *I got two down and three more to go.*

(HAPTER 41
BOSS HEAD

THE THINGS PEOPLE would do for boss head never ceased to amaze me. I was guilty myself. I was addicted to a bitch and I couldn't let her go.

When I made it to Ginger's house, she had the door cracked open for me. I walked in and heard the sound of Sade playing. I just looked at Ginger. *I don't know what it is about her, but she has me gone, and it's cool. I'm a freak anyways. I need two pussy-lickers in my life.*

"Hey, Sissy, you want something to drink?" she asked me. Ginger never played fair. *If she ain't popped that shit in my drink, maybe I wouldn't be such a freak.*

"Yes," I said. Ginger went to her bar to pour me a shot of Patron. She reached in her drawer and opened it all the way. I know she was looking for them pills she be popping.

"You looking for these?" I asked as I held up the pills. Her face turned red in embarrassment. "You know, Ginger, you a dirty bitch!" I yelled. She just looked at me. "And to tell you the truth, the way you eat pussy, you didn't have to drug me. I think ya head game is boss—best I ever had—but I don't like getting played."

"Sissy, I'm sorry."

"Bitch, I ain't Sissy," I said. She looked at me. "It's me, bitch, the one ya put in jail."

Her facial expression changed. I could tell she got scared. "Emerald!" she yelled.

"Yup, it's me, baby."

She backed away from me cause she knew firsthand I'd kick a bitch's ass good. "What you goin' do to me?"

"You know, Ginger, I thought long and hard about that. I was gonna put ya ass in jail wit ya husband. Oh, yeah, S.L. gone to jail, and he's gonna be there a while. But you know, a bitch got feelings for ya. I love the way you make me feel, and I'm kind of strung out on you. So I thought, 'Why send her to jail and let her lick another bitch's pussy, when she could be here licking mine?' I done fucked wit a lot of people, and boss head is hard to come by these days. When I talked it over with our friend Angel—you remember Angel?"

I called Angel's name, and she came walking through the door. Ginger's face turned pale.

"She thought the same as me, so you got two choices," I advised her. "One, I'll put ya ass in jail or kill you, whichever way I feel. Or door number two, you come show me and Angel how sorry you are for betraying us."

Ginger walked my way. I knew she'd take door number two. Ginger would never make it without S.L., and she didn't want to be behind bars. She was too high-class for that.

Before she fell to her knees, I pulled her by her hair and let her know, "Bitch, you better eat dis pussy like ain't no tomorrow coming."

Ginger dropped down to her knees and laid me down. She ate me alive. Shit, I can't even explain the shit. All I know is that I saw the stars, sun, and moon. I even got jealous cause Angel was screaming louder than me! But it was cool.

Ginger is goin' be my bitch until I'm done wit her ass. Before I left, I slapped her ass with my pimp hand to let her know her ass was gonna die if she fucked me again. She might have crossed me once, but if she crossed me twice, her ass was grass.

CHAPTER 42
THE RUN

IT WAS A cold and brisk morning. I didn't want to wake up. I felt like I was having déjà vu. I had felt this same way the very first time I made a drop for Dollar. My stomach was turning knots from being scared.

This was a big chance for me to take. I was going all the way out to Michigan. I didn't know a soul there. Plus, if I got caught, I was a goner. They would lock your ass up for a nose full of coke, so I knew I would be under the cell. For some reason, I felt like something bad was going to happen to me.

I got dressed and went straight to Sissy's truck. I'd loaded up her car last night, so all I needed to do was take off.

"You ready? You got all the stuff right?" Dollar asked me.

"Yeah, I'm ready. I got it all."

"Cool. I've been looking for S.L. for four days. I can't find him nowhere. So I thank you for packing that up. I know you didn't want to. When you get there, call me. Drive slow and be careful."

"Bye," I said.

"I love you, Sissy," Dollar said. I just rolled the window up and pulled off on his ass. *Love that bitch, nigga, I don't care.*

I threw in my 2Pac CD and jammed all the way there. I hadn't taken this ride in a long time, but I still knew it like the back of my hand.

When I made it there, I popped the trunk and jumped out. My hands were sweating, I didn't know why. I'd done this many times before. After the man searched me, we walked to the back of my truck. I lifted up my latch and unzipped one of the bags to show him the product.

"Hey, baby," a cracked-out bag lady said to the man.

"Get your ass away from here!" he yelled.

"Come on, daddy, I need a hit. I'll suck on your dick, baby. Come on, just a little."

I was scared outta my mind. I had a feeling something was gonna happen. The lady wouldn't move her crackhead ass down the street. I wanted this crackhead bitch to move before she made the police come and I went back to jail. *Shit, I'll set it off up in dis bitch first.*

"Bitch, get your ass outta here before I put a cap into yo' ass," he said to her.

"Come on, daddy, I can suck you right now," she moaned as she started scratching all over herself. She reached under her dress and my heart started pounding like a drum.

"All I want is some blow," she said as she pulled out a nine and pointed it at us. "Bitch, give me the yayo and the money now!" she demanded.

I shot a look at him to see what he wanted me to do. He shook his head at me and reached down and grabbed his strap. By the time he got up, six niggas with big choppers rushed the garage.

I almost pissed on myself. My heart was racing. I shoulda followed my first mind. They taking all the shit away. This was not in the plan. *What do I do?* I knew I wasn't finna die for this shit. Getting Dollar back wasn't worth me dying.

"The yayo and the money now!" she yelled again, pointing her gun at my head. I didn't want them to kill me, so I threw them the two black duffel bags of drugs I had. "That's all I got, I swear," I pleaded.

"Nigga, give me the cash now," one of the others demanded as he cocked back his chopper.

The man threw him the money and looked pissed. He looked at me and I just stared at him. I coulda fainted. "Bitch, you set me up!" he said.

"I swear, nigga, I didn't! These probably yo' damn boys!"

The guys opened the bags to check the money. "Thank you, bloodclot. I have a message for you from Dirty. He say suck his dick and he'll see you in hell." *Boom!* One shot to the head killed him dead. All his blood splashed on me.

"Please don't kill me," I begged. They took the bags and jumped back into the car and pulled off. As soon as they pulled off, I ran to my truck as fast as I could and backed out. I was so glad I still had my car running.

I was hysterical and I couldn't think straight. *Dollar goin' be pissed off about this shit!* I called him right away as I made a run for the expressway, driving as fast as I can.

"Sissy?" he answered.

"Dollar, it didn't go good!"

"What?" he yelled.

"When I got there, it was these guys with these big guns and they took everything."

"Please tell me you're kidding me."

"I'm sorry, Dollar. I was so scared. I thought I was going to die."

"Shit!" he yelled as he slammed his hand into the wall. "Where you at now?"

"I'm so sorry, Dollar, don't be mad at me, I didn't know what to do."

"They took all six bags of drugs?"

"Yeah, they took it all. I'm so sorry."

"I know, baby, it's not your fault. Just come home."

"I'm scared," I said. "They blew his head off right in front of me. I don't want to be there. I'm scared."

"What? Where you want to go?"

"Let's just get a room tonight and we can figure this out."

"Cool, where?" Dollar asked.

"At the Essence."

"Fine. How long you gonna be?"

"About three hours. I'll call you when I get there."

I hung up the phone and pushed Sissy's truck to the max. I had to get back to Chicago ASAP.

CHAPTER 43
REUNITED

I CHECKED INTO the hotel and got my key. I got the biggest room they had. I wanted to soak my body in their garden tub. I heard they had a swing in this joint, and I needed to get fucked in it.

I opened my door and the room was fly and romantic—somewhere I could take a nice young fella back to. They had a rain shower and a bench. There were so many different places to get fucked on in this room. Shit, I needed a good fuck to take my mind off all this bullshit that just happened.

I soaked in the tub for a half-hour, got out, and lotioned myself up. The taps on the door let me know Dollar had arrived right on time.

"Hey, baby," I said to him as I pulled him into the room.

"Hey, I'm glad you okay," he said. "Now tell me what happened."

"I took the guy to the back of the car and some crackhead came up asking for a hit. Then she pulled out a gun and six other guys came from nowhere. I was so scared. I thought I was gonna die."

Dollar held me close to him and rubbed my hair. "It's okay, long as you are safe."

"What we goin' do now?"

"I don't know. I can't get in touch with S.L. I'll figure something out. You know, when it rains, it pours." That was an understatement.

I took off his coat and shoes. I took the gun that I knew he would have. I put all his things on the sink and came back over and kissed him on the lips.

"Dollar, I got something to tell you."

"What, baby?" he said, all excited like I was fin to tell him I was carrying his seed or something.

I rubbed my hand across his face, down to the small of his back. He loved to be touched like that. I rubbed my hands up his big arms, making him shiver. "Baby, tell me," he moaned.

I took a step back and looked at him. "I'm not who you think I am."

"What?" he said, looking confused.

"I'm not Sissy."

"Oh, you want to role-play wit ya man. I'm wit it. I need something to take my mind off this shit." Dollar lay back and placed his arms behind his head. "So...who are you, baby? Beyoncé? Cause you know I love me some Beyoncé."

I just smiled at him, really cute. "No, baby, I'm Emerald."

"Emerald?" he said as he sat up. "Naw, baby, pick somebody else. What, you tryin' to kill the mood?"

The mood, nigga? I got ya mood. "No, seriously, nigga, I'm Emerald."

He sat up and looked at me. My facial expression told him I was serious. "Sissy, stop playing with me like that."

"Nigga, you wish Sissy could fuck you like I did."

His facial expression changed. He was nervous now. "Sissy, this shit ain't funny. Stop fucking playing."

"Will the real Sissy please stand up?" I yelled.

Sissy came outta the bathroom with her hands tied behind her back and her mouth taped shut. Dollar's eyes grew big when he saw us both there and Slim pointing his nine at him.

I snatched the tape off of Sissy's mouth and she let out a loud scream. "So you two kids are in love and shit," I said.

Dollar's mouth hung open. "Emerald?"

"Yup, it's me, nigga. You thought you left a bitch for dead, huh?"

"Emerald, please don't hurt us," Sissy cried.

"Aw, shut the hell up, I'm not. I thought for a whole year about what I'ma do to you two. Prayed about it, too. I'ma let y'all go free, live all happily ever after. I don't care."

They both looked at me like I was joking. I took Sissy's keys and threw them to her. "There go your car keys and your phone. Nice ride. You two go and have a good life and lots of little Dollars too."

Slim untied Sissy's hands and she went and hugged Dollar. *What a nice reunion.* "Y'all better go before I change my mind and go westside in this bitch."

Dollar slid into his shoes and grabbed his coat and started walking out the door. "Dollar," I called after him. He turned around and looked at me. "What goes around comes back around eventually."

When the door shut, I locked it and put the latch on the door. Slim was looking at me all sideways. "What's your problem?" I asked him.

"You told me you wasn't gonna fuck him."

Oh lord, here we go. "Nigga, get your mind off that old shit and come over here and beat this pussy up in this swing."

186

"No, seriously, Emerald, did you suck his dick too?"

"Did that bitch you had me stuck out in the cold for suck yo' dick?"

He just looked at me. He knew he didn't want to go there with me. *An eye for an eye, nigga.* I climbed my big ass into the swing and gave my orders. "I want you to beat it, then eat it. Beat it, then eat it, you hear me?"

He just looked up at me, dropped to his knees, and followed my orders.

(HAPTER 44
BOOMERANG

I COULDN'T BELIEVE my eyes. How in the hell did Emerald get outta jail and nobody said nothing? I should have gone back there and kicked in the hotel door and blasted the both of them. But I knew I had to be smart with my moves. If Emerald pulled all this off, she was not working alone. I had to check my sources to see what the word was on the street about her.

I called up my nigga that worked in the county to see what he knew.

"Hello," Chico answered.

"Man, why you ain't tell me that bitch was out?"

"What bitch you talking bout, Papi Chulo?"

"Emerald, that bitch that took my bid."

"Yo, I was told she got transferred for stabbing up your chica baby momma. That's what they told us. I told you that, bro ham."

"Well, I just seen her, so that's not true. I need you to find out everything you can, ASAP. I don't got no fucking time to waste. I need that like yesterday. I got a lot of missing money and heads gonna roll if I don't get it back."

"I'll put in some calls. I don't know. I checked her file myself. It said she was transferred out to Joliet. I even called the warden out there and he told me she was there. I need until the morning to find out what I can."

"Don't fuck with me, Chico. If I go down, we all going, you hear me?"

"I hear you. Calm down. Let me find out what I can and I'll call you first thing."

"You heard from S.L.? He's been missing."

"No, I haven't talked to him in a minute."

"Call me back first thing, nigga!" I yelled as I hung up the phone.

My head was pounding. I needed an aspirin. Was S.L. working with this bitch or what? I needed to get in contact with his ass right now. I knew his bitch had to know something. I was going over there to see what was up. I didn't want to talk to her over the phone. I didn't trust no-fucking-body right now. Everybody could be compromised.

I pulled into the gas station so I could get into the car with Sissy and speak to her. I needed to know everything she knew—what happened and how long she'd been gone. I jumped into the car, reached in, and rubbed

Sissy's face. She was all black and blue.

"I'm so sorry, baby. How did this happen? How long you been gone?" I asked.

"That bitch Emerald goin' get it!" Sissy yelled as she looked at her face in the mirror. "She had me locked in that basement for two weeks, feeding me crackers and water. That bitch gonna see me and I'ma beat her ass!"

"Two weeks?" I yelled. My stomach knotted up. I got even sicker to know Emerald had been in my house all this time. "I did not know, Sissy. I swear. I'm so sorry. Did that nigga touch you?"

I swear, if he raped her I'm gonna find him and clap his bitch ass.

"No," Sissy said. "He didn't touch me."

"Shit!" I yelled as I slammed my hand against the dashboard. "That bitch played me. Did you hear anything about S.L.?"

"No, Emerald only came there twice. They just had me locked in the basement."

I gotta go over to S.L.'s house. I gotta try to find him so I can go and get our money back.

"Dollar, I want you to come home."

"I'll be there within the hour. I promise," I said.

"You think it's safe? What if she come back to kill us?"

"Listen, I got some money over my mom's crib. After I leave Ginger's house, I'ma go and pick it up. Then, in the morning, we can bounce outta here, okay?"

"Okay, Dollar, I love you."

"I love you too." I kissed Sissy goodbye and jumped into my 2008 Maserati Gran Turismo. I had six hundred over at my momma's crib. I was gone take half of that and get Sissy out of here. *But me, I ain't leaving until I get my fucking money or work back.*

I rang S.L.'s bell like I was stupid. "Who the fuck is it?" Ginger yelled.

"It's me, bitch, open the door."

I busted through Ginger's door with fire in my eyes. "Bitch, where's S.L.?"

"Bitch! Nigga, don't come over here with that shit. I don't know where the fuck he at! He's not answering his phone and he ain't came home."

"You call the police?"

"No, I figured he might be with his bitch on the other side of town. I'm pretty sure you know her."

"So, you seen any old friends lately?" I questioned her so I could read her face.

"Old friends? Now, you know I ain't got no damn friends."

I looked at her. Ginger was a master at getting people to believe her. "So you ain't seen or heard from Emerald?"

"Emerald?" She frowned up her face. "How she goin' contact me from jail? I don't accept no fucking collect calls."

I followed her as she poured herself a drink and went on and on about being scared to see Emerald. "All right then," I said. "If you hear from S.L., tell him to call me, ASAP."

"Okay."

I let myself out. Either Ginger was a good-ass liar or she had no clue Emerald was out. And I wasn't telling her I had my own problems.

When I made it home, Sissy was waiting up for me looking scared.

"Dollar, can we go now?" she asked.

"No. In the morning I gotta make some calls and get you a place. I can't do that until the morning. We safe. I alerted all the guards outside and I got my nine in the drawer." I pulled Sissy close to me in the bed so she could feel safe.

"I want you inside me," she whispered in my ear. Her talking to me like that reminded me of Emerald, and I wasn't excited. I knew I needed to make her feel safe, like I had everything under control.

I slid inside her, making her cringe as she put her nails in my back. "I miss you, Dollar," she moaned in my ear.

I had to be honest: Emerald's pussy had felt much better than Sissy's. I shoulda known Sissy wasn't rocking my world like that. But even though Emerald was better in the bed, Sissy's pussy was good enough for me. I loved her and I'd die before I let Emerald try to hurt her. Sissy was all I needed, and I had to get her away before these walls came crashing down. I knew Emerald was up to something. *She not goin' let us get away with doing her dirty.*

After I put her to bed, I stared at the walls for hours. I didn't know what she could be planning. I knew that little bitch was up to something. I wasn't worried about her coming here—she wouldn't get in. I gave more orders not to let anybody on the property.

I finally dozed off in the wee hours of the night after I wrecked my brain until I couldn't think.

💲 💲 💲

The fog was so thick outside you couldn't see a thing. I hated it when the fog was this bad. The gusting winds blowing seventy miles an hour didn't make it any better.

"I want three officers in the back, two on the side, and a team through the front," Officer Jordan said as she gave her direct orders. "I want this done clean and accurate. I've been on Mr. Miller's ass for six years now. I'm too close to nailing his ass to have any fuck-ups. You hear me?"

"Yes, ma'am," the officers all said in unison.

"Lieutenant David, are you sure everything's in place?" she asked him.

"Yes, I'm sure."

The DEA had Dollar's house surrounded. "On the count of three. One, two, three!" Dollar's front and back door came tumbling down and the DEA rushed in the house.

Dollar and Sissy woke up and got handcuffed to the floor. After an hour of searching, the DEA recovered ten kilos of drugs and two unregistered handguns. They also recovered over three hundred thousand in cash, and Sissy's truck had two kilos of drugs under her seat in a stash spot.

"Good job," Officer Jordan said to me as I got out of the back seat of her car. I had planned this out to a T. I knew Officer Jordan wanted Dollar, and after two years of planning, I got her what she wanted.

The corroboration at the station was only to protect my identity, and getting David to have the warrant issued was easy. My little videotape helped with that. I walked over to the police car that Dollar was in, and me and Angel got in on each side of him.

Dollar looked at me and then Angel and hung his head low.

"Hey, papi," Angel said to Dollar.

"You know, Big Daddy, I didn't know you would be stupid enough to come home," I said. "But I figured, what the hell, I was stupid enough to take your jail time, right?"

Dollar wouldn't look up. He just kept his head down and didn't speak.

"The cat got your tongue now, nigga?" I yelled.

Dollar was a lost cause, and I was happy he was goin' be where he belonged. "Oh yeah, Dollar, your nappy-headed sister goin' be in jail too. You know, the one you didn't tell me about? Her ass is grass too, and tell S.L. I said hi when you get there, you dirty bastard."

As Dollar and Sissy pulled off on their journey to jail, I felt so much better. What goes around comes around, just like a boomerang.

CHAPTER 45
THE NEW ME

Two Months Later

THE BIRDS CHIRPING outside my window were working on my last nerve. The launch of my Secret Garden collection was coming up. I had to start from scratch because of Joseph's crazy ass, but my life had been settled and I'd never been in a better space. Besides splitting my time between my two Johns, everything else was good. I knew I needed to settle down with somebody, but I just couldn't figure out who. They both made me happy, but they both were giving me ultimatums to choose one.

"What are you thinking about?" John asked me.

"Nothing. Going over some ideas for the line, that's all. You hungry?"

"Yeah, I would like some of those blueberry pancakes you make me."

"No problem," I smiled as I kissed John on his lips.

I went into the kitchen and turned on the TV to watch Judge Mathis. "Just in…" said the Channel Seven news anchor, Robin Robertson.

"Vonzel Miller and his mother, along with his sister, will stand trial tomorrow. Mr. Miller has twenty-six counts of fraud against him, as well as his sister and mother. His mother suffered a mild stroke from an allergic reaction to some food she ate, but is expected to recover and stand trial. Mr. Miller was arrested initially on drug charges when a home raid turned up ten kilos of cocaine. He was arrested along with his wife Sissy Jones-Miller and taken into custody two months ago. The pair was later charged, along with his mother and sister, with credit card fraud, falsifying documents, and tampering with witnesses. We will be live at the trial for coverage. Robin Robertson, Channel Seven News. Back to you, Dave."

I flipped the TV to Judge Mathis. I didn't want to watch that depressing shit.

My cell phone rang, and I really didn't want to answer it. Juggling two men was very hard, especially when you had good pussy like mines.

"Hello," I answered quietly so John wouldn't notice I was talking.

"Why you talking so low?" he asked me.

"I'm not talking low. Good morning," I said trying to change the subject. It was like the War of the Roses between these two.

Slim no longer wanted me to call him by his street name, so when I said, "John," they were both like, "Huh?" It made it good when I fucked them, cause if I yelled, "Oh, John!" it didn't matter which one I was talking about. That was the good thing about it.

"I need you to come to the shop," he said. "Did you order the booths like I asked?"

"Yes, I did." When I turned around to put John's pancake on his plate, he was sitting down and reading the paper. *Fuck.* I really didn't feel like stroking nobody's ego today. It was getting tiresome. Now I know how niggas feel when they jump off be pressuring them to leave their wifey. It will give you a damn headache. "I ordered them. Let me find the receipt and I'll call you back."

"Why you rushing me off the phone?"

"I'm not. I need to get into the shower anyway." I tried my best not to make eye contact with John.

"Yeah, I know that motherfucker over there. I ain't stupid."

"John, I'll call you back, okay?" I hung up the phone on him, but I knew I would hear his mouth later. They both felt a certain way when I was on the phone with one of them.

"Here you go, Big Daddy," I said as I handed John his plate of food and gave him a kiss.

"I thought we talked about no phone calls in my presence."

"I know. I'm sorry. He needed something."

"I don't care. You need to respect our time. I don't blow up your phone when you're with him, do I?"

I looked at him. He knew damn well he called me every other minute if he thought I was with him. I didn't feel like arguing. I had enough on my plate, and I just didn't have the energy. "I'm sorry. It won't happen again."

"I'm telling you, Emerald, I care for you, I really do. But I can't take this shit too much longer. You need to make your mind up fast, or I'm going to stop messing with you. I don't need the headache, and I don't like sharing my pussy."

John had been tripping for the last couple of months, trying to talk all street to me like he gangster. I guess he called himself trying to compete with my other love. "Okay, soon, I promise."

"I'm not joking with you!" John yelled as he pushed his chair back and threw his napkin over his food. "Excuse me. I need to go."

I started to cuss his ass out for having me cook for him and his ass didn't even eat it. *Bastard.* At this point, I was so ready to end the drama in my life. They both were killing me slowly. Like they weren't fucking nobody else. I knew for a fact they both had a bitch on the side, so they could stop popping that "I want you for myself" noise.

John got dressed and walked right out the door without giving me a kiss or saying goodbye. I had to make a choice, and soon. I couldn't keep dealing with this stress. I didn't want to keep misleading them, and they both deserved to have a dedicated woman.

I got dressed and went over to Angel's place. I needed to talk with her. I made it down to Angel's condo and the smell of food roamed the hallway. She was always cooking something. Angel opened the door with her apron on as usual.

"Girl, you is Betty Crocker for real," I joked.

"Whatever, I'm fixing my man a cake and I thinking about what I'm cooking him for dinner."

"You got your housewife role down for real."

"Yeah, I love it, girl. Guess what!"

"What?" I asked.

"Black got me a building. He took me there yesterday. It needs to be fixed up, but it's mine. I can finally have my own restaurant." Angel's face lit up like a light bulb. She had a glow on her that you needed sunglasses to block out. She was really happy with Black, despite Dollar hurting her like he did. She had managed to trust again.

"I don't know how you do it."

"Do what?" she asked as she gave me a sample of her homemade cherry frosting.

"That's good. Make me some and a cake. I need to take it over to John tonight. I need to make up with him." Angel had gotten her chef certificate while she was doing her time, so now she cooked up a storm. "You know, I don't know how you trust Black and be happy, especially since he a street nigga like Dollar."

"Firstly, he not like Dollar at all. He does what he do, but he never would put me in any kind of harm. He's home at a decent hour and he gives me his time, not just his money."

"Yeah, but he still from the streets. That's my problem with John. I can't get past that aspect to want to deal with him. I don't know how you can do it."

"Well, I had to forgive myself first, because when you're hurt, you blame everybody including yourself. You keep screaming, 'Why, why, why?' But you have to tell yourself, 'I forgive me for being so blind. I forgive myself for making so many bad choices.' I forgave myself. I was angry at the world for what Dollar did, saying, 'Fuck a nigga,' but that was the hurt talking. Once I forgave myself and learned from my mistake, I was able to move on and be happy."

It sounded kind of crazy, but right at the same time. "Forgive your own self?" I asked.

"Yeah, look yourself in the mirror and have a talk. I had a long talk with myself, and no, I ain't crazy, but I needed to heal. I accepted the fact that I was just young and got had, you know? I had to let my own self know it's okay to cry and forgive. I let all that hurt and past go. All that hoing we was doing, it didn't make that hurt go away. I mean, we got paid, but we was still angry. It was when I accepted responsibility for my actions that I was truly able to move on with my life. We both played a part in what happened to us. You can't look for no man to take away the pain of being hurt. You got to ask God to do it for you. Forgive the bad choices that you've made and move on with better ones. I'm happy. I'm in love. I don't worry about what Black's doing when he's gone. You'll be crazy. I trust him to do the right things by us and our life. I'm a grown woman now, and I know when shit ain't right, and I know how to open my mouth and talk about it. At this point in our life, we both have money in the bank, so leaning on a man to take care of us is just played out. We was just young and dumb, and we had to grow up, that's all. In this world all, you need is peace of mind and Jesus. That can get you through anything."

After I heard Angel speak, my heart started pounding. I'd never seen her in this space. I knew it had been a rocky ride for the both of us. *I almost lost our friendship being stupid. I do need friends, and I do need to forgive myself.* Angel was right. She'd definitely grown into her womanhood. I couldn't hate on her. I needed to get to that space as well.

I said, "You know, John snapped on me about John calling me while he was there. He's like, 'Oh, I'm not putting up with this shit no more.'"

"Which one you talking about? We need to make them up some code names. You be having me all confused. We'll call white John JW and black John BJ," she said as she laughed with her goofy self.

"Well, I'm talking about JW. He got all fresh at the mouth with me."

"Girl, I don't understand it myself. Black was asking me about it. When we all went out last weekend with BJ, he was like, 'John seems like a cool nigga, but he letting Emerald pimp him out like a sucker.' He like, 'Ain't no way a nigga in his right mind goin' share some pussy.'"

"They'll share the snapper, please believe me. It's mean enough."

"Yeah, for how long? They're both very handsome guys. You and I both know that they can find a woman in the blink of an eye."

"I know, I know. But it's hard, you know, cause I like them both. It's hard for me to choose."

"I think you should pick BJ," Angel said. "Ain't nothing like a big dick and some boss head to make the bad times good."

"I don't know, Angel. It's just so confusing. I can't explain it. In a way, they both good for me, and they both have money and good credit. BJ just has a much bigger dick."

"Well, God bless the big dicks. I thank him every night for mines. Cause you know we ain't got no time for the little ones, period."

"Right." I laughed. Shit, I could give her a big amen on that one. "Well, I'm going to see my sister off to her new home. Please make sure you take the cake up to my place. I need it."

"Okie dokie," said Angel.

CHAPTER 46
FORGIVING ME

I COULDN'T GET my mind off what Angel was saying about me forgiving myself. I never really took ownership of what happened to me. Maybe I needed to man up and face my own self in the mirror and heal myself.

When I parked, I let down my visor and looked into the mirror. As I took a good look at myself, I saw a different person, not the same little girl I was at sixteen. When I looked at myself, I saw a new woman.

"I forgive you," I said, feeling crazy as hell. *What am I doing?* I closed up my visor because I felt stupid talking to myself. *I can do this.* I pulled my visor back down. "I forgive you," I said loudly, and everybody that passed me looked at me like I was crazy. I didn't care. I needed to get this out. "I forgive you for being so blind. I forgive you for being young, dumb, and stupid. I forgive you for prostituting your body."

Tears streamed down from my eyes. The more I came clean and grasped the reality of what I'd done, the more the tears flowed. I'd been hurting my own self. I had to let go and move on. The only other person I needed to ask to forgive me was God.

Once I asked God to forgive me, I felt so much pressure fly away. It was like a weight lifted off me and I felt free. Although it may seem stupid or small, you have to forgive yourself for letting yourself get hurt before you can move on with your life.

I really didn't need to go inside and speak with Sissy or Dollar, but since I was there, I figured I might as well rub it in their faces. I only had a little bit of Jesus in me right now.

I signed in and waited for the guards to bring Dollar down. Since I got the juice in here, I got us a private room. After fifteen minutes of waiting, Dollar entered the room in his orange jumpsuit and looked at me and hung his head low.

"Orange makes you look real sexy." I smiled.

"I'm going back up," he said as he pushed through the guards, but they made him sit down.

"What, you not happy to see me, Big Daddy?"

"What do you want, Emerald?"

"Do I sense attitude from you? Now, how is it going on the inside? You cool? You need anything?"

"You know, I underestimated you, Emerald. I never knew you had a brain."

"Real funny. I only tried to be what I thought you wanted, but I've never been a complete fool."

"I see. I guess you got lucky and stashed away some of my money," he said.

"Please, if that's what you think? I have my own money."

"So, tell me how you managed to get outta jail and set us up."

"Well, I don't owe you anything, but if you want to know, it was a simple plot," I said. "Sissy was an easy target. She's not street-smart. I followed Sissy for a whole year, and she didn't even know it. I studied her like an SAT test. Her every move, I got down to a T. And you—I broke right into your house and fucked you and you didn't even know it."

"The picture from your party," he said as his mouth hung open.

"I knew then that I could get away with fucking you and you wouldn't know if I was Sissy. And me getting out was priceless—not a soul knew it. You looking at an eight-figure bitch right now, no chump change."

"And my momma?"

"That bitch? Please, she put her own self in jail, and your ugly-ass sister. The thing with computers is that even though you delete things, it's still there. How was I to know y'all schemed so many people? I ain't losing no sleep. You can believe that."

"And the nuts…did you do that?"

I looked at him and thought about my answer. If there's one thing I've learned, it's not to confess your sins to anyone. "Nope, I didn't do that. How would I know that?"

"And my money?" he asked.

"What money?"

"Don't play, Emerald."

"You watch *The Wire*?" I asked him.

"Yeah, why?"

"Well, I like *The Wire*. They get real grimy on there—give you all kind of ideas on that show. But what I won't do is tell you shit. I don't owe you nothing, Mr. Miller. Karma is a motherfucker, ain't it?"

"You know, Emerald, I got to give you credit. Out of all the girls, I never thought you would be the one to bring me down."

"Greed brought you down, not me."

"Well, Emerald, I don't know my fate, but I want you to know, if it means anything to you, that I did love you, but I just got caught up in the life. But I did care for you."

"You know, Dollar, I came down here to talk with you. I wanted to believe I needed to have a face-to-face with you, ask you, 'Why me?' and feel like I got closure from you. But I don't need it, boo-boo. I forgave myself, and that's all that matters right now. You loving me means nothing to me. I don't need you."

"Well, I just wanted you to know that."

"Please spare me the drama," I said as I got up. "It's just business, right?"

Dollar looked at me and his face turned pale. "Emerald," he called to me, and I turned to see what he wanted. "*The Wire*, the episode when Omar robbed ol' dude and took the money and blow."

I just smiled at him. "What?"

"So, the drugs, what you goin' do with them?"

"I have no clue what you're talking about."

I left Dollar for the last time in my life. I would never look back at him or think about our past. That chapter of my life was closed.

When I saw Sissy, my stomach turned. Even though she hurt me, I could tell jail had taken a toll on her. I didn't want her here, but she had to pay the piper like everybody else. She had bags under her eyes and her skin looked pale.

She came and sat down across from me, and a chill went through my body. "What do you want?" she asked me as she rolled her bag-filled eyes.

"Damn, it looks like you ain't been getting no sleep. Is they in here trying to lick yo' kitty kat?"

"Fuck off," she said.

"Wow, no remorse. Is Dollar worth all of this, girl?"

"He's my husband, and it ain't nothing you can do about it."

"I don't want to. You can have his sorry broke ass."

"I'll see you again, Emerald," Sissy said as she jumped outta her seat.

"So you gangster now?"

"Fuck you, bitch. I'll see you again, and when I do, I'ma make you pay."

"Yeah," I said as I stepped outta my seat and got into her face. "So you want to face off with me, bitch? You making threats?"

"No, a promise. When I get out, it's on."

"Then I'll be waiting. If you want to go to war, then we can. Face off."

"I ain't scared."

"I'ma make sure my good friend Roxy take care of you while you're in here. You just remember, I'm the only family you got."

"My last name is Miller," she said and walked away from me.

I didn't even feel bad anymore. She was gonna have to learn the hard way like I did. *I could have Roxy hem her up and beat the shit out of her, but I'm not. If Sissy wants to go to war with me, then I'll be waiting on her ass.*

CHAPTER 47
JOHN

New Year's Eve

THE TRIAL FOR Sissy and Dollar dragged out cause they tried to fight it, but in the end, Dollar got fifteen years and Sissy got three. Dollar stood up for his wife and family and took all the blame. He didn't want them in jail, but all their hands were dirty, so they had to go down too.

I didn't care if they got only a year. I wanted them to feel that same pain I felt when them bars was slammed in my face.

Ms. Price hadn't fully recovered from her stroke, so she was doing her time in a mental ward. Who knew nuts could make somebody have a stroke? S.L. got off fairly easy with two years. His dad was Jewish and he had the best lawyers money could buy.

As for Ginger, I let her manage one of my stores and fell through to her place anytime I felt like it. I paid her a nice salary, so she could still live good while her husband was away. I couldn't have my bitch out here looking bogus.

The last two years of my life had been this big emotional roller coaster ride. I promised myself some changes in my life for the new year. I wanted to settle down and be loved by one man. I needed to start my year off the right way.

When I looked back over my life, I'd slept with so many men I had to get tested for AIDS and STDs. When my tests came back negative, I was jumping for joy. I was so blessed. There are so many diseases out here. Sleeping around is the dumbest thing you can do.

I looked over my shoulder and saw John sleeping like a baby. I thought about being married to him. My feelings were deep for him, but I didn't know if he was the one. I promised them both that I would choose today who I wanted to be with. I'd never had to make such a hard choice, especially when I liked them both for different reasons. But it was that night. I had to make a choice to bring in the new year with one of them.

"What you thinking about, baby?" John asked me.

"Everything, but I'm cool."

"Look, Emerald, I want you to marry me," he said as he pulled out a five-carat princess-cut diamond ring. "I know you promised to make your choice today, but I want to marry you, not just make you my girlfriend."

My heart started racing. I couldn't believe it. *Marry me?* "John, I don't know. I don't know if me and you will work."

"We will work. Haven't I always been there for you?"

"Yes."

"Then I will always be there."

"What about your family?" I asked.

"What about them? My mom will come around."

"I don't know, John."

"Just think about it."

Once John left, my head started pounding. Should I pass up a chance at getting married? A part of me wanted to settle down and be a wife. *This could be my only chance at getting married, and I think I'm ready. I think my mind is made up.* I took a good look at the ring. The diamonds that John picked sparkled like my eyes.

I put my ring in my drawer and got dressed. The grand opening for the barber shop was in an hour, and I couldn't be late.

I made sure I was looking extra fly, cause I had to represent. When I made it to the shop, it was packed already. I was so proud of him changing his life around and leaving them streets alone. This was a major plus for him. He had big dreams, and I believed he could be whatever he wanted to be.

"Hey, baby," I said to him as I hugged him.

"Hey, sexy, you look good enough to eat."

"I hope so. Maybe later." I giggled. He just smiled at me.

When I walked through the barber shop, I couldn't believe it was the same dump we got nine months ago. I had put my foot into decorating this place. I had plasma TVs on the walls, oversized booths, video games—everything was state-of-the-art.

"It all came together, huh, baby?" he said.

"Yeah, it did. I'm so happy for you."

"I couldn't have done this without you. I love you, Emerald," John said to me. It kind of made me tingle, because I really felt he meant it.

John had gone to barber school and gotten his license. It only took him five months. I was surprised he had a long client list already.

After hours of laughing and talking with his friends, I was too ready to get out of there. "Baby, what time you coming to my place?" I asked.

"I don't know. That depends on you," John said.

"What?"

"You know what today is."

"I know, and I got until twelve o'clock."

He just looked at me and smiled. He kissed me softly on my forehead, and it made me shiver. "So, you want to use me up and leave me!"

"No, it's not like that, baby."

John got down on one knee in front of everybody. My heart started racing. "Emerald, I don't ever want to lose you. I thought long and hard about asking you to spend the rest of your life with me. Are you the one? I even asked myself, why do I even bother with you? My life had this empty spot, and when I met you, I felt that spot was filled. When you're away from me, I can't sleep. I want us to grow old together. I'm so in love with you. I never thought I would feel this way about a woman. I never loved anybody this much besides my mother. I know you've been hurt and I ain't trying to hurt you. I want you in my life forever. Will you marry me?" John opened a box and showed me a ten-carat pink canary princess-cut diamond ring, blinging so hard it almost blinded me.

I started crying so hard I was shaking. Something inside me wanted to say yes to him, but he reminded me so much of Dollar. I didn't know if he would be good for me. I looked at him on his knees, looking so sexy and strong. "God, why?" I cried to myself. *They both asked to marry me. What am I to do? I can't make myself lie to him.* "Baby, I don't know what to say. I love you too, but married? Can I think about it?"

"Don't make me wait too long. I'm your husband, Emerald. God has already written it."

John blew my mind. *I'm so confused. Who do I choose? I have feelings for both of them. I care about them both.*

I told John to stay home and enjoy himself. I knew that if he gave me his long stroke from the back, I would pick him, no questions asked. I needed to think with a clear head.

I lay awake in my bed, putting together a list of both Johns' pros and cons. I would choose whoever had the most pros to be my husband.

CHAPTER 48
ONE YEAR LATER

MY STOMACH WAS turning butterflies. Angel told me it was okay to feel like this cause I was getting married. I was nervous, and I couldn't stop wondering if he was having second thoughts about marrying me. I paced the floor like a madwoman in my forty-thousand-dollar Vera Wang wedding gown.

"Bitch, would you calm down?" Angel said to me.

"How can I be calm? What if I'm making a mistake?"

"A mistake about what?"

"Getting married! What if I'm too young? Maybe I haven't experienced enough yet," I said.

"Bitch, you're twenty-three and done had plenty of dick in your days. Shit, you even had a tag-team. What more could you do?"

"I don't know, Angel. What if I picked the wrong guy?"

"Your heart wouldn't let you get this far if he was the wrong guy," she said.

"I don't know, Angel." I was tripping hard. I sat down so the lady from MAC could finish my makeup.

"Bitch, relax. I like who you picked, wit his sexy ass."

"Girl, I don't know. I'm making a mistake. I can feel it."

"Girl, lighten up!" Angel said. "You picked somebody that you can spend the rest of your life with, and that's it."

"Whatever!"

"Damn, I hope I don't turn into Bridezilla next month when I get married," she said.

"Oh, I didn't tell you that I got the guy from the *Sun-Times* to come to the grand opening of your restaurant for a review." Angel and Black had worked day-in and day-out getting her restaurant off the ground. I was so proud of her. The grand opening was in a week, and I couldn't wait.

"How you do that?"

"I'm still connected."

"Oh, thank you, Emerald!" Angel yelled. She planted a big kiss on my cheek. She deserved to be happy and have a booming restaurant. I'd do what I could to help her.

"Um-hmm. Am I still Bridezilla?"

"Yeah," she laughed. "Emerald, seriously, you picked a great guy. I know you guys are going to be happy together."

"I hope you're right, Angel."

"I am."

Once the lady finished my makeup, I took a good look at myself in the mirror. I felt like a princess. This was the right thing to do. I'd been around the block, and now it was time for my husband and I to explore new things.

Ms. Peaches had agreed to be Derrel today. He was walking me down the aisle to the altar. Deep down inside, I wished my daddy was here to walk me down the aisle, but Ms. Peaches would do. He'd been protecting me since I met him.

When I walked out the back, he looked at me. "You look like a princess," he said. "You ready to get married?"

"Yes," I said as I flashed a smile. I had gone all out for my wedding, and it was costing a pretty penny, too. *But fuck it, it ain't tricking if you got it, and I'm rich. I damn sure got it!* I heard Brian McKnight's "Never Felt This Way" start playing, and my heart started pounding. I looked at Ms. Peaches with fear on my face.

"Look, Emerald, I woulda told you if you was making a bad choice," he said. "Don't I always keep it real?"

"Yes."

"He's good for you, Emerald, trust him."

I grabbed Ms. Peaches's arm and he looked at me. "I got a surprise for you," he said.

"What?"

"I'm not walking you down the aisle," he said.

"What?" I yelled. "You promised me."

"I know, but he should take you."

I turned around, and my father was standing behind me in a white tux. I couldn't believe it. I started crying.

"Girl, stop crying," Ms. Peaches said as he wiped my eyes.

"When did you get out?" I asked my dad.

"I'll tell you all about it later. Right now, I have to take you to meet your husband." I grabbed my dad's arm, and he turned and looked at me. "It wouldn't be right if Derrel didn't walk with you as well."

I grabbed Peaches's arm and headed down the aisle to meet my future husband. *I feel like the coldest bitch in here. Naw, scratch that, I am the coldest bitch in here.* When we made it to the altar, my heart started pounding again.

"Who gives this woman away?" the preacher asked my father and Peaches.

"I do," they both said.

We turned and faced each other, and my hands started sweating. John flipped my veil over my face and looked at me like he never had before. I saw a tear form in his eye, and he was making me want to cry.

"Emerald, do you take this man to be your lawfully wedded husband? Do you promise to honor and cherish him through sickness and in health, for richer or for poorer, for better or for worse, to have and hold, until death do you part?"

My stomach was bubbling. *What if he doesn't say "I do" about me? That's a lot of shit he just kicked...for richer or for poorer? I don't know about no poorer shit.* "I do," I said.

"John, do you take this woman to be your lawfully wedded wife? Do you promise to honor and cherish her through sickness and in health, for richer or for poorer, for better or for worse, to have and hold, until death do you part?"

"I do."

"The rings, please." When we got our rings, the preacher prayed over them. We both said a speech, placed them on our hands, and the preacher looked into the crowd. "If any man knows why these two should not accept these vows, speak now, or forever hold your peace."

I looked out into the crowd and nobody said a word. They ass knew better. They woulda got they ass kicked up outta here. "Well, if we have no takers, by the power vested in me, you can now kiss your bride."

John reached in, and we kissed each other so passionately. I was his wife now. I had never thought the day would come in my life when I'd feel so complete.

We had a Hawaiian luau for our reception, and we went all out. We had hula girls dancing, a tiki bar, all Hawaiian food, and an open bar. It was great.

When I looked at John before they announced us, all my doubts went out the door. I knew I'd picked a good man who was gonna take good care of me. Angel was right. My heart wouldn't lead me wrong. I'd loved John from the moment he touched my body. I knew he was the one. I kissed my husband on his soft lips. He was all mine, and I was happy.

206

The DJ put on a drumroll. "Please, everybody, get outta your seats and help me welcome Mr. and Mrs. Wells!"

When we entered the room, all my butterflies flew away. I was Slim's bitch now. We danced the night away until it was time for him to remove my garter. I sat down in the chair and the DJ played "Sex Is On My Mind," and Lord knows I couldn't wait to get my husband in our limo. We hadn't had sex in four weeks. I'd been going through withdrawal.

Why did I pick Slim over John? John was a good man, and they pretty much tied in the pros and cons area. I had to think about it. There are two kinds of men in the world—the kind that can break you and the kind that can make you. John was the kind that could do either if he wanted. He could build me up or he could break me down, take all my money, and wipe me out just like that.

His mother didn't care for me since all that stuff went down at the art gallery, and that's her right, but I'd rather not deal with another bitch-ass mother-in-law. Ms. Price was enough. John would have had too much control over me. He was very demanding, and business and personal relationships don't mix sometimes. We'd have gotten a divorce within the first year. So I didn't want to take the chance of letting Slim walk outta my life for another relationship that might work.

I'd learned so much through my journey in life, but the most important thing I learned was that a man can only do to you what you let him. I let Dollar get away with doing whatever he wanted to. I put myself through half of that shit. Once I stopped pointing the finger at him and looked, there were three fingers pointing back at me, I was able to see my mistakes. I shoulda slapped my own self silly for all that shit I put up with. Dollar was a dirty nigga, but I couldn't look at all men the same.

I knew what I would and wouldn't take from my husband. As a woman, I had learned to demand my respect; if you don't, they goin' treat ya ass just like you let 'em. I would never let another man walk over me and get away with doing me dirty. And till I reached my grave, love or no love, I would always put *Money Over Niggas*.

That was a small portion of my decision to choose Slim. Besides that, I was a hardcore freak. I needed to be fucked right. I was a nympho. I needed it in the morning, noon, and night. When I looked at my list, two major points stood out to me: Slim had a ten-inch dick and John had a seven-inch dick. I made sure I was right, too. I went to Lover's Lane and bought a cock-measuring tape.

It didn't matter how many pros John had over Slim; I couldn't get over them three inches of dick that I would be missing. So I did what any other bitch would do in my situation—I picked the big dick and prayed to the good Lord that this marriage was gonna work. Sex is fifty percent of a relationship, and if it's not right, somebody gonna be cheating. *Besides that, I ain't got no time for the little dicks, period.* I thanked God for a fine husband who knew how to blow my back out.

So, me and my husband faded off into the sunset, headed to Fiji to have a big honeymoon. The wedding and honeymoon cost us three hundred thousand dollars, but it was cool. We had come into lots of cash all of a sudden. My life couldn't have been any better. My dad was home, and I was in love. Who could ask for more?

I stared at the sunset, praying to God, *Please don't let Slim turn on me. Please let him be the one. God, please help me to be the best wife I can be. Please bless our marriage. God, I'm willing to do what it takes to make us work. I know we will be happy as long as we don't tell **Lies** and keep **Secrets**. We'll be forever.*

STAY TUNED FOR THE SEQUEL
LIES AND SECRETS
COMING SOON

Excerpt from upcoming novel Lies and Secrets

I waited outside Angel's house in my 2010 Aston Martin DBS, courtesy of my husband. I was the only bitch in Chicago pushing one of these bitches, despite the two-hundred-and-fifty-thousand-dollar price tag. Slim got it custom-painted a pretty deep purple, which is my favorite color. He also had my headrest embroidered with "Ms. Wells" and the inside tricked out. My plush cream butter leather bucket seats had purple stitching that matched my paint perfectly. My sound system knocked so hard you could hear it miles away. My ride was sick. Slim had gotten it for me as a Valentine's Day present.

I was listening to some tracks from Slim's new artist, Poe Boy. Most of the tracks were fire, but there were a couple that were hot garbage. *I'ma make sure I tell his ass to scratch these two.* "Angel needs to hurry her ass up!" I yelled, popping my fingers to the music. I was on my way out to Bed, Bath, and Beyond to shop for some dishes, and I didn't want to get behind schedule.

"Damn, late-ass!" I yelled at Angel.

"Hey, I'm sorry," Angel said as she closed the door and threw her Bojari purse down.

"That's fly. When you get that?"

"Black got it for me last week," she said.

"So, how's the restaurant coming?"

"It's great. I'm opening up a new one in two months."

I was glad Angel's restaurant had taken off; she deserved to be success-ful like me. Once we made it to Bed, Bath, and Beyond, I went straight to the dishes. I wanted some of those Cornell dishes that don't break. After the sales associate convinced me to get fifteen hundred dollars' worth of pots, pans, and dishes, I was ready to go.

"What you finna do?" I asked Angel as I dropped her off at her house.

"Go in and get my husband dinner ready."

"Man, he got you trained." I laughed.

"Please. You know you getting Slim dinner ready too."

"I know."

Slim always came home before he went to the studio, so I tried to be a good little wifey and have his dinner ready for him. I washed my new dishes and started to cook my chicken and broccoli meal. That was my husband's favorite.

I turned on my Keyshia Cole CD and started jamming. "If he don't love you the way he should, then let it go," I sang, feeling Keyshia Cole's words. I grabbed my pot off the stove to pour the water off my rice.

"Emerald," a voice crept at me, scaring the shit out of me.

I turned around. "Slim, baby, you scared me."

"I'm sorry, baby. Guess what? I ran into my brother today."

"Brother? You ain't never tell me about a brother."

"I know, cause we stopped talking, but he showed up today at my shop and I wanted him to meet you. We made up with each other since I stopped hustling and all."

"Where is he?" I said, walking over to the sink.

"Right here," his brother said.

I turned around and my heart skipped a beat. The whole left side of my body froze up. My hands started shaking so bad I dropped my glass pot and it broke into pieces. "Shit," I said as I reached down and tried to pick up the broken pieces. I couldn't believe it. My brain was scrambled and I couldn't think. *Oh my God.*

"Hi," I said to him.

"Hi. You look so familiar to me," he said, smiling.

"Oh, I have a sister that looks just like me," I said as I paced the floor back and forward. The scent of his cheap-ass Cool Water cologne started making me nauseous and lightheaded.

"No, I swear I know you. What's your name?"

"My bad, dog. This is my wife, Emerald," Slim said to him. "Emerald, this is my brother…"

Stay tuned.

Do you want to know who popped back into Emerald life? Head over to www.nwhoodtales.com and unlock the entire chapter for only 99 cents or wait until July of 2009.

Stay Tuned!

Coming Soon To A Hood Near You!

Upcoming Titles From NWHoodTales
Misery luv's Company 12-2008
STEP YA HEAD GAME UP! 12-2009
Secrets and Lies 07-2009

Also Upcoming from
NWHoodTales:

Step Ya Head Game Up

Excerpt from Upcoming Novel

Step Ya Head Game Up!

Whoever said pussy is power ain't never lied. I found that out at the young age of eleven. I ran my finger across my clit slowly and got such a wonderful feeling. I did it again, but a little faster, and damn! A bitch was feeling like something was taking over my body. I didn't want that feeling to stop. I sped up a little faster and my legs began to shake. "Ohh," I moaned. Something was happening that I liked. Then a gush came out of me. I was too young then to know I made myself have an orgasm. I knew that if I could make myself feel good, I damn sure wouldn't have a problem making a man feel good.

Now I'm much older and I understand the meaning of "Pussy Is Power." Men can't survive without it. Women definitely rule the world. I can fuck a man so good that he'd disown his mother, stop talking to his sister, and kill his brother if he thought he'd got a piece. Yup, pussy is power: you just gotta use it the right way. Giving boss head is a way to a man's heart, pockets, whatever. Head is the new pussy, so bringing your A game is a must every time. Boss head can turn the hardest thug soft in a matter of minutes.

Please believe me: if ya snooze ya lose. First impression means everything; ain't no room for half stepping. When you lay that nigga down for the first time, you better bring it. Let that nigga know you ain't the bitch from down the street or the ho from up the block. Show him you that bitch that's gone get him right; show him you dat boss *wifey*-type bitch! Let that nigga know ain't no need to keep searching, that you're definitely that girl he's been looking for!

It's just like a job interview. You say and do the right things to get the job. We have the power right in the palms of our hands, so don't be scared to use it. Use the powers that the good Lord blessed you with; don't run from it. Trust me, I know everybody ain't blessed by the good Lord to be a boss bitch, so if ya unsure or if ya brain game is lame, don't worry: there's always room to *Step Ya Head Game Up!*

Coming Soon to a Hood Near You.

About the Author

Author Nichelle Walker hails from the fabulous city of Chicago. Nichelle found her love for writing early in life. During her high school years she penned several successful screenplays, short stories and her first novel. While matriculating through college to attain a degree in Accounting, Nichelle put her love for writing on the back burner only to find herself constantly wanting to write and tell her story. While on a three week break from school and unhappy with losing touch with her creative passion, she wrote her highly anticipated novella Doing His Time. Not wanting to wait on a publisher to decide her fate, Nichelle founded her own publishing company NWHoodTales Publishing. Nichelle Walker is excited to introduce her company and her novella to the world and show why her company's motto is "We Keep Them Pages Turning".

Meet me at MySpace and let me know what ya think.
http://www.myspace.com/nichelle2007
Also hit me up at www.nwhoodtales.com
And my new Blog site where you can read all the latest Gossip.
www.nwmasssmedia.com
www.girlsdorock.org

Every little girl dreams of meeting Prince Charming and living happily ever-after. But in the hood the Prince Charming are ballers and we dream of living happily ever "Rich!"

Now imagine being swept off your feet and upgraded from a nobody into a ghetto superstar. Imagine a life of nothing but the best; clothes, jewels, whips and homes. Just picture your life as baller's bit*h! Ask yourself how much are you willing to sacrifice to be the hottest chick in the game?

When Emerald found her ghetto Prince Charming Dollar he quickly upgraded her into a overnight ghetto superstar. Spoiling her with the hottest whips, the finest clothes, the fliest jewels and an unlimited cash allowance. Emerald represented a baller's chick to the fullest; she lived, breathe and swore by the hustlers anthem "Balling!"

The night Dollar asked Emerald to marry him; she knew all her blood, sweat and spit had paid off. She'd be forever fly; Emerald knew the life of a baller's wife could only get more luxurious. But when a drop goes bad and Emerald back is pushed against the wall. How much will she be willing to sacrifice to stay at the top spot?

We Keep Them Pages Turning

Name: _____

Address: _____

City/State: _____

Zip: _____

QTY	TITLE	PRICE
	Money Over Men $15.00/book	$
	Doing His Time $14.95/book	
	Shipping & Handling $3.95/book	$
	***Discount if applicable	– $

TOTAL $_____

***NWHood Tales will give a 25% discount to all books
shipped to a prison or county jail.
Enter in appropriate line above.

Mail payment and form to:
NWHood Tales
516 N. Ogden Avenue #131
Chicago, IL 60622